SHADOW IN THE NORTH

Also by Philip Pullman
THE RUBY IN THE SMOKE

Shadow in the North

Philip Pullman

ALFRED A. KNOPF

New York

This is a Borzoi Book published by
Alfred A. Knopf, Inc.

Copyright © 1986, 1988 by Philip Pullman
Jacket illustration copyright © 1988 by Linda Benson
All rights reserved under International and Pan-American Copyright Conventions. Published in the United States by Alfred A. Knopf, Inc., New York. Distributed by Random House, Inc., New York. Originally published in Great Britain as *The Shadow in the Plate* by Oxford University Press in 1986. Copyright © 1986 by Philip Pullman.

Manufactured in the United States of America
First American Edition
2   4   6   8   10   9   7   5   3   1

Library of Congress Cataloging-in-Publication Data
Pullman, Philip, 1946— .
Shadow in the north.
Sequel to: The ruby in the smoke.
Summary: In 1878 in London, Sally, now twenty-two and established in her own business, and her companions Frederick and Jim try to solve the mystery surrounding the unexpected collapse of a shipping firm and its ties to a sinister corporation called North Star.
[1. Mystery and detective stories.   2. London—
Fiction]   I. Title.
PZ7.P968Sh   1988   [Fic]   87-29846
ISBN 0-394-89453-7
ISBN 0-394-99453-1 (lib. bdg.)

Contents

1

Unsolved Mysteries of the Sea

ONE SUNNY MORNING IN THE SPRING OF 1878, THE STEAM-
ship *Ingrid Linde,* the pride of the Anglo-Baltic shipping line, vanished in the Baltic Sea.

She had been carrying a cargo of machine parts and
a passenger or two from Hamburg to Riga. The voyage
had been uneventful; the ship was only two years old,
well found and seaworthy, and the weather was gentle.

A day out from Hamburg, she was sighted by a
schooner plying in the opposite direction. They ex-
changed signals. A barque, in the same part of the sea,
would have seen her two hours later if the *Ingrid Linde*
had kept to her course. But the barque saw nothing.

She vanished so swiftly and so completely that
journalists of the time scented something as delicious
as the lost continent of Atlantis, or the *Mary Celeste,* or
the Flying Dutchman. They got hold of the fact that
the chairman of the Anglo-Baltic line and his wife and
daughter were on board, and filled the papers with
accounts that it was the little girl's first voyage; that,
on the contrary, she wasn't a little girl, but a young
lady of eighteen, with a mysterious disease; that there

was a curse on the ship, laid by a former sailor; that the cargo consisted of a deadly mixture of explosives and alcohol; that in the captain's cabin was a fetish idol from the Congo, which he had stolen from an African tribe; that in that part of the sea there was a gigantic and unpredictable whirlpool that appeared without warning and sucked ships down into a monstrous cavern at the center of the earth—and so on, and so on.

The story became quite famous. It was resurrected occasionally by writers who specialized in books with titles like *Strange Horrors of the Deep*.

But without facts, even the most inventive journalism peters out in the end, and there were no facts at all in this case—just a ship that had been there one minute and vanished the next, and the sunshine, and the empty sea.

ONE COLD MORNING a few months afterward, an old lady knocked on the door of an office in the financial heart of London. Painted on the door were the words S. LOCKHART, FINANCIAL CONSULTANT. After a moment, a voice—a female voice—called out "Come in," and the old lady entered the room.

S. Lockhart—the *S* stood for Sally; she was a remarkably pretty young woman of twenty-two, with blond hair and deep brown eyes—stood up behind her cluttered desk. The old lady took one step into the room and then hesitated, because standing on the hearth in front of the coal fire was the biggest dog she had ever seen—as black as night and, to judge from its shape, a mixture of bloodhound, Great Dane, and werewolf.

"Down, Chaka," said Sally Lockhart, and the great beast sat peacefully. His head still came up to her waist. "It's Miss Walsh, isn't it? How do you do?"

The old lady shook the hand held out to her. "Not altogether well," she said.

"Oh, I'm sorry," said Sally. "Please—sit down." She cleared some papers off a chair, and they sat on either side of the fire. The dog lay down and put its head on its paws.

"If I remember correctly, I helped you with some investments last year," Sally said. "You had three thousand pounds—isn't that right? And I advised you to go for shipping."

"I wish you had not," said Miss Walsh. "I bought shares in a company called Anglo-Baltic, on your recommendation. Perhaps you remember."

Sally's eyes widened. Miss Walsh, who'd taught geography to hundreds of girls before she retired and who was a shrewd judge, knew that look well; it was the expression of someone who's made a bad mistake and has just realized it, and who is going to face the consequences without ducking.

"The *Ingrid Linde*," said Sally. "Of course. . . . And wasn't there a schooner that sank as well? I remember reading about it in *The Times*—oh, dear."

She got up and took a large book of newspaper clippings from the shelf behind her. While she leafed through it Miss Walsh folded her hands in her lap and looked around the room. It was neat and clean, though the furniture was threadbare and the carpet worn, and there was a cheerful fire in the hearth, and a kettle hissing beside it. The books and the files on the shelves and the map of Europe pinned to the wall gave the place a businesslike look of purpose.

As for Miss Lockhart, she was looking grim. She tucked a strand of blond hair behind her ear and sat down, book open on her lap.

"Anglo-Baltic collapsed," she said. "Why didn't I notice . . . ? What happened?"

"You mentioned the *Ingrid Linde*. There was another ship—a schooner—that was lost too. And a third ship was impounded by the Russian authorities in St. Petersburg. I don't know why, but they had to pay an enormous fine to have the ship released. . . . Oh, there were a dozen things. When you advised me to buy into it, the firm was prospering. I was delighted with your advice. And a year later it was finished."

"It changed hands, I see. I'm reading this for the first time; I cut out things like this so as to have them for reference, but I don't always have time to read them. Weren't they insured against the loss of the ships?"

"There was some complication; Lloyd's refused to pay out—I didn't understand the details. There was so *much* bad luck, and so suddenly, that I almost began to believe in curses. In a malevolent fate."

The old lady was gazing into the fire, holding herself perfectly upright in the worn armchair. Then she looked at Sally again.

"Of course, I know that's nonsense," she went on more briskly. "Being struck by lightning today doesn't prevent you from being struck again tomorrow; I'm quite familiar with the theory of statistics. But it's hard to keep a clear head when your money is vanishing and you can neither see why nor prevent it. I've got nothing left now but a tiny annuity. That three thousand pounds was a legacy from my brother and a lifetime's savings."

Sally opened her mouth to speak, but Miss Walsh held up her hand and went on. "Now, please understand, Miss Lockhart, I do not blame you. If I choose to speculate with my money, I have to take the risk that I shall lose it. And at the time, Anglo-Baltic was an excellent investment. I came to you in the first place on the recommendation of Mr. Temple the lawyer, of Lincoln's Inn, because I have a lifetime's interest in the emancipation of women, and nothing pleases me more than to see a young lady such as yourself earning a living in this enterprising way. So I come to you again to ask for your advice: is there anything I can do to recover my money? I strongly suspect, you see, that it's not bad luck; it's fraud."

Sally put her book of clippings down on the floor and reached for a pencil and a notebook.

"Tell me everything you know about the firm," she said.

Miss Walsh began. She had a clear mind, and the facts were marshaled tidily. There weren't many of them; living as she did in Croydon, with no connections to the world of business, she'd had to rely on what she could gather from the newspapers.

Anglo-Baltic had been founded twenty years before, she told Sally, to profit from the timber trade. It had grown modestly but steadily, carrying furs and iron ore as well as timber from the Baltic ports and machine tools and other industrial products from Britain.

Two years ago, it had been taken over, Miss Walsh thought, or bought out—could that happen? She wasn't sure—by one of the original partners, after a dispute. The firm had leaped ahead, like a locomotive when the brakes are taken off; new ships were ordered, new contracts were found, a North Atlantic connection was built up. Profits rose remarkably in the first year under the new management, persuading Miss Walsh—and hundreds of others—to invest.

And then came the first of the apparently unconnected blows that brought the company to liquidation in just as short a time. Miss Walsh had details about all of them, and Sally was impressed again by the old lady's command of the facts—and of herself, because it was clear that she was now on the brink of poverty, having expected to live out her retirement in modest comfort.

Toward the end of Miss Walsh's account, the name Axel Bellmann came into the story, and Sally looked up.

"Bellmann?" she said. "The match manufacturer?"

"I don't know what else he is," said Miss Walsh. "He didn't have any great connection with the company; I happened to see his name in a newspaper article. I think he owned the cargo the *Ingrid Linde* was carrying when it sank. *She* sank. I could never get used to calling ships *she*, could you? Some kind of machinery. Why do you ask? Do you know of this Mr. Bellmann? Who is he?"

"The richest man in Europe," said Sally.

Miss Walsh sat silently for a moment. "Lucifers," she said. "Phosphorus matches."

"That's right. He made his fortune in the match trade, I believe. . . . Though there was some kind of scandal, now that I think of it. I heard some gossip a year ago, when he first appeared in London. The Swedish government closed down his factories because of the dangerous working conditions in them."

"Girls with necrosis of the jaw," said Miss Walsh. "I've read about them, poor things. There are some wicked ways of making money. Did my money go into that, then?"

"As far as I know, Mr. Bellmann's been out of the match business for some time. And we don't know of his connection with Anglo-Baltic, anyway. Well, Miss Walsh, I'm grateful to you. And I can't tell you how sorry I am. I'm going to get that money back—"

"Now, don't say that," said Miss Walsh, in the sort of tone she must have used with frivolous girls who imagined they could pass examinations without working for them. "I don't want promises, I want knowledge. I very much doubt whether I shall ever see that money again, but I am curious to know where it's gone, and I am asking you to find out for me."

Her manner was so severe that most young women would have quailed. But Sally wasn't like that—which was why Miss Walsh had been able to come to her in the first place; and she said hotly: "When someone comes to me for financial advice, I don't find it acceptable that I should lose all their money for them. And I don't want to be patronized when it happens. This is a blow to me, Miss Walsh, as much as it is to you. It's your money, but it's my name, my reputation, my livelihood. . . . I intend to look into the affairs of Anglo-Baltic and see what happened, and if it's humanly possible, I shall recover your money and give it back to you. And *I* very much doubt that you'd refuse to take it."

There followed a glacial silence from the old lady, and a look that spoke thunder; but Sally sat firm and stared her out. And after a moment or two a twinkling warmth appeared in Miss Walsh's eyes, and she tapped her fingers together.

"Quite right too," she said.

Both of them smiled.

The tension passed out of the room, and Sally got up. "Would you care for some coffee?" she said. "It's rather primitive to make it on the fire, but it tastes all right."

"I'd like that very much. We always used to make coffee on the fire when we were students—I haven't done it for many, many years. May I help?"

Within five minutes, they were talking like old friends. The dog was waked and made to move out of the way, the coffee was brewed and poured out, and Sally and Miss Walsh discovered the companionship that only women who'd had to struggle for an education could experience. Miss Walsh had taught at the North London Collegiate College, but she had never taken a degree; nor had Sally, for that matter, although she had studied at Cambridge and done well on the examination. The university let women do that much; they just didn't give them degrees.

But Sally and Miss Walsh agreed that the time would come, though it was hard to say when.

Eventually Miss Walsh stood up to go, and Sally noticed her neatly darned gloves, the frayed hem of her coat, and the brightly polished old boots, now badly in need of resoling. It was more than money she'd lost; it was the chance of living in modest comfort and without worry after a lifetime of helping others. Sally looked at her and saw that, despite her age and anxiety, the old lady's posture was firm and straight and dignified; Sally found herself standing straighter too.

They shook hands, and Miss Walsh turned to the dog, who had sat up expectantly when Sally stood.

"What an extraordinary beast," she said. "Did I hear you call him Chaka?"

"Chaka was a Zulu general," Sally explained. "It seemed appropriate. He was a present, weren't you, boy?"

She rubbed his ears affectionately, and the great animal turned and licked her hand with an enveloping tongue, his black eyes glowing with adoration.

Miss Walsh smiled. "I'll send on all the documents I've got," she said. "I'm most grateful to you, Miss Lockhart."

"I haven't done anything yet except lose your money for you," said Sally. "And it might turn out to be no more than it seems—things often do. But I'll see what I can learn."

SALLY'S BACKGROUND was unusual, even for one who lived an unusual life, as she did. She had never known her mother, and her father, a military man, had taught her a great deal about firearms and finance but very little about anything else. When she was sixteen he had been murdered, and she found herself drawn into a web of danger and mystery. Only her skill with a pistol had saved her—that, and a chance meeting with a young photographer named Frederick Garland.

With his sister, Frederick had been running their uncle's photographic business, but for all his skill with a camera, he was quite unable to manage the financial side of it. They were on the verge of ruin when Sally appeared—alone, and in deadly danger. In exchange for their help, she took over the running of the business, and her talent for bookkeeping and accounts had saved them from bankruptcy.

The business had prospered. Now they employed half a dozen assistants, and Frederick was able to turn his attention to private detection, where his real interest lay. In this he was helped by another old friend of Sally's—Jim Taylor, who'd been an office boy in her father's firm and who had a taste for sensational novels of the sort known as penny dreadfuls and the most scurrilous tongue in the city. He had a vivid imagination and a quick ear, and he'd developed an actor's ability to vary his native Cockney accent to fit a multitude of circumstances. He was two or three years younger than Sally. In the course of their first adventure Jim and Frederick had fought, and killed, the most dangerous thug in London. They'd been nearly killed in the process, but each of them knew that he could rely on the other to the death.

The three of them—Sally and Fred and Jim—shared a great deal. Frederick would have been willing to share more. He was quite frank: he was in love with Sally, he always had been, and he wanted to marry her. Her feelings were more complicated. There were times when she felt she adored him, that no one could be more fascinating and brilliant and brave and funny; and there were times when she felt furious at him for wasting his talents fiddling with bits of machinery, or disguising himself and prowling about London with Jim, or generally behaving like a little boy who didn't know how to occupy himself. As far as love was concerned, if she loved anyone it was Fred's uncle Webster Garland, officially her partner in the photographic business: a gentle, untidy genius who could create extraordinary poetry out of light and shade and human expression. Webster Garland and Chaka: yes, she loved them. And she loved her work.

But Fred—well, she'd never marry anyone else, but she wouldn't marry him. Not until the Married Women's Property Act was passed.

It wasn't that she didn't trust him, she'd said a hundred times; it was a matter of principle. That one moment she could be independent, a partner in a business, with money and property that was her own; and that the next, after a clergyman had pronounced them married, every single thing that was hers would become (in the eyes of the law) her husband's instead—that was intolerable. Frederick protested in vain, offered to draw up legal agreements swearing that he'd never touch her property, begged and pleaded and got angry and threw things, and then laughed at himself and at her. She wouldn't budge.

As a matter of fact, it wasn't as simple as she

claimed. There had been a Married Women's Property Act passed in 1870, which had removed some of the injustices, though not the worst ones; but Frederick knew nothing of the law and didn't know that Sally's property could legally remain hers under certain conditions. But because Sally was uncertain of her feelings, she stuck to this principle—and rather dreaded the passing of a new act, since it would force her to decide one way or the other.

Recently this had led to a quarrel and a coolness between them, and they hadn't spoken or seen each other for weeks. She'd been surprised to find how much she missed him. He'd be just the person to talk to about this Anglo-Baltic business. . . .

She cleared away the coffee cups, rattling them crossly as she thought of his flippancy, his facetiousness, his straw-colored hair. Let him come to her first; she had real work to do.

And with that, she settled down at the desk with her book of clippings and began to read about Axel Bellmann.

2

The Wizard of the North

SALLY'S FRIEND JIM TAYLOR SPENT A GOOD DEAL OF HIS time (when he wasn't cultivating his criminal acquaintances, or betting money on horses, or flirting with chorus girls and barmaids) writing melodramas. He had a passion for the stage. Frederick's sister Rosa (now married to a most respectable clergyman) had been an actress when they first met, and she'd fired an interest already stoked by his long and devoted reading of such penny magazines as *Stirring Tales for British Lads* and *Spring-Heeled Jack, the Terror of London*. He'd written several bloodcurdling plays since then and, not wanting to waste his genius on second-best companies, he'd sent them to the Lyceum Theatre, for the consideration of the great Henry Irving. So far, though, he'd received nothing back but polite acknowledgments.

He spent his evenings in the music hall—not in the audience, but where it was far more interesting: backstage, among the carpenters and the stagehands and the lighting crew, not to mention the artists and the chorus girls. He'd worked in several theaters,

learning all the time, and on the evening of the day
Miss Walsh called on Sally he was doing various jobs
behind the scenes in the Britannia Music Hall in
Pentonville.

And it was there that he came across a mystery of his
own.

One of the artists on the bill was a conjurer by the
name of Alistair Mackinnon—a young man who'd
sprung to extraordinary fame in the short time he'd
been appearing on the London stage. It was one of
Jim's jobs to call the artists from their dressing rooms
shortly before they were due to come onstage, and
when he knocked on the door of Mackinnon's room
and called out "Five minutes, Mr. Mackinnon," he
was surprised to hear no answer.

He knocked again, louder. Still there was no reply,
and Jim, knowing that no performer would miss a call
if he could humanly help it, opened the door to see if
Mackinnon was actually there.

He was: in evening dress and chalk-white make-up,
his eyes like black stones. He was gripping the arms of
a wooden chair in front of the mirror. Beside him stood
two other men, also in evening dress: one a small,
mild-looking man with spectacles, the other a heavily
built character who tried, as Jim looked in, to conceal
a life preserver—a short stick loaded with lead—
behind his back. He'd forgotten the mirror; Jim could
see the weapon perfectly.

"Five minutes, Mr. Mackinnon," Jim said again, his
mind racing. "I thought you might not have heard."

"All right, Jim," said the magician. "Leave us,
please."

With a casual glance at the other two men, Jim nodded and went out.

What do I do now? he thought.

IN THE WINGS a number of stagehands stood silently, waiting for the act onstage to finish so that they could change the scenery. Above them in the flies the gasmen waited for their cue; it was their job to change the colored gelatin in front of the flaring gas jets or to turn the jets up and down according to how much light was wanted on stage. Some of the other artists on the bill were waiting too, for Mackinnon was a phenomenal performer and they wanted to watch his act. Jim picked his way through the darkness and the half-light as the soprano onstage came to the final chorus of her song, and took his place by a great iron wheel beside the curtain.

He stood there, light and tense, his fair hair slicked back from his forehead and an anxious look in his green eyes, and tapped his fingers on the wheel; then he heard a whisper beside him.

"Jim," came Mackinnon's whisper out of the darkness. "Can you help me?"

Jim turned around and saw the magician hanging back in the shadows, his dark eyes the only features visible in the pale blur of his face.

"Those men . . ." Mackinnon went on, and pointed up through the proscenium to a box, where Jim saw two figures settling themselves and caught the gleam of the little man's spectacles. "They're trying to kill me. For God's sake, help me get away as soon as the curtain's down. I don't know what to do. . . ."

"Shhh!" said Jim. "And keep back. They're look-ing."

The song came to an end, the flute in the band trilled in sympathy, and the audience clapped and whistled. Jim's hands tightened on the wheel.

"All right," he said. "I'll get you out. Watch out the way—"

He started to swing the great wheel over, and the curtain descended.

"Come off this side," he said over the noise of applause and the rumbling of the pulleys, "not the other. Anything you want out of the dressing room?"

Mackinnon shook his head.

The instant the curtain touched the stage, off came the colored gelatins above, flooding the stage with white light; up rolled the painted backdrop of a fashionable drawing room; and the crew in the wings leaped into activity, unfolding a large velvet screen and bracing it behind, lifting onstage a slender table that seemed oddly heavy for its size, and unrolling a wide Turkish carpet. Jim darted forward to straighten the edge of the carpet and held the screen while another hand adjusted the weight behind it. The whole process took no longer than fifteen seconds.

The stage manager gave a signal to the gasmen, and they slotted new gelatins into the metal frames, lowering the pressure in the jets simultaneously to dim the light to a mysterious rose. Jim sprang back to his wheel; Mackinnon took his place in the wings as the master of ceremonies came to the end of his introduc-tion, and the conductor raised his baton in the orches-tra pit.

A chord, a burst of clapping from the audience, and Jim hauled on the wheel to raise the curtain. Mackinnon entered, transformed. The audience fell silent as he began his act.

Jim watched for a moment or two, amazed as always by the way this figure, so furtive and unhealthy in real life, could become so powerful onstage. His voice, his eyes, his every movement embodied authority and mystery; it was easy to believe that he commanded hosts of invisible spirits, that the tricks and transformations he performed were the work of demons. . . . Jim had seen him a dozen times and had never been less than awestruck. He tore himself away reluctantly and slipped under the stage.

This was the quickest way from one side to the other. Jim moved between beams, ropes, a demontrap, and all kinds of pipework without a sound and emerged on the other side as a burst of clapping rose from the audience.

He dusted himself off and went through a little door into the auditorium, and then through another to the stairs. He reached the top—and shrank back into the shadow, because standing outside the door of the box where Mackinnon's pursuers had gone was a third man, a rough-looking bruiser, obviously put there to keep watch.

Jim thought for a moment, then stepped forward into the gaslit, gilt, and shabby-plush corridor and motioned the man to bend forward. Frowning, he did so, and cocked his head as Jim whispered.

"We've had word as Mackinnon's got some mates in," Jim told him. "They're going to try and spring him out the front. Any minute now he'll do a disappearing trick and get away under the stage and come out the back of the audience, and then his mates'll whip him away in a cab. You go on down to the front of the house, and I'll nip in and tell the boss."

Wonderful what you could do with a bit of cheek, thought Jim as the bruiser nodded and lumbered away. Jim turned to the door. This was risky; someone might come along at any moment. But it was all he could do. He took a bundle of stiff wire from his pocket, crouched by the keyhole, and twisted the wire inside it till he felt something move; then he withdrew the wire, bent it more accurately, inserted it again and, under cover of the applause, locked the door of the box.

He straightened up just in time, as the front-of-house manager came along the corridor.

"What are you doing here, Taylor?" he said.

"Message for the gentlemen in this box," said Jim. " 'S all right, I'm off backstage now."

"It ain't your job to take messages."

"It is if Mr. Mackinnon asks me, ain't it?"

Jim turned and left. Back down the stairs, through the baize door—how far was Mackinnon through his act? Another five minutes, Jim reckoned; time to have a look outside.

Ignoring the curses and instructions to watch his bloody feet, he shoved through the press of stagehands and artists and made his way to the stage door. It opened into an alley behind the theater; the wall on the other side was the back of a furniture depository, and there was only one way out.

There were two men leaning against the wall. As the door opened, they looked up and stepped out farther onto the pavement.

"Wotcher," said Jim affably. "Bleedin' hot in there. Waitin' for Miss Hopkirk, gents?" Miss Hopkirk was the soprano; her admirers often waited at the stage door with flowers or proposals, or both.

"What's it to you?" said one of the men.

"Just being helpful," said Jim easily.

"When's the show finish?" said the other man.

"Any minute now. I better be getting back. Evenin'," he said, and went back inside.

He rubbed his chin; if the back was blocked, and the front was risky, there only remained one way out—and that was risky too. Still, it might be fun. He ran through the area backstage until he found four workmen seated in a little pool of light, playing cards on an upturned tea chest.

"Here, Harold," he said. "Mind if I borrow your stepladder?"

"What for?" said the oldest man, not looking up from his hand.

"Bird's-nesting."

"Eh?" The workman looked up. "Mind you bring it back."

"Ah, well, that's the problem. How much did you win on that tip I gave you last week?"

Muttering, the older man laid down his cards and got up. "Where are you going to take it? I need it in ten minutes, soon as the show's over."

"Up in the flies," said Jim, drawing him away and explaining what he wanted. He peered over the workman's shoulder; Mackinnon's act was coming to an end. Scratching his head, the other man slung the stepladder over his shoulder and climbed up into the darkness as Jim hurried back to the wheel, just in time.

A chord from the orchestra, a storm of applause, a bow, and the curtain came down. Leaving the chaos of objects that had appeared onstage—a sphinx, a bowl of goldfish, dozens of bunches of flowers—Mackinnon sprang into the wings, where Jim seized his arm and thrust him toward the ladder.

"Climb! Go on!" Jim said. "There're blokes out front and back, but they won't catch us this way. Go *on!*"

Mackinnon had changed again: in the shadows of the wings, he looked furtive once more and, in his white make-up, bizarre and sickly.

"I can't," he whispered.

"Can't what?"

"I can't go up there. Heights . . ." He looked around, trembling.

Jim shoved him toward the ladder impatiently. "Get up and stop fussing, for Gawd's sake. Blokes go up and down here hundreds o' times a day. Or d'you want to go out and take your chance with that pair of cutthroats I saw in the alley?"

Mackinnon shook his head feebly and started to climb. Jim twitched a corner of the side curtain across to conceal what they were doing—he didn't want Mackinnon's exit revealed by a stagehand who didn't know what they were up to. Jim scrambled up after him, and they came out on a narrow, railed platform stretching right across the stage, where the gasmen were busy dousing their jets and recovering the gelatins. The smell of hot metal was nearly as powerful as the heat itself, and together with the sweat of the gasmen and the size from the canvas backdrops, it prickled the nose and made the eyes water.

But they didn't linger: another short ladder led to a swaying iron walkway, hung with pulleys and ropes. The floor was an open iron grille, and through it they could see all the way down to the stage, where the carpenters were busy moving sidepieces and flats into position for the melodrama that was due to start playing the following day. It was dark up here, all the light being directed downward, but it was just as hot, and the ropes—some taut, some loose and hanging—and the great balks of timber that took the weight of the scenery, and the suggestion of further levels of platform, tunnel, and vault in an infinite recession into the darkness, and the yawning abysses below, where sooty figures manipulated fire, all made Jim think of a picture of hell he'd once seen in a print shop window.

Mackinnon was swaying, clinging with both hands to the railing.

"I can't!" he was moaning. "Oh, God, let me down!"

His voice had become much more Scottish than his usual upper-class drawl.

"Don't be soft," said Jim. "You won't fall. Just a little bit farther—come on . . ."

Mackinnon stumbled blindly along where Jim directed him. At the end of the walkway, Harold the workman was waiting with his stepladder and put out his hand to guide the performer. Mackinnon seized it with both his hands and clung tight.

"It's all right," said Harold. "I got yer, sir. Take hold o' this."

He guided Mackinnon's hands to the stepladder.

"No! Not more climbing! I can't—I can't do it—"

"Shut up," said Jim, who'd heard a disturbance below. He peered over the railing but saw only the swaying curtains and the ropes. "Listen."

Voices were raised, though they could not make out the words.

"We got about two minutes before they find their way up here. Hold on to him, Harold."

Jim swarmed up the stepladder and unfastened a small window high in the darkness of the dusty brickwork. After propping it open he slipped down again and pushed Mackinnon toward the stepladder. This, to be truthful, was rather risky; the ladder spanned the gap between the end of the platform and the wall, and to get through the window it was necessary to let go and reach up into the darkness with both hands. If you fell . . . But there was a clatter from below. Someone was climbing the first ladder.

"Get up," said Jim. "Don't stand there wetting yourself. Get up and get through that window. Move!"

Mackinnon had heard the noise and set his feet on the stepladder.

"Thanks, Harold," said Jim. "You want another tip? Belle Carnival for the Prince of Wales Handicap."

"Belle Carnival, eh? I hope I get better odds than the last one," grumbled Harold, holding the ladder steady.

Jim put his hands on the ladder on either side of Mackinnon's trembling body.

"Go on! Get up, for Christ's sake!"

Mackinnon moved upward, step by step. Jim stayed close behind, urging him on. When they reached the top, he felt the other man sag downward, unable to go any farther, and hissed up at him, "They're coming! They're on their way! Five great big blokes with knives and coshes! Now reach up till you find a window and pull yerself through. There's a three-foot drop the other side onto the roof next-door. Both hands—go on, that's the way. Now *pull*—"

Mackinnon's feet left the ladder and kicked wildly at the air, nearly sending Jim to his death; but after a second or two of frantic scrabbling, Mackinnon's legs disappeared upward, and Jim knew he was through.

"All right, Harold?" he called down softly. "I'm going up now."

"Hurry up, then" came the hoarse whisper.

Steadying himself against the wall, Jim felt for the window, then found the sill and pulled. Another second or two and he was halfway through, and then he tumbled out onto the cold, wet lead under the open sky.

Mackinnon was being sick beside him.

Jim got up carefully and took a step or two away. They were in a little gully between the wall of the theater, which reached up another seven feet or so to the edge of the roof, and the triangular pitched roof of the pickle factory next-door. A series of these triangular sections, like waves in a child's drawing of the sea, led away for sixty feet or so, glinting wetly in the light from the low sky.

"Better now?" said Jim.

"Aye. Heights, you know."

"What's it all about? Who are those blokes?"

"The wee man's called Windlesham. It's a complicated matter. . . . There's murder involved."

He looked uncanny: chalk-white face with black eyes and lips, black cloak, white shirt front; he looked bleached and inhuman. Jim looked at him closely.

"Murder?" he said. "Whose murder?"

"Can we get down from here?" said Mackinnon, looking around.

Jim rubbed his chin, then said, "There's a fire escape at the other end of this roof. Don't make too much noise—there's an old feller on watch inside, guarding the pickles."

He shinned up the sloping side of the first section and dropped silently down on the other. They were about six feet in height, and slippery with the recent rain; Mackinnon slipped and fell twice before they reached the fire escape. *What am I doing this for?* thought Jim, helping Mackinnon up and marveling at his frailness. He was as light as a child.

But he'd meant it about the murder. He was terrified, and not only of heights.

The fire escape was a slender iron staircase bolted to the side of the factory. It led down to a yard that was dark, fortunately, and this side of the building was quiet. Trembling, sweating, ghastly with fear, Mackinnon inched himself over the edge of the roof and found the first step, then went down on his backside, eyes shut tight. Jim reached the ground ahead of him and took his arm.

"Brandy," Mackinnon was muttering.

"Don't be soft," said Jim. "You can't go into a pub dressed like that—you wouldn't last five minutes. Where d'you live?"

"Chelsea. Oakley Street."

"Got any money on you?"

"Not a penny. Oh, God . . ."

"All right, come with me. I'll take you somewhere you can change your clothes and have a drink—and we'll talk about this murder business. Sounds a prime lark to me."

Mackinnon, drained of will and even of the capacity for surprise, showed no reaction as the young stage-hand with the green eyes and the rough clothes led him around into the street, hailed a cab, and in the most authoritative manner imaginable, gave an address in Bloomsbury.

3

The Photographers

JIM PAID OFF THE CAB IN BURTON STREET, A QUIET LITTLE
row of three-story shops and houses not far from
the British Museum, and while Mackinnon glanced
around nervously, unlocked the door of a neat, double-
fronted shop with GARLAND AND LOCKHART, PHOTOG-
RAPHERS painted over the window. He led Mackinnon
through the darkened shop into a warm, well-lit room
behind it.

This was furnished as an odd mixture of laboratory,
kitchen, and shabbily comfortable sitting room. A
bench laden with chemicals stood along one wall; a
sink occupied one corner, and a battered armchair and
sofa stood on either side of a black-leaded range. A
pungent reek filled the air.

Most of the reek came from the short clay pipe
being smoked by one of the two men in the room. He
was about sixty years old, tall and powerfully built,
with stiff gray hair and a beard of the same color. He
looked up from the table as Jim came in.

"Hello, Mr. Webster," said Jim. "Wotcher, Fred."

The other man was much younger: mid-twenties,

about Mackinnon's age. He was lean and sardonic-looking; his expression was a vivid mixture of sharp humor and a cool, intelligent thoughtfulness. Just as Mackinnon compelled attention, so did something about this man—though it might have been the dramatically disordered fair hair, or the broken nose.

"Greetings, O strange one," he said. "Oh, I beg your pardon, I didn't see you . . ."

These last words he directed to Mackinnon, who was standing in the doorway like a phantom. Jim turned to him.

"Mr. Webster Garland and Mr. Fred Garland, photographic artists," he said. "And this is Mr. Mackinnon, the Wizard of the North."

They got up to shake hands. Webster said enthusiastically, "I saw you perform last week—marvelous! At the Alhambra. You'll have a glass of whiskey?"

Mackinnon sat down in the armchair while Jim perched on a stool by the bench. As Webster poured the drinks Jim said, "We had to get out over the roof. The thing is, Mr. Mackinnon had to leave in a hurry, and he's left his normal clothes in the dressing room, not to mention his money and other bits and pieces. I can probably pick 'em up in the morning, but he's in a fair bit of trouble by the look of things. So I thought we might be able to help."

Seeing Mackinnon's doubtful look, Frederick said, "This is Garland's Detective Agency, Mr. Mackinnon. We've tackled most things in our time. What's your problem?"

"I'm not sure I . . ." Mackinnon began. "I don't know whether it's a suitable case for a detective

agency. It's . . . very vague, very . . . shadowy. I
don't know . . ."

"It can't do any harm to hear it," said Jim. "There
won't be any fee if we don't take it on, so you've got
nothing to lose."

Webster raised his eyebrows slightly at the coldness
in Jim's voice. Jim had begun to be irritated by
Mackinnon, by his shifty, furtive manner, by his
unpleasant combination of the helpless and the sly.

Frederick said, "Jim's right, Mr. Mackinnon. No
engagement, no fee. And you can trust our discretion.
Whatever you tell us here will stay secret."

Mackinnon looked from Frederick to Webster and
back again and made up his mind.

"Aye," he said. "Very well. I'll tell you about it, but
I'm not sure whether I want any detecting done. It
might be best to let the whole thing blow over. We'll
see."

He drained his glass, and Webster filled it again.

"You mentioned murder," Jim prompted.

"I'll come to that. What d'ye know about spiritualism, gentlemen?"

Frederick raised his eyebrows. "Spiritualism?
Funny you should say that. A man asked me today to
look into some spiritualist affair. Fraud, I expect."

"There are many frauds, aye," said Mackinnon.
"But there are some who have a genuine gift for the
psychic, and I'm one. And in my profession it's a
handicap, despite what you might think. I try not to
let the two things overlap. What I do on stage looks
like magic, but it's only technique. Anyone could do
what I do if they practiced.

"But the other side, the psychic side . . . that's a gift. What I do is called psychometry. D'ye know the term?"

"I've heard it, yes," said Frederick. "You take an object and you can tell from it all sorts of things—is that right?"

"I'll show you," said Mackinnon. "Have you got something I can try it with?"

Frederick reached across the bench where he was sitting and picked up a little circular object of brass, not unlike a heavy pocket watch without a face. Mackinnon took it, sat forward, and held it in both hands, eyes shut, frowning.

"I can see . . . dragons. Red, carved dragons. And a woman . . . Chinese. She's dignified and very still, and she's watching, just watching. . . . There's a man on a bed or a couch of some sort. He's asleep. No, he's moving, he's dreaming. He's crying out. . . . There's someone coming. A servant. A Chinaman. With a . . . with a pipe. He's crouching down. . . . He's got a taper from the lamp. . . . He's lighting the pipe. There's a sweet smell, sickly . . . opium. There, it's gone now." He opened his eyes and looked up again. "Something to do with opium," he said. "Am I right?"

Frederick ran his hands through his hair, too amazed to speak. His uncle sat back and laughed, and even Jim felt impressed—by the brooding atmosphere Mackinnon evoked, by his still concentration, as much as by what he said.

"You've hit the bull's-eye," said Frederick, leaning forward and taking the brass object from his hand. "D'you know what this is?"

"I've no idea," said Mackinnon.

Frederick wound up a small key in the side of it and pressed a button. From inside the mechanism a long thin ribbon of whitish metal unwound itself, coiling in a heap on the bench in front of him.

"It's a magnesium burner," he said. "You set the end alight and it burns down, and the spring shoves it out at exactly the same rate, so that you have a constant light for taking pictures by. I last used this in an opium den in Limehouse, taking pictures of the poor devils who smoke the stuff. . . . So that's psychometry, eh? I'm impressed. How does it happen? D'you see a picture in your mind, or what?"

"Something like that," said Mackinnon. "It's like having a dream when you're awake. I can't control it. It comes into my mind at the oddest times. And this is the point: I've seen a murder, and the murderer knows I have, but I don't know his name."

"Good start," said Frederick. "Promising. You'd better tell us all about it. More whiskey?"

He filled Mackinnon's glass, and sat back to listen.

"It was six months ago," began Mackinnon. "I was performing in a private house for a nobleman. It's something I do from time to time—more as a guest, you understand, than a hired entertainer."

"You do it without a fee, you mean?" said Jim. He was finding Mackinnon's condescending manner and high, slightly grating, genteel Scottish voice increasingly hard to bear.

"There is a professional charge, naturally," said Mackinnon stiffly.

"Who was the nobleman?" said Frederick.

"I would rather not say. A man of great prominence

in political life. There is no need for his name to be mentioned.

"As you wish," said Frederick affably. "Please go on."

"I was invited for dinner on the evening of the performance. That is my usual practice. I am one of the guests; that is understood by all. While the ladies withdrew after dinner and the gentlemen remained in the dining room, I went into the music room of this particular house and prepared the items I needed for my performance.

"I noticed that someone had left a cigar case on the lid of the piano, and I picked it up, meaning to put it out of the way somewhere, and at once I had the strongest psychometric impressions I've ever experienced.

"It was a river in a forest—a northern forest, with dark pines and snow, and a lowering, dark gray sky. There were two men walking together on the bare ground by the bank, talking angrily. I couldn't hear them, but I could see them as clearly as I see you now, and suddenly one of them took his stick, drew a sword out of it, and ran the other man through and through—not a moment's warning—in and out of his chest three, four, five, six times. I could see the dark blood on the snow.

"When the may lay still, the killer looked around for a clump of moss and wiped his sword clean, then bent and took the dead man by the feet and dragged him away toward the water. The snow was beginning to fall. And then I heard a splash as the body fell into the water."

He paused and sipped his whiskey. Either it's true,

thought Jim, or he's a better actor than I take him for, because Mackinnon was sweating with fear, and his eyes were haunted. But then, damn him, he was a performer—that was his profession. . . .

Mackinnon went on. "I came to myself after a few moments and found I was still holding the cigar case. Before I could put it down, the door of the music room opened and in came the very man I'd just seen. He was one of the guests—a big, powerful man, with smooth fair hair. He saw what I was holding and came up to take it from me, and our eyes met, and he *knew* what I'd seen. . . .

"He didn't speak to me, because at the same moment a servant came into the room. He turned to the servant and said, 'Thank you, I've found it now,' and with a last look at me, he went out again. But he knew.

"I went through my performance that night, and everywhere I looked I seemed to see that sudden furious stabbing and the dark blood gushing out onto the snow. And his smooth, powerful face was looking at me all the time. Well, naturally, I didn't let my host down. The performance was a great success—I was generously applauded by everyone there; and several gentlemen were good enough to say that the great Maskelyne himself had never done better. When I'd finished, I gathered my materials and left at once instead of mingling politely with the guests, as I usually did. You see, I was beginning to be afraid of him.

"Ever since then I've lived in fear of meeting him again. And one day recently that wee man with the glasses—Windlesham—came to me and said that his employer would like to meet me. I knew who he meant, though he wouldn't say his name. And this evening he came again, with a gang this time—well, you saw them, Jim. He said that he was obliged to take me to his employer to settle a question of mutual interest—that was how he put it.

"They want to kill me. They're going to take me and kill me, I'm certain of it. What can I do, Mr. Garland? What can I do?"

Frederick scratched his head.

"You don't know the man's name?" he said.

"There were a lot of guests that night. I may have been told his name, but I can't remember. And Windlesham wouldn't say."

"What makes you think they want to kill you?"

"This evening he said if I didn't agree to come with them after the show, there would be extremely serious consequences. If I were an ordinary person, I'd go into hiding. Change my name, perhaps. But I'm an artist! I have to be visible to earn my living! How can I hide? Half of London knows my name!"

"That should make you safer, then," said Webster Garland. "Whoever he is, he'd hardly dare to harm you if you're in the full glare of public attention, surely?"

"Not this man. I've never seen such ruthlessness on any human face. And besides, he's got powerful friends—he's wealthy and well connected. I'm just a lowly conjurer. Oh, what can I do?"

Suppressing the suggestion that came to his mind, Jim got up and left the room for a breath of fresh air.

He was finding it more and more difficult to control his irritation with the man. It was hard to pin down why, but he'd seldom met anyone he disliked more.

He sat in the backyard and shied bits of gravel through the unglazed window of the new studio Webster was having built until he heard a cab being called to the front door. When he thought Mackinnon had gone, he went back inside, where he found Webster lighting his pipe with a spill from the fire and Frederick winding the magnesium back into the pocket burner.

Frederick looked up and said, "Nice little mystery, Jim. Why'd you get up and leave?"

Jim flung himself down into the armchair. "He was getting on my nerves," he said. "And I don't know why, so don't ask. I wish I'd left him to it instead of risking me neck hauling him over the rooftops. *I canna stand the heights! Oh, let me doon, let me doon!* And his blooming snobbishness. *Of course, Ai'm treated as quaite one of the guests.* . . . Great shivering Tomnoddy. You ain't taken him on, have you, Fred? As a client, I mean?"

"He didn't want to be taken on—quite. It's *pro*tection he wants, not *de*tection, and I told him we didn't deal in that. But I've got his address, and I said we'd keep our eyes open on his behalf. I don't know what else we can do at this stage."

"Chuck him out for a start," said Jim. "Tell him to take a jump at himself."

"Whatever for? If he's telling the truth, it's interesting, and if he's lying, it's even more interesting. I take it you think he's lying."

"Course he is," said Jim. "I never heard such a package of whoppers in all me life."

"You mean the psychometry?" said Webster, settling back on the sofa. "What about his little demonstration? I was impressed, even if you weren't."

"You're an easy mark, you are," said Jim. "I pity you if you ever come up against the three-card trick. He's a conjurer, ain't he? He knows more about cunning little bits o' machinery than even Fred here. He knew what that thing was, and he saw that photograph you're so proud of up there, and he put two and two together and had you gaping like a pair of yokels."

Webster looked up at the mantelpiece, where Frederick had pinned a print of one of their pictures from the opium den, and then laughed and flung a cushion at Jim, who fielded it neatly and tucked it behind his head.

"All right," said Frederick, "I give you that one. But the other story about the forest and the murder in the snow—what d'you make of that?"

"You poor cod," said Jim. "You didn't believe that, did you? I despair, Fred. I thought you had a bit of milk in your coconut. Since you can't see what's obvious, I'll have to tell you. He's got something on this geezer, this guest at the dinner party. Blackmail, see. Naturally the bloke wants to get him out the way, and I don't blame him. And if you don't like that for an explanation, try this one: He's been playing goose and duck with the feller's wife, and he's been found out."

"That's what I like about Jim's mentality," said

Frederick to Webster, "if that's what it is: it goes straight for the basic. No unnecessary frills, no higher motives—"

Jim jeered. "You *did* believe him! You're getting soft, mate, and no error. Sally wouldn't fall for a tale like that. But, then, she's got a head on her shoulders."

Frederick's face darkened. "Don't talk to me about that ranting jade," he said.

"Ranting jade! That's a good 'un. What was it you called her last time? A fanatical, narrow-minded calculating machine. And she called you a feckless, feather-brained fantasist, and you called her—"

"Enough, damn it! I want nothing more to do with her. Tell me about—"

"I bet you go and see her before the week's out!"

"Done. Half a guinea I don't."

And they shook hands.

"*Do* you believe him, Fred?" said his uncle.

"I don't have to believe him to wonder about his case. As I said a moment ago—only Jim doesn't remember—if he's lying, it makes the whole business more interesting, not less. In any case, I've got spiritualism on my mind at the moment. When this kind of coincidence comes up, I always take it as a hint there's something going on."

"Poor old Fred," said Jim. "The decay of a fine mind. . . ."

"What about spiritualism, then?" said Webster. "Is there anything in it?"

"Plenty," said Frederick, refilling his glass. "There's fraud, there's gullibility, there's fear—not so much fear of death as fear of there being nothing after it—there's loneliness, there's hope, there's vanity; and maybe in the middle of it all there's something real."

"Get away," said Jim. "It's all poppycock."

"Well, if you want to find out, tomorrow night there's a meeting of the Streatham and District Spiritualist League—"

"Load o' rubbish!"

"—which might interest your broad, sympathetic, and ever-open mind. Especially as there's something odd going on. Care to come along and have a look?"

4

Nellie Budd

FREDERICK WASN'T THE ONLY PERSON TO BE INTERESTED IN spiritualism, by a long way. It was one of the burning concerns of the time. Humble parlors, fashionable drawing rooms, and university laboratories alike all echoed to the sounds of rapping and knocking as spirits with nothing better to do tried to communicate with the living; and stories circulated of even stranger manifestations—ghostly voices, spirit trumpets, and mediums who could exude a mysterious substance called ectoplasm. . . .

It was a solemn business. Was there life after death? Were phantasms and apparitions really there? Was mankind on the verge of the greatest discovery in history? Many earnest people took it all very seriously, and no one was more earnest than the Streatham and District Spiritualist League, which was meeting in the house of Mrs. Jamieson Wilcox, widow of a most respectable grocer.

Frederick had been invited by one of the members, a city clerk who was perturbed by some things he'd heard in the course of a séance. The man insisted that

Frederick should disguise himself; he was embarrassed at spying on his friends, but he'd told Frederick that there were great issues involved, matters of enormous financial implication, and he dared not ignore it. Frederick readily agreed. He became a scientist for the evening, and Jim went as his assistant.

"The only thing you have to do," Frederick told Jim, "is listen. Remember every word. Ignore the flying tambourines and the ghostly hands—they're two a penny at a do like this. Just concentrate on what the medium says."

His hair was slicked down, and a pair of owlish glasses sat oddly on his broken nose. Jim, interested despite himself, carried a small brass-bound box and a battery case, and grumbled all the way to Streatham about the weight.

By seven o'clock Mrs. Jamieson Wilcox's front parlor was crowded: twelve people packed in like dates, hardly able to move. All the smaller items of furniture had been moved out for the occasion, but that still left a substantial table, a piano, three armchairs, a laden whatnot, and a sideboard on which a black-draped portrait of the late Mr. Jamieson Wilcox was kept company by a solemn pineapple.

The room was warm, not to say hot. The gaslights on the ornamental brackets were turned up high, and a coal fire burned in the grate. The assembled spiritualists put out a good deal of fleshly heat themselves, fortified by the meat tea they had consumed earlier, and the odors of tinned salmon, cold tongue, potted shrimp, beetroot, and blancmange lingered heavily in the air. There was a good deal of brow-mopping and fanning, but no one would have considered for a moment removing a jacket or loosening a tie.

The meeting proper was due to start at half past seven, and as the time drew near, a stout and commanding gentleman opened his watch and coughed loudly to attract everyone's attention. This was Mr. Freeman Humphries, retired draper and chairman of the league.

"Ladies and gentlemen!" he began. "Friends and comrades in the search for truth! Let me begin on your behalf by proposing a vote of thanks to Mrs. Jamieson Wilcox for the substantial and delicious repast we have just enjoyed." There were murmurs of assent. "Next, may I welcome Mrs. Budd, the well-known medium and clairvoyant, whose messages so impressed and consoled us on her last visit." He turned and bowed slightly to a plump, dark woman with a roguish eye, who smiled back at him saucily. He coughed again and shuffled his notes. "And finally I am sure you would all like to make the acquaintance of Dr. Herbert Semple and his associate, of the Royal Institution. I call upon Dr. Semple, then, to explain the purpose of this meeting tonight and to say something about his research."

This was Frederick's cue. He stood up and looked around the crowded room at the shopkeepers and clerks and their wives, at the pallid young man with the sniff and the pallid young woman with the jet necklace, at Mrs. Budd the medium (whose eyes traveled admiringly down his frock-coated form), at Mrs. Jamieson Wilcox, at the pineapple.

"Thank you, Mr. Humphries," he began. "Capital

tea, Mrs. Wilcox. First rate. Well, ladies and gentlemen, I'm very grateful to you for inviting me. My
assistant and I have been interested for some time in
the investigation of the trance state, particularly in
relation to the electrical conductivity of the skin. This
box"—Jim lifted it onto the table, and Frederick
opened it to disclose a copper coil, a mass of twisted
wire, brass terminals, and a large glass dial—"is an
improved version of the electrodermograph, invented
by Professor Schneider of Boston."

He passed a length of wire to Jim to connect to the
batteries, and then uncoiled four more lengths, each
ending in a little brass disc. They were all connected
to the copper coil.

"These wires are attached to the medium's ankles
and wrists," he explained, "and the resistance is
shown on the dial. Mrs. Budd, may we connect you
up?"

"You can connect me to your apparatus anytime,
dear," she said brightly.

Frederick coughed. "Ahem . . . good. Could one
of the ladies perhaps oblige by fastening the wires
to Mrs. Budd's ankles? It's a delicate matter, I
know . . ."

But Mrs. Budd was having nothing to do with
delicacy.

"Oh, no," she said, "you do it, love, so's I don't get
electrified. Besides, you've got the gift, haven't you? I
knew it as soon as I saw you, dear. You've got
spirituality shining out of you."

"Oh," said Frederick, aware that Jim was grinning
widely at him. "Well, in that case . . ."

Trailing wires, he plunged beneath the tablecloth while the ladies and gentlemen of the Spiritualistic League, caught between the impropriety of a young man's actually touching a pair of female ankles and the evident spirituality of both parties, coughed and talked and looked genteelly elsewhere. After a minute Frederick emerged and pronounced the wires attached.

"And very gentle you done it, too," said Mrs. Budd. "I hardly knew you was touching me. Such artistic fingers!"

"Well," said Frederick, delivering a sharp kick to Jim's ankle. "Shall we try the apparatus?"

He threw a switch, and the needle sprang away from the stop and trembled at the center of the dial.

"Fancy that," said Mrs. Budd. "It doesn't even tingle."

"Oh, there's no danger, Mrs. Budd; the current is very mild. Now, ladies and gentlemen, shall we take our places at the table?"

Chairs were drawn up, and the spiritualists and their guests jammed themselves as comfortably as they could around the table. Frederick sat on one side of Mrs. Budd with the electrodermograph in front of him, and before he could escape, Jim was seized by a strong, beringed hand and planted firmly on the other.

"Lights, Mrs. Wilcox, if you please," said Mr. Freeman Humphries, and the hostess turned down the gaslights one by one before taking her place. Only the faintest glow now filtered down. A hush fell over the company.

"Can you see your apparatus, Dr. Semple?" enquired a spectral voice.

"Perfectly, thank you. The needle is coated with luminous paint. Ready when you are, Mrs. Budd."

"Thank you, dear," she said placidly. "Join hands, ladies and gentlemen."

Hands felt for one another and lay palm to palm around the edge of the table. The circle was joined. Frederick peered down at the box, his right hand folded in Mrs. Budd's warm, moist one, his left clutching the bony fingers of the pallid young woman on his other side.

Silence fell.

After a minute Mrs. Budd gave a long, shuddering sigh. Her head had fallen forward and she seemed to be slumbering. Suddenly she woke up and began to speak—in a man's voice.

"Ella?" she said. "Ella, my dear?"

It was a rich voice, a fruity voice, and more than one person in the circle felt the hairs prickle on their necks in response. Mrs. Jamieson Wilcox started and said faintly, "Oh! Charles—Charles! Is it you?"

"It is indeed, my dear," answered the voice—a man's voice, a voice no woman could imitate, a voice with sixty-seven years of port and cheese and raisins in it. "Ella, my dear, though the veil has parted us, let not our love grow cold. . . ."

"Oh, never, Charles! Never!"

"I am with you night and day, my dear. Tell Filkins in the shop to mind his cheese."

"Mind the cheese—yes—"

"And pay heed to our boy Victor. I fear he may be falling in with low companions."

"Oh, dear! Charles, what can I—"

"Fear not, Ella. The blessed light is shining—the golden land beckons, and I must depart. Remember the cheese, Ella. Filkins is not sufficiently careful with his napkins. I go . . . I depart . . ."

"Oh, Charles! Oh, Charles! Farewell, beloved!"

A sight, and the spirit of the grocer departed. Mrs. Budd shook her head as if to clear it; Mrs. Jamieson Wilcox wept discreetly into a black-edged handkerchief, and then the circle was resumed.

Frederick looked around. In the dimness it was impossible to make out anyone's features, but the atmosphere had changed: people were excited now, tense with expectation and ready to be convinced. This woman was good. Frederick had no doubt she was faking, but he hadn't come here to listen to dead grocers talk about cheese.

And then it happened.

Mrs. Budd gave a convulsive little shudder, and began to talk in a low voice—her own voice, this time, but brimming with fear and horror.

"The spark . . ." she said. "There's a wire, and the counter going round—hundred and one, hundred and two, hundred and—no, no, no . . . Bell. Bells. The bellman. Such a pretty ship, and the little girl dead . . . It isn't Hopkinson, but they're not to know. No. Keep it in the shadows. Sword in the forest—oh, blood on the snow, and the ice—he's still there, all in a glass coffin . . . The Regulator. Three hundred pounds—four hundred—North Star! There's a shadow in the north . . . a mist all full of fire—steam, and it's packed with death, packed in pipes—steampipes—under the North Star—oh, horrible . . ."

Her voice trailed away, with infinite sadness, into silence.

This was what Frederick had come to hear, and though he didn't understand it, her tone made his flesh creep. She sounded like someone in the toils of a nightmare.

The other spiritualists sat with reverent attention. No one moved. But then, with a loud sigh, Mrs. Budd woke up, and took charge again.

A loud chord resounded from the piano. Everyone jumped, and the three silver-framed photographs on the top vibrated in sympathy.

A furious rapping came from the center of the table. Heads jerked in surprise, only to be lifted upward toward a pale, tremulous glow that was materializing on the ceiling. Mrs. Budd, eyes closed, seemed to be at the center of an invisible storm. Frederick was aware that she was controlling it all, but it was still impressive: the curtains waved, the strings of the piano jangled wildly, and then the heavy table under its damask cloth began to heave and sway like a boat on a surging sea. A tambourine on the mantelpiece jingled once and then fell with a crash onto the hearth.

"A physical manifestation!" cried Mr. Humphries. "Keep still, everyone! Observe the phenomena! The spirits will not harm us—"

But evidently the spirits had other intentions regarding the electrodermograph, because there was a sudden blinding flash from it, with a loud crack and a smell of burning. Mrs. Budd cried out in alarm, and Frederick leaped up hastily.

"Lights! Lights, if you please, Mrs. Wilcox!"

As the hostess, in all the confusion, turned up the nearest gaslight, Frederick bent over the medium, unfastening the wires from her wrists.

"Wonderful result!" he was saying. "Mrs. Budd, you've surpassed all my expectation! An unparalleled reading—you're not hurt? No, of course you're not. Machine's broken, but that doesn't matter. Couldn't take the reading! Went right off the dial! Marvelous!"

Beaming with triumph, he nodded at the bewildered spiritualists, who were blinking in the light. Jim disconnected the wires from the battery while Mrs. Budd rubbed her wrists.

"Sorry and all that, Mrs. Wilcox," Frederick went on. "Didn't want to break up the séance, but d'you see, this is scientific proof! When I publish my paper, this meeting of the Streatham and District Spiritualist League will be seen to mark a turning point in the history of psychical research. No, that wouldn't surprise me at all. Wonderful result."

Gratified by this, the circle broke up, and Mrs. Jamieson Wilcox, whose nature turned automatically to sustenance at moments of crisis, suggested a nice cup of tea all around. It was soon brought in; Mrs. Budd was surrounded by a small group of admirers, and Frederick and Mr. Humphries conversed earnestly by the fire while Jim packed the electrodermograph away, with the help of the prettiest girl in the room.

Presently some of the guests rose to leave, and Frederick rose with them. He shook hands all around, detached Jim from the girl, and paid an especially appreciative tribute to Mrs. Budd before leaving the house.

A thin, nervous, middle-aged man left at the same time, as if by chance, and walked with them toward the station. As soon as they turned a corner Frederick stopped and took off his glasses.

"That's better," he said, rubbing his eyes. "Well, Mr. Price. Is that what you expected? Does she always do that?"

Mr. Price nodded. "I'm sorry about your machine," he said. He had the air of being sorry about most things.

"Nothing to be sorry about. What d'you know about electricity?"

"Nothing at all, I'm afraid to say."

"Nor do most people. I could wire up this box to a cucumber and tell 'em it contained the soul of their uncle Albert, and if the needle jumped, they'd never know the difference. No, this is a camera."

"Oh! But I thought you had to have chemicals and all sorts . . ."

"Used to with the old wet-collodion plates. Had to slap the stuff on fresh every time. This is loaded with a gelatin plate—new invention. Much more convenient."

"Ah."

"And the flash was deliberate. Can't take photographs in the dark. I look forward to seeing Nellie Budd up to her tricks when I develop the plate. . . . But that stuff about sparks and shadows and the North Star. That was different."

"Indeed, Mr. Garland. That was what alarmed me in the first place. I've seen Mrs. Budd four times now, and each time she's gone into a trance like that, quite different from the rest of the performance, and she's come out with details of matters I know about in the city—financial dealings, things like that—highly confidential, some of them. It's inexplicable."

"Did you recognize any of that stuff tonight? Who's this Hopkinson, for instance?"

"That name means nothing to me, Mr. Garland. Her colloquy was dark and obscure tonight. Only the business about the bells, and North Star . . ."

"Well?"

"She said *the bellman*, if you remember. Well, that's the name of my employer—Mr. Bellmann. Axel Bellmann, the Swedish financier. And North Star is the name of a new company he's formed. What I fear is that word will get out, you see, Mr. Garland, and suspicion attach to myself. . . . A clerk has only his good name for recommendation. My wife's not very well, and if anything should happen to me, I dread to think . . ."

"Yes, I understand."

"I'm afraid the poor lady—Mrs. Budd, I mean—is under the control of a disembodied intelligence," said Mr. Price, blinking under the gaslight in the slight drizzle.

"Quite possibly," said Frederick. "Well, you've certainly shown me something interesting, Mr. Price. Leave it with us—and stop worrying."

"ALL RIGHT," said Jim in the train, ten minutes later. "I changed me mind. There *is* something in it."

Frederick, balancing the camera on his knees, had just written down what Nellie Budd had said in her strange trance, at Jim's dictation. Jim was good with words; he'd remembered it all. And he'd spotted something odd.

"It links up with Mackinnon!" he said, reading it back.

"Don't be daft," said Frederick.

"It bloody does, mate. Listen. *Sword in the forest— oh, blood on the snow, and the ice—he's still there, all in a glass coffin . . .*"

Frederick looked doubtful. "Could be. I don't understand the glass coffin, though. I thought that was the Sleeping Beauty. Blood on the snow . . . that's what's-her-name, Snow White or Rose Red or someone. Fairy tales. But I thought you didn't believe him?"

"You don't have to believe it to see a connection, do you? It *is* part of the Mackinnon business. Betcher ten bob."

"Oh, no. I'm not taking bets where Mackinnon's concerned. He sounds as if he's likely to pop up all over the place. Look, I want to get this plate developed. You take the batteries to Burton Street, and I'll take a cab to Piccadilly and call on Charlie."

5

A Financial Consultation

S. Lockhart, the financial consultant, was working late. The city outside her office was dark and quiet, and her coal fire was burning low. A great deal of paper was scattered about the carpet, some of it crumpled and thrown toward the wastepaper basket, the rest of it arranged in rough piles according to some complicated system. Sally herself sat at the desk, scissors and paste at one elbow, a mass of newspapers, letters, certificates, and files at the other, while an atlas opened at a map of the Baltic countries occupied the blotting pad.

Chaka lay in his place in front of the fire, his great head lolling sideways, his forefeet occasionally twitching as he dreamed.

Sally's hair was giving her trouble; it would not stay up, and she frequently had to push it out of her eyes with an impatient hand. Her eyes were strained. She looked up for the twentieth time at the gaslight, measuring its distance from the desk and wondering whether it would be worth the effort to push the desk closer and disarrange the papers on the floor, and then decided it wouldn't. She turned back to the atlas with a magnifying glass.

Suddenly the dog sat up and growled.

"What is it, Chaka?" she said softly, and listened. After a moment there came a knock on the distant street door, and Sally got up, lit a candle from the gaslight, and fitted it into a little lantern to keep it from drafts.

"Come on, boy," she said, taking a key from the table. "Let's go and see who it is."

The massive creature got to his feet and stretched, yawning redly, before padding after her down the two flights of stairs. The empty building loomed dark and silent around the little moving pool of light, but she knew it well; it held no terrors.

She unlocked the street door and looked coldly at the figure on the step.

"Well?" she said.

"Do you want me to go through it all on the doorstep?" said Frederick Garland. "Or am I invited in?"

She moved aside without a word. Chaka growled, and she put a hand on his collar as Frederick moved ahead of her up the stairs. Neither of them spoke.

When they reached her office, Frederick dropped his hat and coat on the floor and put the camera down carefully before pulling one of the chairs closer to the fire. The dog growled again.

"Tell that brute I'm friendly," he said.

Sally stroked the dog's head, and Chaka sat down alertly by her side. She remained standing.

"I'm busy," she said. "What do you want?"

"What do you know about spiritualism?"

"Oh, really, Fred," she said in exasperation. "Is this some silly game? I've got work to do."

"Or a man called Mackinnon? A magician?"

"Never heard of him."

"All right, another man. His name's Bellmann. And something called North Star."

Her eyes widened. She felt for her own chair and sat down slowly.

"Yes, I've heard of him," she said. "What's it all about?"

He told her briefly about the séance in Streatham and handed her the paper with Jim's writing on it. She blinked and screwed up her eyes.

"Did Jim write this?" she said. "I can usually read his writing, but—"

"He wrote it on the train," Frederick told her. "You ought to get this place fitted out with some decent lights. Here, let me read it to you."

He did so. When he'd finished, he looked up and saw an expression of distant excitement on her face.

"Well?" he said.

"What do you know about Axel Bellmann?" she said.

"Hardly anything at all. He's a financier, and my client works for him. That's all I know."

"And you call yourself a detective?"

She spoke scornfully but without malice and bent to sort through some papers at her feet. Her hair fell forward again; impatiently she shook it out and then looked up at him, her cheeks flushed and her eyes bright. He felt the familiar wave of helpless love, followed by the equally familiar wave of angry resignation. How could this untidy, half-ignorant financial obsessive have such a power over him?

He sighed and saw she was holding out a paper. He took it and read her clear, swift handwriting:

AXEL BELLMANN—BORN SWEDEN(?) 1835(?)—FIRST CAME TO PROMINENCE IN BALTIC TIMBER TRADE—MATCH FACTORIES IN GÖTEBORG, STOCKHOLM—FACTORY IN VILNA CLOSED DOWN ON GOVERNMENT ORDERS FOLLOWING FIRE IN WHICH THIRTY-FIVE WORKERS DIED—SHIPPING INTERESTS: ANGLO-BALTIC STEAM NAVIGATION COMPANY—MINING, IRON FOUNDING—BUYS CHEAPLY COMPANIES THAT ARE FAILING, CLOSES THEM DOWN, SELLS OFF THEIR ASSETS—FIRST CAME TO ENGLAND 1865—OBSCURE SCANDAL INVOLVING MEXICAN RAILWAYS—DISAPPEARED—BELIEVED JAILED IN MEXICO, 1868–9—NEXT HEARD OF IN RUSSIA WITH PARTNER ARNE NORDENFELS IN SCHEME AGAIN INVOLVING RAILWAYS(?)—NO TRACE OF NORDENFELS AFTER BELLMANN ARRIVED IN LONDON 1873, APPARENTLY WITH LIMITLESS FUNDS—PAPERS GAVE HIM NICKNAME THE STEAM KING—PROMOTED NEW COMPANIES, PRINCIPALLY MINING, CHEMICALS—FINANCIAL INTERESTS IN STEAM POWER, RAILWAYS, ETC.—NORTH STAR?—UNMARRIED—ADDRESS: 47 HYDE PARK GATE; BALTIC HOUSE, THREAD NEEDLE STREET.

Frederick handed back the paper. "He sounds a shifty sort of character. Why are you interested in him?"

"I've got a client who lost all her money in the Anglo-Baltic shipping company. It was my fault, Fred; it was awful. I advised her to invest in it, and a few months later it collapsed. There was no warning at all. . . . I looked into it, and I think he did it deliberately. Just wiped it out. There must have been thousands of people who lost their money in that company. It was very cleverly done; you'd never suspect. But the more I look, the more I feel things aren't right. It's too vague to be sure about, but there's something nasty going on. This man Nordenfels . . ."

"His partner in Russia? The one there's no trace of?"

"Yes. I found out something today; I'll have to add it to that paper. Nordenfels was a designer of steam engines. He designed the engine of the *Ingrid Linde*— that was an Anglo-Baltic steamship that vanished on the way to Riga. It wasn't properly insured, and that was one of the things that ruined the company. But Nordenfels just vanished; there's no trace of him after he was seen in Russia."

Frederick scratched his head and leaned back, stretching his legs out carefully to avoid Chaka.

"And why's there a question mark after *North Star?*"

"Simply because I don't know what it is. That's why this séance of yours is so exciting. What did she say, again?"

She took the paper from him and peered closely.

"It isn't Hopkinson, but they're not to know. . . . And then she says *the Regulator.* This is amazing, Fred. This company—North Star—no one knows what it is or what it's for; certainly the papers don't. The only thing I've managed to find out is that it's somehow connected with a machine, or a process, or *something,* anyway, that's called the Hopkinson Self-Regulator."

"Steam engines have regulators," Frederick said.

"And he's called the Steam King, is he, this Bellmann character?"

"He used to be. I think he had someone working for him, a journalist perhaps, who'd put pieces about him in the papers—not real news but short pieces to make him seem interesting and important. To make him seem like someone worth investing in. And when he first came here, five or six years ago, and set up his first companies, that was what they used to call him. But they haven't used that name for some time now. And the stories they print are more like real news—not that there are many of them. He's hardly visible. But he's the richest man in Europe—and he's wicked, Fred. He destroys things. How many other people did as my client did and put their money into his company, only for him to ruin it deliberately? I'm going to fix him. I'm going to make him pay."

Her fists were clenched on her knees, and her eyes were blazing. The great dog growled softly at her side.

"But what about this spiritualism business?" Frederick said after a moment. "Is this medium—Mrs. Budd—is she genuinely picking up the stuff out of the ether or is she lying? I can't make it out."

"I don't know about her," said Sally. "But I knew some people at Cambridge—scientists—who were investigating it. There's something in it, I'm sure. She could be reading your client's mind, I suppose. He must have all the information at his fingertips."

"Possibly . . . though he didn't know anything about this spark business. Or three hundred pounds. Seems a pitiful sum of money if we're talking about the richest man in Europe."

"It might not be money," said Sally.

"Weight? Is he fat, then?"

"Steam engines," she said.

"Ah. Pressure. Three hundred pounds per square inch. Impossible. Perhaps that's what this self-regulator does. Prevents the pressure from building to that level. But there are valves for that sort of thing. Interesting stuff, Lockhart. I had another client only yesterday—well, not really a client. Jim brought him home from the music hall—conjurer chap. He's having visions or something—psychometry, he calls it—and he reckons he's seen a murder. I don't know what he thinks I can do about it. . . ."

"Hmm." Sally seemed to be thinking of something else. "Are you going to take this séance business on?" she said.

"You mean, as a case? I have done that already. I'm going to see Nellie Budd as soon as I've got the photograph developed, and see what she's got to say. Why?"

"Just don't get in my way."

He sat up angrily. "Well, I like that! I could say the same to you, you snooty frump, if I wasn't too polite. As it is, I'll hold my tongue. Don't get in my way, indeed!"

She smiled. "All right. Pax." Then the smile faded, and she looked tired again. "But please, Fred, be careful. I *must* get that money back. And if you find out anything useful, I'd be grateful to hear about it."

"Let's work together. Why not?"

"No. We'll get more done separately. I mean it."

She wouldn't budge, Frederick knew; and after a

few minutes he got up to leave. She saw him downstairs, with the huge black dog padding ahead of them into the darkness. Frederick turned on the step and held out his hand, and after a second's hesitation she took it.

"We'll share information," she said, "but that's all. Oh, by the way . . ."

"What?"

"I saw Jim this morning. You owe him half a guinea."

6

Lady Mary

FREDERICK LAUGHED.

"Well? What is it?" said Webster from the bench. It was the morning after the séance, and Frederick, having handed over half a guinea to a triumphant Jim, was developing the photograph of Nellie Budd.

"She's got four hands," said Frederick. "The light's good, too."

"Can't rely on it," said his uncle. "Stick to magnesium, that's my advice." He dried his hands and came to peer closely at the print Frederick was holding. "My word, she's up to a trick or two, isn't she?"

The medium was caught perfectly—one hand lifting up the edge of the table while the other was pulling at a string or thread connected to the curtains. Jim, on the far side of her, was clutching what looked like a stuffed glove.

"Seems silly now," Frederick said. "But the one I was holding felt just like a hand at the time. Look at Jim's face . . ."

Jim's cheerful features were caught in an expression halfway between a respectable piety and the alarm of someone about to lose his trousers. Webster laughed.

"Worth your half-guinea, that," he said. "What are you going to do with this now you've got it? Go and put the old girl out of business?"

"Oh, no," said Frederick. "I liked her too much for that. If the members of Streatham and District Spiritualist League are daft enough to fall for this, good luck to Nellie Budd, I say. I think I'll print a set and sell 'em. Call it *Apprehension, or Jim and the Spirits*. No, I'll just use it as a calling card when I go to see her."

FREDERICK HAD intended to go that same day, but at midmorning something happened to put it off: Mackinnon arrived, wrapped in a long cloak and wide-brimmed hat to avoid being recognized, but attracting more attention as he slipped through the shop in this furtive rig than if he'd turned up with a regiment of cavalry.

Webster was busy in the studio and Jim was out, so Frederick saw him alone in the room behind the shop.

"I need your help," said Mackinnon urgently as soon as they were sitting down. "I've got a private engagement this evening, and I'd like you to be there. In case, you know, the man . . ."

"A private engagement?"

"A charity performance at Lady Harborough's. A hundred people or so. They pay their five guineas and it goes to a hospital fund. I give my services free, of course. With a nominal charge for expenses."

"Well, what d'you want me to do? I told you I wasn't in the protection business. If you want a bodyguard—"

"No, no, not a bodyguard. I'd feel safer with someone else to watch out for him—it's no more than that. If he tries to contact me, you could engage him in conversation. Distract him, d'ye see?"

"I don't even know what he looks like. You're being confoundedly vague about all this, Mr. Mackinnon. You think he's pursuing you because he knows that you've seen a vision of him killing someone, but you don't know who, and you don't know where, and you don't know when, and you don't know what his name is, and you don't know—"

"I'm hiring you to find out all that," said Mackinnon. "If you can't do it, I'd be obliged if you'd recommend another detective who can."

He looked austere and commanding, and a little ridiculous in his bohemian cloak and hat. Frederick laughed.

"Very well," he said. "Since you put it like that, I'll do it. But I'm not bodyguarding you, mind. If this fellow tries to poke a sword through you, I shall whistle and look out the window. I've had my fill of brawling."

He rubbed his nose, which had been broken during a fight six years before on a lonely wharf in Wapping—a fight he'd been lucky to survive.

Mackinnon said, "You'll come, then?"

"Yes. But you'll have to tell me what to do. D'you want me to act as your assistant onstage, or what?"

Mackinnon's expression showed what he thought of that idea. Instead he produced an invitation card.

"Show this at the door, and pay your five guineas, and you can come in with the guests," he said.

"Evening dress, naturally. Just . . . look around. Watch the others. Be where I can see you easily. I'll find a way of letting you know who he is—if he's there. I don't know if he's coming or not. And if you see him, find out who he is. Well, you know what to do."

"Sounds easy enough," said Frederick. "There's only one flaw in it, which is that it'll be five of your guineas I hand over, not mine."

"Of course," said Mackinnon impatiently. "That's understood. Ye'll be there, then. I shall rely on you."

IF YOU CALLED at Burton Street and sat for a portrait, the photographer who'd take it, as likely as not, would be a dark, solidly built young man by the name of Charles Bertram, of whom Webster Garland thought very highly: he was imaginative and skillful, and his portraits caught a real air of life and movement. Charles Bertram had cause, as Sally had, to appreciate the casual bohemian democracy of the Garlands, for his father was a baron and he was an Honorable; and he'd have been doomed to remain an aristocratic amateur if he hadn't met Webster. But in the company of artists and technicians, only ability mattered, and Charles Bertram had plenty of that, so he took his place in the establishment with Jim the stagehand, and Frederick the detective, and Webster the genius, and occasionally Sally the financial consultant.

He wasn't just training to be a working photographer, of course. Taking portraits at two shillings and sixpence a time was no great mark to aim at. He and Webster were working at something much more ambitious: nothing less than the capture of movement itself on a photographic plate. He'd put some of his own money into the business, and they were having a larger studio built in the yard behind the shop, ready for the time when their experiments demanded more space. But in the meantime he helped around the shop and took his share of the odd jobs that arose— including, this morning, fitting a new lens to the main studio camera.

Frederick was in the kitchen, scribbling down his thoughts about Mackinnon and Nellie Budd and wondering if the two things did connect as Jim suspected, when Charles put his head around the door and said, "Fred?"

"Hello, Charlie," said Frederick. "Know anything about spiritualism?"

"Not a thing, I'm glad to say. Look, could you give me a hand with the new Voigtlander? I need someone to stand and . . ."

"Pleasure. And then you can do something for me," said Frederick, going with him into the cluttered, heavily-draped room they used as a studio.

When Charles's task was finished, Frederick explained the job he had on hand that evening for Mackinnon.

"Sounds a slippery sort of blighter," said Charles. "I saw him myself a week or two ago—at the Britannia. Jim told me to go. Astonishing skill he's got. . . . And he's being chased by someone, you say?"

"He says."

"It's Mephistopheles. Mackinnon's sold his soul, and the devil's coming to claim it."

"I wouldn't be at all surprised. But look, Charlie, you know all these people—Lord This and the Countess of That—you couldn't come along, could you, and point 'em out? Give me a race meeting or an opium den and I know where I am, but the English upper classes are a closed book to me. You busy tonight?"

"No. I'd be glad to come. Think there'll be a roughhouse? Should I take a pistol?"

Frederick laughed. "You know the manners of your peers, dear boy," he said. "If that's the usual form at a charity function, you'd better come prepared. But if people start throwing things, I shall nip out smartish, and I've told Mackinnon so."

LADY HARBOROUGH'S house in Berkeley Square was thronged when they arrived. They presented the invitation to a footman, paid their entrance money, and were shown into an overheated salon where gaslights and chandeliers blazed and glittered on the jewels of the women and the studded shirt fronts of the men. Double doors opened into a ballroom, where a small orchestra was playing discreet waltzes behind a stand of potted palms, almost drowned by the bray of aristocratic voices.

Charles and Frederick stood by the entrance to the ballroom and took glasses of champagne from a waiter.

"Which is Lady Harborough?" said Frederick. "I suppose I ought to know who she is."

"The old trout with the lorgnette," said Charles. "Over there by the fireplace, talking to Lady Wytham. I wonder if her daughter's here? She's a stunner."

"Whose daughter?"

"Wytham's. That's Lord Wytham talking to Sir Ashley Hayward—the racing man."

"Ah, yes. I know Hayward. By sight, that is. I won a tenner on his horse Grandee last year. So that's Lord Wytham, is it? The cabinet minister?"

Lord Wytham was a tall, gray-haired man with a strangely nervous look; his eyes flicked this way and that, he chewed his lip, and from time to time he lifted a hand to his mouth and gnawed at a finger like a hungry dog.

Near Lady Harborough, still and silent, sat a girl who Charles told him was Lady Mary Wytham. A couple of young men were talking loudly in the group around her, and she smiled politely every so often, but for most of the time she sat with her eyes cast down and her hands folded in her lap. As Charles had said, she was beautiful—though Frederick thought, as he felt the breath catch in his throat at his first glimpse of her, that *beautiful* wasn't quite the word. The girl was astoundingly lovely, with a grace and shyness and delicate coral coloring that made him want to reach for his camera—except that nothing, surely, could catch the bloom on her cheeks or the nervous animal tension in the line of her neck and shoulders.

Well, perhaps Webster could. Or Charles.

But it must be a strange family, he thought, for the father and daughter to share this controlled desperation. Lady Wytham, too, had a haunted air: she was handsome rather than beautiful like her daughter, but her eyes were dark and preoccupied in the same tragic way.

"Tell me about Wytham," he said to Charles.

"Well, now: seventh earl, seat on the Scottish borders somewhere, President of the Board of Trade—at least he was, but I gather Disraeli's moved him out of the Cabinet. Lady Mary's his only child; don't know much about her people. In fact, that's about all I do know. He's not the only politician here—look, there's Hartington as well . . ."

Charles mentioned half a dozen other names, any of which, Frederick supposed, could have belonged to Mackinnon's pursuer. But he found his eyes drawn back again and again to the slim, still figure of Lady Mary Wytham on the sofa by the fire in her white evening dress.

They had time for another glass of champagne, and then the main entertainment was announced. The double doors into the ballroom were thrown open to reveal a wide curve of chairs, several deep, which had been laid out facing a little stage. A velvet curtain was hung across the back of it, and the front was lined with ferns and little palms.

The orchestra had gone, but a pianist was waiting by the instrument that stood below the stage. The audience took five minutes or so to settle themselves; Frederick made sure that he and Charles were sitting close enough to the stage for Mackinnon to see them clearly, and with a clear run to the door if they should need it. He explained this to Charles, who laughed.

"You're making it sound like one of Jim's yarns," he said. "We'll have Spring-Heeled Jack leaping in next, or Deadwood Dick holding us all up and demanding our money. What are you actually expecting?"

"I haven't the faintest idea," said Frederick. "Nor's

Mackinnon, and that's half the problem. Look— here's our hostess."

Lady Harborough, assured by her staff that all the guests were ready, was on the platform, making a short speech in which she described the valuable work her hospital fund was doing. It seemed to consist largely of rescuing unmarried mothers from poverty and subjecting them to slavery instead, with the additional disadvantage of being preached at daily by evangelical clergymen.

However, the speech didn't last long. Lady Harborough was helped down from the stage; the pianist took his place, unfolded his music, and played a sinister series of arpeggios in the bass; and then the curtain was drawn aside, and Mackinnon appeared.

He was transformed. Jim had described it, but Frederick hadn't really believed him; now he blinked in amazement to see the furtive, shadowy figure he knew become so dominating and powerful. He was wearing his chalk-white make-up—bizarre at first sight, but in fact a brilliant stroke, because it allowed him to be at various times sinister and comic and appealing—a skull, or a clown, or a Pierrot.

And his appearance was an important part of the total effect. He didn't just perform tricks: he turned flowers into goldfish bowls, plucked cards from the empty air, and made solid silver candlesticks disappear just as ordinary magicians did. But the tricks weren't the end of his performance—they were the means. The end was the creation of a world. It was a world in which nothing was fixed, everything was changeable; in which identities merged and dissolved, qualities such as hard and

soft and up and down and sorrow and joy changed into
their opposites in the twinkling of an eye and became
meaningless; and in which the only reliable guide was
suspicion, the only constant theme mistrust.

It was a world, thought Frederick, that was more
than a little devilish. For there was no delight in
Mackinnon's performance, no sense of innocent play.
He scorned the thought as he felt it—was he getting
superstitious now?—but there it was: Mackinnon had
summoned up shadows, even if one could laugh at
them in the light.

Then came a trick in which Mackinnon needed to
borrow a watch from someone in the audience. As he
announced this, he looked directly at Frederick, and
his dark eyes flashed; and Frederick, understanding at
once, unhooked his own watch chain from his waistcoat and held it up. Half a dozen other hands were up,
but Mackinnon leaped down gracefully and was at
Frederick's side in a moment.

"Thank you, sir," he said loudly. "Here's a gentleman with faith in the benevolence of the world of
wonders! Does he know what terrible transformations
will befall his timepiece? No! Will it come back to him
as a chrysanthemum, perhaps? Or as a kippered
herring? Or as a pile of tangled springs and cogs?
Stranger things have happened!" And then, almost
before Frederick was aware of it, he heard a whisper:
"Beside the door. Just come in."

A moment later Mackinnon was on the stage again,
wrapping the watch up in the folds of a silk handkerchief with many flourishes and declamations. Did
Frederick imagine it, or was there a hysterical edge to

Mackinnon's voice now? He seemed to be speaking
more quickly, his gestures seemed more exaggerated,
less controlled. . . . As soon as he could manage it,
Frederick turned around unobtrusively to look where
Mackinnon had indicated.

On the chair nearest to the double doors sat a large,
powerfully built man with smooth blond hair. He was
watching the stage with impassive, wide-set eyes; one
arm lay along the back of the empty chair next to him,
and his whole aspect was one of watchfulness and
command. Despite his faultless evening dress there
was something brutal about him. No, thought Frederick, not brutal, because that meant animal; and this
man was mechanical.

Now why did he think that?

He found himself staring and turned back to the
stage. Mackinnon was completing some intricate piece
of business with the watch, but his mind wasn't on it.
Frederick saw his hand shake as he passed the handkerchief to and fro over the little table he was working
on, and saw, too, that his eyes kept flicking up to look
at the man by the door.

Frederick turned himself sideways in the chair,
crossing his legs, as if he were looking for a more
comfortable position. He could just keep Mackinnon
and the man by the door in his field of vision, and as
he watched, the blond man beckoned with a discreet
finger to a servant. The footman bent to listen, and
the visitor looked up at Mackinnon again and seemed
to be saying something about him—or asking—at any
rate. Frederick saw that Mackinnon had seen it, saw
the servant nod and leave the room, and saw Mackin-

non falter. Now there were only three people in the whole ballroom who mattered, it seemed: the blond man, and Mackinnon, and Frederick watching their strange duel of wills.

But the audience was aware now that something was wrong. Mackinnon's patter had dried, the handkerchief hung loosely in his hand, and his face looked ghastly; and then he dropped the handkerchief altogether and staggered backward.

The music stopped. The pianist looked up hesitantly. Mackinnon stood clutching the curtain in the electric silence and managed to say:

"Beg pardon—indisposed—must leave the stage—"

And then he twitched the curtain aside and vanished behind it.

The audience was too well bred to react with excitement, but there was certainly a stir of comment. The pianist, using his initiative, began to play some bland waltz or other, and Lady Harborough got up from her seat at the front and held a whispered consultation with an elderly man, possibly her husband.

Frederick tapped his fingers on the arm of his chair, and then made up his mind.

"Charlie," he said quietly. "That fellow by the door—fair hair, big build. Find out who he is, could you? Name, rank, number, everything you can."

Charles nodded. "But what are you—"

"I'm going detecting," said Frederick.

He left his seat and made his way to Lady Harborough. She was standing by the piano with the elderly man at her side, and she looked as if she was about to summon a servant. The rest of the audience—most of them—were politely looking the other way and talking to each other as if it were the most natural thing in the world.

"My lady?" Frederick said. "I don't like to interrupt, but I'm a doctor, and if Mr. Mackinnon's indisposed, it might be helpful if I saw him."

"Oh! What a relief!" she said. "I was about to send out for a physician. Do go with the footman, Doctor . . ."

"Garland," said Frederick.

A stiff footman, hair powdered white, calves bulging in his white stockings, blinked impassively and gave a slight bow. As Frederick followed him out of the ballroom, he heard Lady Harborough give orders for the orchestra to be brought back in, and he saw Charles Bertram in conversation with someone in the row behind.

The footman led Frederick through the hall and along a corridor to a door near the library.

"Mr. Mackinnon was using this as a dressing room, sir," he said.

He knocked at the door, but there was no reply. Frederick stepped past him and turned the handle. The room was empty.

"Wasn't there a footman in the hall?" said Frederick.

"Yes, sir."

"Would you go and ask him if he saw Mr. Mackinnon coming out of the ballroom?"

"Certainly, sir. But he wouldn't have come that way, if you don't mind me pointing it out, sir. He'd've more likely gone through the drawing room, coming out the back of the stage like what he did, sir."

"Yes, I see. But if Mr. Mackinnon wanted to step outside for a breath of air, he'd have gone through the hall, wouldn't he?"

"I daresay he would, sir, yes. Should I go and ask?"

"Yes, do."

While the footman was out of sight, Frederick quickly glanced through the room. It was a small sitting room of some kind, with one gaslight glowing by the mantelpiece, and Mackinnon's cloak and hat flung over the back of an armchair near the fire. There was a wicker case standing open by the table, and a tin of grease paints next to a small hand mirror—but there was no Mackinnon.

After a minute or so, the footman knocked at the door behind Fredrick.

"Seems as if you were right, sir," he said. "Mr. Mackinnon ran to the front door and went straight out."

"I dare say he'll be back when he feels better," said Frederick. "Well, there's nothing to be done here. Could you show me the way back?"

IN THE BALLROOM, the servants were removing the chairs while the orchestra reassembled on the stage. Footmen were passing through the crowd with more champagne; it was as if time had jumped backward an hour and Mackinnon had never started his performance.

Frederick looked around for the blond man, but he was nowhere in sight. Nor was Charles. Frederick took a glass from the nearest footman and wandered through the room, watching the faces of the guests. Pretty insipid lot, by the look of 'em, he thought. Smooth and bland and superior . . . He wondered what the time was and then remembered that Mackinnon had his watch. If it still was a watch, and not a rabbit or a cricket bat, he thought morosely.

Then he saw Lady Mary Wytham and stopped to look at her. She was sitting not far from the piano, and her mother was beside her, and they were both smiling politely at someone Frederick couldn't quite see; there was a potted palm in the way. He moved to one side, then looked again, casually, and saw the blond man.

He was sitting opposite them, with his back to Frederick, talking easily. Frederick couldn't quite hear him, but didn't want to move any closer; he felt exposed enough as it was. With a pretense of nodding his head in time to the music, he watched Lady Mary closely. There was a shadow of that same desperation he'd noticed earlier in her eyes, and she didn't speak at all: when there was a remark to be made in reply, her mother made it. Lady Mary was listening, but dutifully, and from time to time she would glance around quickly and then look back. Frederick wondered how young she was; at times she looked about fifteen.

Then the blond man stood up. He bowed to the women and took the hand which Lady Mary unsurely moved toward him and kissed it. She flushed but smiled politely as he turned and left.

As the man went past him, Frederick had an impression of great physical force, of smooth power like a huge volume of water sliding through a sluice, of pale hair and prominent gray-blue eyes, and then the man was gone.

Frederick thought of following him but dismissed the idea at once; the man was bound to have a carriage, and by the time Frederick found a cab he'd be out of sight. In any case, Charles Bertram was coming toward him.

"Did you find Mackinnon?" said Charles.

"No. He's the original will-o'-the-wisp," said Frederick. "He'll turn up again. He'd better, dammit; I want my watch back. What about the fellow with the fair hair? He's just been flirting with Lady Mary Wytham."

"Has he, now?" said Charles. "That's interesting. I heard some gossip about Wytham himself just now— it seems the old boy's on the verge of bankruptcy. I don't know how true that is, mind you. And the fair-haired man's a financier—something big in railroads and mines and matches. A Swede. His name's Bellmann."

7

A Strange Proposal

NEXT MORNING, BEFORE FREDERICK HAD HAD A CHANCE TO tell her about Mackinnon's connection with her case, Sally arrived at her office to find a client waiting for her.

At least she thought he was a client. His name, he told her, was Windlesham; he was a mild-mannered little man with gold spectacles, and he waited most politely until she had settled Chaka and taken off her coat and hat. Then he sprang a surprise.

"I represent Mr. Axel Bellmann," he said. "I think his name is known to you."

She sat down slowly. What did this mean?

"It has come to Mr. Bellmann's attention," he went on, "that you have been making persistent and un-friendly inquiries into his affairs. He is a busy man, with numerous important interests and responsibilities, and such unfounded and ill-formed rumors as those you are attempting to spread, while trivial in the extreme, can only cause considerable annoyance and inconvenience. In order to spare you the embarrass-ment of a formal communication, and the pain of a legal threat, Mr. Bellmann has sent me to convey his displeasure in person, in the hope that you will take it to heart and see the foolishness of continuing in the unproductive path you have sought to follow."

He folded his hands and smiled at her gently.

Sally's heart was racing. She could think of only one thing to say.

"Did you learn that off by heart? Or were you making it up as you went along?"

The smile left his face.

"Perhaps you have not understood," he said. "Mr. Bellmann—"

"I understand very well. Mr. Bellmann is frightened, and he wants to frighten me. Well, I'm not going to be frightened, Mr. Windlesham. I have a particular reason for making my inquiries, and until I'm satisfied, I'll go on with them. And what precisely is this legal threat you mentioned?"

He smiled again. "You're too intelligent to expect me to tell you that at this stage. Mr. Bellmann will decide whether or not to use that weapon when I tell him of your response."

"Tell me," she said, "what's your particular function in Mr. Bellmann's company?"

He looked mildly interested in the question. "I am Mr. Bellmann's private secretary," he said. "Why do you ask?"

"Curiosity. Well, you've told me a lot, Mr. Windlesham. I know I'm on the right track now. I wonder what's making Mr. Bellmann so anxious? Could it be the *Ingrid Linde*?"

It was a shot in the dark—but it struck home. Mr.

Windlesham drew breath sharply, and a scholarly frown appeared on his brow.

"I really would advise great care," he said. "It is very easy for the inexperienced person to make serious errors in the interpretation of quite innocent facts. If I were you, Miss Lockhart, I would stick to financial consultancy, I really would. And may I say"—he rose, gathering stick and hat—"as a private person, how much I admire your enterprise? I have always taken a keen and sympathetic interest in the woman question. Stick to what you know, Miss Lockhart. I wish you every success. But don't let your imagination run away with you."

He raised his stick in salute. Chaka, not understanding, leaped to his feet and growled, but the mild little man didn't flinch.

Well, thought Sally as he left, he's got nerve. What do I do now?

WHAT SHE DID DO, as soon as he had gone, was put on her coat and hat and walk to the office of her friend Mr. Temple the lawyer.

Mr. Temple was an ironical old gentleman who moved in a faint perpetual fragrance of buckram and seedcake and snuff. He had been her father's lawyer and had helped her when Captain Lockhart was killed six years before; Sally had so impressed him with her knowledge of the stock market and her grasp of financial affairs that he had overcome his old-fashioned reservations and had helped her to set up first her partnership with Webster Garland and second her own business.

She told him briefly about the background of the case and described Mr. Windlesham's visit that morning.

"Sally," he said when she'd finished, "you will take care, won't you?"

"That's what *he* said. I thought you'd come up with something more original!"

He smiled and tapped his snuffbox.

"The great strength of the law," he said, "lies in the fact that so little of it *is* original. Thank heaven. Tell me what you know about North Star."

She summarized all she knew, which was not much. She left out Nellie Budd, however; she thought Mr. Temple was hardly likely to be impressed by trance revelations from the world of spirits. She wasn't even sure if she was.

"I don't know whether it's manufacturing, or mining, or what it is," she ended. "There's a connection with a chemicals firm, but that's all I know. What do you think could make them want to keep it secret?"

"Chemicals," he said thoughtfully. "Nasty, smelly things that leak and poison the water and . . . Does he still make matches?"

"No. There was a government investigation in Sweden, and his factory was closed down; but it turned out he'd sold it the year before, so he wasn't responsible."

"Well, now. I happened to come across the name North Star in another context a day or so ago. A man at my club was talking about cooperative societies, trade unions, and what-have-you, and he mentioned some new firm up in Lancashire that's been organized on odd lines—didn't quite follow what he was saying, wasn't really listening, as a matter of fact—don't go to my club for lectures on sociology—but the gist of it was that this firm had set out to organize the lives of its workers down to the last detail. Like Robert Owen. Total control, you see. It sounded appalling to me. But the point was that it was called North Star."

Sally sat up and smiled. "At last!" she said.

"I beg your pardon?"

"A clue. What does this firm do?"

"Ah, that he didn't know. Something to do with railways, he thought. . . . Would you care for a glass of sherry?"

She accepted, and watched the little motes of legal dust floating in the ray of sunshine that slanted through the old window while he poured the drink. Mr. Temple was an old friend, and she'd dined at his house many times, but she still didn't feel quite at ease when they stopped talking about business. Things that other young women could do easily— make small talk, dance gracefully, flirt with a stranger at dinner while unerringly picking up the right knife and fork—were difficult and embarrassing still, and hampered by the memory of humiliating failures. Away from her balance sheets and her files she was really at home, truly herself, only in the cheerful haphazardness of the Garlands'. She sipped the pale brown nectar, tongue-tied, while he leafed through the papers she'd brought.

"Nordenfels . . ." said Mr. Temple. "Who's he? His name's come up more than once."

"Ah. Bellmann had a partner called Nordenfels—he

was a designer, an engineer. I came across an article only yesterday in the *Journal of the Royal Society of Engineers* where his name was mentioned. He invented a new kind of safety valve, apparently; it worked at higher temperatures, or higher pressures, or something. I must look it up in more detail. But he disappeared—Nordenfels, I mean—oh, three or four years ago. Perhaps they just parted company. But I've got a feeling about him. . . ."

"Hmm," said Mr. Temple. "I'd avoid feelings if I were you. Go for facts and figures. You're on the track of something with this Anglo-Baltic business—that's quite clear. Have you checked the insurance on the *Ingrid Linde?*"

"It's on that yellow sheet—all in order. It's not an insurance fraud." After a minute she went on: "This Mr. Windlesham mentioned a legal threat. Could he mean an injunction?"

"I doubt it very much. The court would have to be satisfied first that the activity he complained of was wrong in itself, which you would deny; and second that the proper remedy for it would not be damages."

"So the legal threat is a bluff?"

"I suspect so. But there are other ways of injuring you, my dear, than by taking you to court, which is why I urge you again: Take care."

"Yes. I will. But I'm not going to stop looking into his affairs. He's up to something *wrong*, Mr. Temple. I know he is."

"You may well be right. Now, I don't want to keep you, but there's a Mr. O'Connor here who's been left a thousand pounds: shall I send him along to you, so that you can tell him how to turn it into something more?"

AT THE SAME TIME, in the financial heart of the city, ex-Cabinet Minister Lord Wytham was sitting in a corridor outside an imposing office, drumming his fingers on his silk hat and getting to his feet every time a clerk came around a corner or out of a door.

Lord Wytham was a handsome man, but with that doe-eyed, distinguished masculine beauty seen these days only in photographs of middle-aged male models. On a real face it looks like weakness. When Frederick had seen him the evening before, his first impression had been of a gnawing anxiety, and if he'd seen him now, that feeling would have been intensified. His fingernails were bitten to the quick, his large, dark eyes were red-rimmed, and his gray mustache was ragged where he'd chewed it. He couldn't sit still for more than a minute; if no one came along the corridor, he'd get up anyway and stare sightlessly at one of the prints on the walls or out the window overlooking Threadneedle Street, or down the marble staircase.

Finally a door opened and a clerk came out.

"Mr. Bellmann will see you now, my lord," he said.

Lord Wytham snatched his silk hat from the chair, picked up his stick, and followed the clerk through an anteroom and into a large and newly furnished office. Axel Bellmann got up from behind the desk and came forward to shake hands.

"Good of you to come, Wytham," Bellmann said, motioning him to an armchair. "Curious evening at Lady Harborough's, was it not?"

His voice was deep and almost unaccented, his face unlined, his blond hair thick and straight. He could have been any age between thirty and sixty. Like his office, he had a factory-finished look about him, being large and smooth and heavy—but it was the smoothness of machined steel, not of pampered flesh. His prominent eyes were direct and disconcerting. They gave no hint of mood, humor, or temper; they rarely blinked, yet they weren't dead. They were electrically intense.

Lord Wytham found himself looking away and fiddling with the rim of his hat. The clerk offered to take it for him, and Wytham handed it over. Bellmann watched as the man placed it on the hatrack and went out; then Bellmann turned back to Lord Wytham.

"Lady Harborough's," he prompted. "Interesting evening, no?"

"Ah. Chap disappearing like that. Yes, indeed."

"Do you enjoy the performance of magic, Wytham?"

"Can't say I've had much experience . . ."

"Really? It is interesting to watch, I find. Perhaps you should have watched more closely."

If that was a curious way of putting it, Lord Wytham did not notice. His eyes, dark and bloodshot, flickered around the room as if he was unwilling to look Bellmann in the face.

"Well, now," said Bellmann, after a few seconds of silence. "Perhaps you are wondering why I invited you to visit me this morning. I understand you have been dismissed from the Cabinet."

Lord Wytham's face became a shade darker. "The

Prime Minister—er—wished to redistribute the port-
folios among . . . ummm . . ." he said, faltering.

"Yes. You were dismissed. So now you are free to
take an active part in the world of business, is that
not so?"

"I beg your pardon?"

"There is no impediment now to your becoming the
director of a company?"

"Well, none. Except . . . No, none. I don't understand, Bellmann."

"Evidently not. I shall explain more fully. I know
your financial position in detail, Wytham. You are in
debt to the extent of nearly four hundred thousand
pounds, because of a combination of foolish investments, bad management, and incompetent advice.
There is no prospect of your paying it back, especially
since you have no job now that you are out of
government, so you are considering bankruptcy as a
final option. Of course, that will mean every kind of
disgrace. Let us look for a moment at your assets: they
consist almost entirely of your London house and your
estate. But they are both mortgaged, are they not?"

Lord Wytham nodded. How did the man know all
this? But he was too sickened to protest.

"And then there is your daughter's property," Bellmann said. "I understand she owns land in Cumber-
land."

"Eh? Yes. That's right. No good to me, though. I
can't touch it—I've tried. Some kind of entail; mother's side of the family, property tied to her, that kind
of thing. Mines and so forth."

"Graphite."

"Is it, by Jove. Something to do with pencils, I know that."

"Her mines have a monopoly of a certain pure form of graphite."

"Wouldn't be surprised. My agent in Carlisle sees to it. Done it for years. They make pencils with the stuff. But there's no money in it; no way out there."

"I see," said Bellmann. "Well, there is no use my asking what you intend to do. It's plain you have no idea." Lord Wytham began to protest, but Bellmann held up his hand and went on. "Which is why I asked you here this morning. I can offer you a position as director of a company I have set up. You are no longer in the government, but your contacts in Whitehall will be of considerable use to me. I shall not be paying you for any business ability you possess, for you have none. The fees you earn as director will be related to the connections you have in the civil service."

"Connections?" said Lord Wytham faintly.

"With officials in the Board of Trade and the foreign office. To be precise, in the matter of export licenses. You know the gentleman concerned, no doubt?"

"Oh, yes. Of course. Permanent secretaries, and so forth. But—"

"I do not expect you to exert influence; you would not be able to. You supply the contacts, and I shall supply the influence. That settles the matter of your income. There remains the problem of the debts. You will not pay those out of a director's fees, I regret to say. However, there is a solution. I wish to marry your daughter."

It was such a startling thing to hear that Lord

Wytham thought he was mistaken and merely blinked.

Bellmann went on. "It has been my intention for some time now to choose a wife. I have seen your daughter, and she will please me. How old is she?"

Lord Wytham swallowed. This was preposterous, it was insane. Damn the man! How dare he? Then came a consciousness of the catastrophe hanging over him, poised like a wave, and he sank back in the chair, helpless.

"Seventeen. I—Mr. Bellmann, you know my position. I—"

"Quite as well as you. Probably better, since you are incompetent where money is concerned, whereas I am not. You have a month to find three hundred and ninety thousand pounds. And you will not find it. I cannot imagine what you will do. Your credit is exhausted."

"I—Mary is—please, Mr. Bellmann. If you could see your way to . . ."

He faltered, having genuinely no idea what he was going to say next. Bellmann sat still, watching him closely with those wide, electric eyes. Then he said, "You understand what I am saying. Your daughter, Lady Mary, will suit me very well. When we are married, I shall make you a payment of four hundred thousand pounds. Three hundred and ninety will cover your debts; the other ten thousand is in consideration of the expense you will be put to to organize the wedding. I think that is quite clear."

Lord Wytham was breathless. He had never been so dazed in his life since falling once while hunting and being knocked unconscious; it was the same sensation now—that of coming into unexpected collision with something much bigger and more powerful than himself. It hurt almost physically.

"I—most persuasively put. Interesting proposition. Have to speak to my lawyer, naturally. I—"

"Your lawyer? What for?"

"Well, this is a family matter. My lawyer will have to examine the proposal. You must see that."

His brain had started to work again. It *was* like a fall; you were dazed, and then you found your bearings. And he saw now that if Bellmann was willing to part with four hundred thousand, he might well disgorge more.

"Yes, I see," said Bellmann. "You want to make a little more, and you think your lawyer better able to get it than yourself. You are undoubtedly right. How much more were you thinking of?"

Again a fall. Bellmann was too strong, too quick; it wasn't fair, Lord Wytham felt . . . But what should he say now? Back off, and he'd look weak; ask for too little, and he'd lose a fortune; ask for too much, and he'd lose everything. . . . His mind scurried like a rat across a line of figures ending in a row of noughts.

"I have to . . . protect myself," he said cautiously. "The estate. The house in Cavendish Square. It all costs . . . Without any capital, I . . ."

Bellmann said nothing. He wasn't going to help. Lord Wytham took a deep breath.

"Two hundred and fifty thousand pounds," he said. It was half the figure he would have liked to ask.

"Very well," said Bellmann. "That sounds satisfactory to me. We agree that the value of your daughter is six hundred and fifty thousand pounds. I shall pay you a check for fifty thousand pounds when the betrothal is announced; that will take care of the most pressing debts and be an earnest for the rest. The remainder of the first figure we agreed, namely three hundred and fifty thousand, will be paid on the morning of the wedding. The extra amount, the two hundred and fifty thousand, will be paid the morning after, subject to my satisfaction with Lady Mary's condition. Do I have to make that any clearer?"

The hardest fall of all, and this time the horse had trampled him into the ground. Bellmann was saying that if Lady Mary was not a virgin, there'd be no extra money. Lord Wytham felt ill and heard himself whisper; this was too cruel, too shameful, too much to bear. People shouldn't act like this. Beaten, dazed, he could hardly think, he felt so confused.

"You will want to speak to my daughter," he said faintly.

"Of course."

"If . . . If she should . . ."

"If she should refuse?" said Bellmann.

Lord Wytham nodded. He couldn't say it.

"If she should refuse my offer of marriage, then of course I would respect her wishes. The matter must be entirely her own choice. Do you not agree?"

"Oh, by all means." Lord Wytham's voice was hardly audible. He knew what was meant.

"Then, with your permission, I shall call at Cavendish Square on Friday morning to put my proposal to Lady Mary. Today is Tuesday. Three days."

Lord Wytham swallowed. In each of his long-lashed eyes there was a tear.

"Yes," he said hoarsely. "Of course."

"Then that is agreed. Now to some business. We shall draw up the contract for your directorship over the next day or so, but in the meantime I shall tell you a little about the company you are joining. I think you will find it interesting. It is called North Star Castings, Limited."

Bellmann bent to take some papers out of a drawer, and while he was looking away Lord Wytham brushed his hand across his eyes. His dismissal from the Cabinet had hurt, but these twenty minutes with Bellmann had taken him beyond pain into a region he'd never dreamed of, where decency and dignity and fairness were blown away like dead leaves. How could he have known that before the morning was out he'd have sold his own daughter—and sold her, what's more (like a flush of poison, the guilty thought), for so much less than he might have done? Suppose he'd asked a million?

But he wouldn't have gotten it. Bellmann knew everything; he'd never beat a man like that. Lord Wytham felt as if he'd sold his soul and found (with the rest of eternity to think about it) that the price he'd gotten for it was no more than a mouthful of ash.

Bellmann spread out some papers on the desk. Lord Wytham composed his weak, handsome face into an expression of interest and leaned forward, trying to listen, as Bellmann began to explain.

8

Declaration of War

JIM'S LATEST MELODRAMA, *THE VAMPIRE OF LIMEHOUSE*, HAD been sent back from the Lyceum Theatre with a note from someone called Bram Stoker, the manager.

"What d'you reckon, Mr. Webster?" he said. "Does he like it, or does he think it's a load of cobblers?"

Webster Garland took the letter and read it aloud.

"Dear Mr. Taylor," he read. "Thank you for letting me see your farce, *The Vampire of Limehouse*. I regret that the company's program is full for the next two years, so we are unable to consider it for production. However, I thought it had an unmistakable vigor and life, though I feel that vampires, as a subject, are played out. Yours, etc. . . . I don't know, Jim. At least he took the trouble to write."

"Perhaps I ought to go and read it to him. He probably missed half the good bits."

"Is that the one with the bloodsucking warehouse-man and the barge full of corpses?"

"Yeah. Farce, he called it. It's a bleedin' tragedy, that one. Farce, my arse . . ."

"*Bleeding*'s the word," said Frederick. "It's thick

with gore from start to finish. It's not a play—it's a black pudding."

"You can laugh, mate," Jim said darkly. "I'll make me fortune yet. I'll have me name in lights."

"Liver and lights, if that play's anything to go by," Frederick said.

It was Wednesday morning, and the shop was busy. Solemn Mr. Blaine, the manager, and the assistant, Wilfred, were serving customers who wanted to buy chemicals, cameras or tripods, while the refined Miss Renshaw at another counter dealt with appointments for portraits and other commissions. In addition to them, the staff consisted of Arthur Potts, a cheerful middle-aged man who loaded the cameras, arranged the studio, carried the equipment when they went out, developed and printed, and helped Frederick make any items that couldn't be bought; and there was a dim boy of Jim's age, called Herbert. They'd taken him on as a general assistant and found he was hopeless—slow, forgetful, and clumsy. But he was the kindest soul in the world, and neither Frederick nor Sally nor Webster had the heart to get rid of him.

As Frederick stood at the back of the neat, prosperous-looking shop, with its busy staff and growing reputation, its well-furnished studio and its air of efficiency and optimism, he thought back to the day Sally had first arrived: diffident, nervous, and in deadly trouble. Frederick had been in the middle of a blazing row with his sister; the place was shabby, half the shelves were empty, and ruin was getting closer by the day. But with the help of a series of comic stereographs which sold surprisingly well, they managed to keep afloat; and when Sally was able to put some money into the business, they began to prosper. They'd given up the stereographs now: the market was diminishing, and *cartes de visite* (small portraits) were the thing these days. But they were running out of space. Soon they'd have to extend the premises, or even open another branch.

Frederick felt for his watch, cursed as he remembered that Mackinnon still had it, and looked up at the clock over the counter. He was half-expecting Sally to call; he had the feeling that she was planning something she hadn't told him about, and it worried him.

The manager was at the counter, writing an order for photographic paper. Frederick went up to him.

"Mr. Blaine," he said, "Miss Lockhart hasn't been in this morning, has she?"

"No, to my regret, Mr. Garland," came the mournful tones of Mr. Blaine. "I wanted to engage her in discussion as to the desirability of hiring some kind of clerical help. I fear that our friend Herbert is not greatly gifted in that department, and everyone else is fully occupied already. What is your feeling on the matter?"

"Good idea. But where would this clerking go on? There's no room to swing a cat in the files room, though I daresay you could skin one in there if it didn't wriggle. We'd need a desk. And a typewriting machine—they're all using 'em now."

"Yes. It may be, Mr. Garland, that an enlargement of the premises would be called for."

"Funny. I was thinking the same thing only a minute ago. But, look here, I'm going out now. If

Miss Lockhart comes in, talk to her about it. And give her my love."

He went to fetch his coat and caught a train to Streatham.

NELLIE BUDD was feeding her cats. Each of them, she explained to Frederick, was the reincarnation of an Egyptian Pharaoh. The lady herself was as earthly as he remembered: deep-bosomed, sparkling-eyed, and given to glances of frank admiration at what she'd no doubt call his manly form.

He'd decided to be open from the start.

"Mrs. Budd," he said, once they were seated on a comfortable sofa in her parlor. "The other night I came to a séance in Streatham and took a photograph of you. What you get up to in the dark doesn't concern me in the least, and if your friends are gullible enough to fall for it, that's their lookout. But it's a nice photograph; there's a false hand on the table, a wire going to the tambourine, and what your right leg's doing I hardly dare think. . . . In short, Mrs. Budd, I'm blackmailing you."

She grinned at him roguishly.

"Go on with you!" she said. Her voice had a touch of the north in it—whether Lancashire or Yorkshire, he couldn't say, since it was smoothed and refined and stagey as well. "A handsome young man like you! You wouldn't have to blackmail me, dear—just ask nicely. What d'you want?"

"Oh, good. I wasn't really going to anyway. I'm interested in what you said in your trance—your real trance. Can you remember what it was?"

She was silent a moment. Her eyes looked troubled, and then it passed and they sparkled again.

"Lord," she said, "you're asking now. That was one of me turns, wasn't it? I've been having me turns for years now. That's what put me on to the medium game—that and Josiah. Me husband, as was, God rest him. Conjurer, you know. He taught me tricks as would amaze you. So when it comes to rattling a tambourine and squeezing hands in the dark, Nellie Budd's got few equals, though I say as shouldn't."

"Fascinating. You're good at avoiding questions, too, Mrs. Budd. What about these turns of yours?"

"Frankly, love," she said, "I haven't the faintest idea. I come all over swimmy and swoony and a minute or two later I come to meself again, but I don't remember what I say. Why?"

Frederick found himself liking her. He decided to show a bit more of his hand.

"Do you know a Mr. Bellmann?" he said.

She shook her head. "Never heard of him."

"Or a company called North Star?"

"Means nothing, I'm afraid, love."

"Look, I'll read you what you said." He took the folded piece of paper with Jim's writing on it out of his pocket and read aloud steadily. When he got to the end, he looked up and said, "Does that mean anything to you?"

She looked amazed. "Did I say all that?" she said. "What a load of nonsense!"

"You really don't know where all this comes from?"

"It's probably—what do they call it?—telepathy. I'm probably reading someone's mind. Lord, I don't know. I've got as much idea about glass coffins and sparks as the man in the moon. What d'you want to know for, anyway?"

"One of the members of the Spiritualist League is a clerk in a city firm, and he's worried about some of the stuff he's heard from you. It seems to be secret business information. He thinks it'll get out, you see, and he'll be blamed for it."

"Well, I'm blowed! This is all to do with business, then?"

"Some of it," Frederick said. "And some we're just not sure of." Then a thought struck him. "You don't know a fellow called Mackinnon, by any chance?"

That took her by surprise. Her eyes widened and she sat back in the sofa.

"Alistair Mackinnon?" she said. Her voice was faint. "The one they call the Wizard of the North?"

"That's him. This man Bellmann I mentioned—he seems to be after Mackinnon for some reason. You wouldn't know anything about him, would you? Mackinnon, I mean?"

She shook her head. "I . . . I've seen him on the halls. Wonderful clever. But not a man as you could trust, I'd say. Not like my Josiah, though Josiah didn't come within a mile of him in the conjuring line. But I don't know nothing about this Bellmann."

"Or . . ." He thought back to the evening at Lady Harborough's. "What about a man called Wytham?"

This time she was really startled. She caught her breath and pressed her hand to her bosom, and he saw she'd gone pale under the powder she wore.

"Wytham?" she said. "Not Johnny Wytham?"

"Do you know someone by that name?"

"Johnny Wytham. Lord Wytham—that's what he is now. He was Johnny Kennet when I knew him—when I was on the halls, that is. He asked me to marry him, and then . . . Ah, well, I had a good man in Josiah. But Johnny Wytham was . . . all grace and fun in those days, and such a handsome man. Lord, he was handsome. What a swell . . ."

She'd have been a stunning girl, thought Frederick; not exactly pretty, but full of life and vigor and fun.

"Look at this," she said, and opened a drawer in a little table. She took out a photograph in a silver frame—a crisp ambrotype of the kind that had been common twenty or more years before. It showed two shapely, smiling girls of twenty or so, dressed scantily in ballet costumes that showed off their well-turned legs. They were identical twins. The caption underneath the caption said MISS NELLIE AND MISS JESSIE SAXON.

"That's me on the left," she said. "Jessie's still on the halls, up north. We were a pretty pair, weren't we?"

"You certainly were. Did your sister know Lord Wytham as well?"

"She knew him, yes, but he was my special . . . Who knows, eh? I might have been Lady Wytham today, if things had worked out different."

"When did you last see him?"

"Funny you should ask," she said. She got up and wandered to the window, as if she were embarrassed. The ginger cat, Rameses, sprang onto the sofa and curled up in the warm spot she'd left. She took a tassel of the curtain and twisted it absently, gazing out into the quiet street.

"Yes?" Frederick prompted.

"It was last summer. Up in Scotland. At—at the races. But we only passed and said hello, and he couldn't talk on account of his family and . . . that's all."

"Is there any connection between him and Bellmann? Or him and Mackinnon? I only mentioned his name because I saw all three of them in the same place the other night."

"No," she said. "I can't imagine. I don't know who this Bellmann is at all . . ."

She was still looking away. Frederick let the silence stretch and then said, "Well, anyway, thank you, Mrs. Budd. If something comes to mind, I'd be grateful if you'd let me know. Here's my address."

He put a card on the table and got up to leave. She turned around to shake hands, and he saw that all her bounce and sparkle had gone: she looked almost like an old woman now, powdered and painted and frightened.

"Look," she said, "I've answered all your questions, and you've told me nothing. Who are you? What are you up to?"

"I'm a private detective," he said. "I'm working on two cases at the moment, and they seem to be joining up in odd ways. You will let me know if you think of anything else?"

She nodded. "I'll try," she said. "I'll try and remember. But you know how it is, these things slip out of your mind. . . . If I think of anything I'll write you a note. All right, dear?"

She showed him to the door with a false, bright smile and said good-bye.

SALLY, MEANWHILE, was going to see Axel Bellmann.

She had decided that she had nothing to lose by taking the initiative, and it might throw him off balance for a short while. It was a tactic her father had taught her. She used it when she played chess with Webster. Sometimes it worked.

She arrived, with Chaka, at Baltic House at ten o'clock. There was a stout commissionaire outside, who saluted smartly and made no move to stop her going in. He had an expression of monumental stupidity; she supposed they ordered commissionaires by girth rather than brain.

The porter inside was quicker on the uptake.

"Sorry, miss," he said. "Quite impossible. No one can see Mr. Bellmann without I have an appointment written in my book here."

He shook his head and started to bar her way.

"Chaka," said Sally, and released his collar.

The huge beast growled and lunged a step or two toward the porter.

"All right! All right! Call him off! I'll see, miss—"

Sally regained her grip, and the man scuttled off to find someone in authority. He came back after a minute with a smooth, mustached young man, who spread his hands and smiled.

"Miss—Lockhart, is it? I do so regret it, but Mr. Bellmann is quite unavailable at the moment—"

"That's all right," said Sally. "I can wait five minutes."

"I say! What a splendid beast! Irish wolfhound?" he said, smiling again. It was a warm, engaging smile, and totally fake. He advanced a manicured hand toward the dog's head. "Unfortunately, it isn't a question of five minutes—my *God!* Help me! Let go—ohh! Ahhh!"

Chaka had casually seized the outstretched hand and was worrying it like a rat.

"I shouldn't worry," said Sally. "He'll let go in a minute. He only likes real meat."

At the sound of her calm voice the dog let go and sat down, pleased, looking up at her happily. The young man staggered to a chair and flopped into it, hugging his hand.

"Look!" he said. "He's drawn *blood!*"

"How very surprising. Perhaps Mr. Bellmann has finished what he was doing a moment ago. Would you go and tell him that I am here and that I would like to see him at once?"

Slack-mouthed, the young man trembled as he got to his feet and hurried out. The porter stayed in the corridor, peering around the door and then retreating again.

Two minutes went by. She looked in her handbag for the card Frederick had given her, with Nellie Budd's address; perhaps she could go and see her afterward. Then she heard footsteps in the corridor and tucked the card into her glove.

The door opened, and a stout middle-aged man came in. From his manner, she could tell that he was someone important in the company, not a well-dressed nonentity like the first man.

Chaka was lying still at Sally's feet. No threats now: another tactic this time. She smiled and held out her hand.

Slightly nonplussed, the man took it.

"I am given to understand that you want to see Mr. Bellmann," he said. "Let me make an appointment for you. Perhaps you can tell me what the matter is about, so that—"

"The only appointment I shall make is to see Mr. Bellmann in three minutes' time. Otherwise I shall go to the *Pall Mall Gazette* and tell them precisely what I know about Mr. Bellmann's connection with the Swedish Match Company's liquidation. I mean it. Three minutes."

"I—"

He gulped, shot his cuffs, and vanished. In fact, Sally knew nothing for certain; there'd been rumors, whispers about irregularities, but nothing concrete. However, it seemed to be working. Two and a half minutes later, she was shown into the presence of Axel Bellmann. He did not get up from his desk.

"Well?" he said. "I warned you, Miss Lockhart."

"You warned me about what, exactly? Let's be clear about it, Mr. Bellmann. What exactly must I stop doing, and what exactly will you do if I don't?"

She sat down calmly, though her heart was beating hard. Bellmann had a massive presence: it reminded her of the stillness of some huge dynamo spinning so fast that it seemed not to move at all. He looked at her heavily.

"You must stop trying to understand matters which are too deep for you," he said after a few moments.

"And if you do not, I shall make it known to everyone who is in a position to help you or to employ you that you are an immoral woman, living on immoral earnings."

"I beg your pardon?"

The expression around his eyes changed unpleasantly: she realized that he was smiling. He reached into a drawer and took out a buff-colored folder.

"I have here a record of visits paid by unaccompanied men to your place of business in North Street. During the past month no less than twenty-four such visits have been made. Only the other night, for example, a man called very late—at half past ten, to be precise—was admitted by yourself, and stayed for most of an hour before leaving. When my secretary, Mr. Windlesham, visited your so-called office yesterday, he noticed that it contained, among other furniture, a large divan. As if that were not enough, you are known to associate with a Webster Garland, a photographer who has made a speciality of photographing—how shall I put it—the nude."

She bit her lip—careful, careful.

"You're quite wrong," she said as calmly as she could. "Mr. Garland specializes in portraiture, as a matter of fact. As for the rest of that absurd nonsense—if that's the worst you can find to fight me with, you might as well give up."

He raised his eyebrows. "How naive you are. You will find out quite soon how much damage an allegation like that can do. A young woman, alone, making money . . . disreputable associates . . ."

He smiled again, and she felt chilly, because he was

quite right. There was no defense against that sort of smear. Ignore it, she thought. Get on.

"I don't want to waste time, Mr. Bellmann," she said. "If I come to see you again, I had better be admitted at once. Now to the point: Your involvement in the Anglo-Baltic Steam Navigation Company has cost a client of mine her life's savings. Her name is Miss Susan Walsh. She was a teacher. A good woman. She's given her life to her pupils and to girls' education. She's harmed no one and done a great deal of good, and now that she's retired she's entitled to live on the money she'd saved. I advised her to invest in Anglo-Baltic.

"Now do you see why it concerns you? You ruined that company deliberately and by stealth. In doing so you lost a great many people money, and they all deserve reparation; but they're not all my clients. I will have a check, please, made out for the sum of three thousand two hundred and forty pounds, to be paid to Miss Susan Walsh. The sum is itemized here."

She dropped a folded piece of paper on the desk. He did not move.

"And I will have it now," she said.

Chaka, at her feet, growled softly.

Suddenly Bellmann moved. He flicked open the paper, read it, and in one movement tore it in half and flung it into a wastepaper basket. His pale face was a shade darker.

"Get out," he said.

"Without the check? I assume you will send it to me. You know where my office is."

"I shall send you nothing."

"Very well." She snapped her fingers, and Chaka got to his feet. "I don't intend to swap allegations with you; it's a silly game. I know enough about you now to make a very interesting article in the papers. North Star, for instance. Nordenfels. What's more, I know where to look next, and look I shall, and when I find out what you're doing I shall publish it. And I will have that money, Mr. Bellmann. Make no mistake about that."

"I do not make mistakes."

"I think you might have done so now. Good morning."

He did not reply. No one came near her as she left the building. It took half an hour in an A.B.C. teashop, a currant bun, and a pot of tea to stop her trembling. Then she found herself wondering, to her considerable annoyance, whether the mistake hadn't been hers after all.

As SOON as she'd gone, Bellmann came out from behind his desk and picked up the card that had fluttered to the carpet from her glove. He'd said nothing as he watched it fall. He stooped to gather it and read:

MRS. BUDD

147 TOLLBOOTH ROAD

STREATHAM

He drummed his fingers on the desk for a moment or two, and then sent for Mr. Windlesham.

9

Lavender

JIM TAYLOR CONSIDERED HE HAD AN INTEREST IN ALISTAIR Mackinnon, much as if he'd bought shares in him. For all the distaste he felt for the man, he couldn't help feeling annoyed when Frederick lost him; and when Frederick retorted that no one could be expected to keep hold of a man who could turn himself into smoke and pour out through a keyhole, Jim said that he must be losing his grip, as he couldn't even keep hold of his own watch. It'd be his trousers next.

So he decided to look for Mackinnon himself. He called at every house in Oakley Street, Chelsea, where Mackinnon had said he lived, and drew a blank; he tried the manager of the music hall he'd rescued Mackinnon from, and was told that no one knew his address; he went to several other music halls in case Mackinnon was appearing under a different name, but he had no luck there either.

Still, he didn't give up. He'd amassed, in his short and scruffy life, an astonishing number of criminal, semicriminal, sporting, theatrical, and even one or two downright respectable acquaintances; and they were all linked by favors owed or owing—racing tips, loans of half a crown, casual hints that the copper on the corner was looking this way, and so on. There wasn't much, Jim reckoned, that he couldn't find out if he wanted to.

So it was that on the evening of the day Sally visited Axel Bellmann, Jim found himself standing elbow to elbow in the four-ale bar of a Deptford pub with a shifty little man in a white muffler, who jumped as Jim tapped his shoulder.

"Wotcher, Dippy!" Jim said. "How are yer, mate?"

"Eh? Oh, it's you, Jim. How do."

Dippy Lumsden looked around furtively, but then he was professionally furtive, being a pickpocket.

"Listen, Dippy," said Jim. "I'm trying to find a bloke. A feller called Mackinnon—a magician. Scotch geezer. He's been on the halls a year or two; you might've seen him."

Dippy nodded at once. "I seen him. And I know where he is, too."

"Eh? Where?"

The pickpocket looked crafty and rubbed his thumb and forefinger together. "What's it worth?" he said.

"Worth Felspar," said Jim. "What you still owe me for, remember?"

Felspar was a horse that had won at twenty to one and had brought them both a tidy sum. Jim had tipped him, thanks to a jockey he knew.

Dippy nodded philosophically. "Fair enough," he said. "He's staying in Lambeth. Dirty little place called Allen's Yard. With a fat old Irish cow called Mrs. Mooney. I seen him last night—I knew who he was cause I seen him at Gatti's Music Hall one night. What you want him for?"

"He nicked a watch. But he ain't in your class, Dippy—don't worry about competition from him."

"Oh. Ah. Righto, mate. But you never saw me tonight, remember. And I never seen him. I gotta look after meself."

"Course you have, Dippy," said Jim. "Another pint?"

But Dippy shook his head. He couldn't afford to stay too long in any one pub, he said, for professional reasons. He swallowed the rest of his drink and left; and after a minute or so of flirtation with the barmaid, so did Jim.

Mrs. Mooney's house was a crazy, stinking, tottering ruin, kept from falling into Allen's Yard only by the fact that there was no room for it to fall into. The little light that reached the court from outside and from the dim windows of the house showed that the floor of it was little better than a cesspool, but that didn't appear to worry the red-haired child who was playing barefoot on the doorstep, teaching her doll manners by smacking its head and toasting a bit of herring over a smoking lantern.

"Mrs. Mooney in?" said Jim.

The child looked up. She sneered at him, and Jim felt tempted to follow the example she was practicing on the doll.

"I says, is Mrs. Mooney in, rat-face?"

She looked more interested. "Lost yer barrel organ?" she inquired. "Where's yer little red jacket and yer tin?"

Jim restrained himself.

"Look, carrot-face, get the murerk, else I'll fetch you a sockdolager what'll lay you out till Christmas," he said.

The brat took a piece of fish out of her mouth and shrieked "Auntie Mary!" before putting it back. She continued to watch Jim contemptuously as he shifted from spot to spot, looking for somewhere dry to stand.

"Enjoying yer little dance?" she said.

Jim snarled and was about to clout her one when a colossal woman rolled into the doorway, blocking almost all the meager light from inside. A powerful wave of gin-laden odor drifted from her.

"Oo's this?" she said.

"I'm looking for Mr. Mackinnon," said Jim.

"Never heard of him."

"Scottish geezer. Skinny bloke with dark eyes. Been here a couple of days, I was told. A conjurer."

"What d'you want with him?"

"Is he in, or ain't he?"

She thought for a fuddled moment.

"He ain't," she said. "And no one can't see him neither."

"Well, tell him when he gets in as Jim Taylor called. Got that?"

"I tell you, he ain't here."

"No, course not. Never thought he was. Only if he turns up one day, tell him I called. Right?"

She considered again and then rolled away without a word.

"Drunken fussock," observed the child.

"You want to mind your manners," said Jim. "Speaking of your elders and betters like that."

She took the fish out of her mouth again, looked at
him steadily for a moment, and then released a flood
of the filthiest, richest, ripest, fruitiest, foulest lan-
guage Jim had ever heard. It went on for an uninter-
rupted two minutes and a half, without repetition. He,
his face, his manners, his ancestry, his clothes, and his
mind were compared unfavorably to parts of his body,
to parts of other people's bodies, to parts of animals'
bodies, to the stink arising from dead fish, to boils, to
intestinal wind, and to several dozen other unpleasant-
nesses. Jim was completely taken aback, and that
didn't happen very often.

He put his hand in his pocket.

"Here," he said, holding out a sixpence. "You're a
virtuoso, you are. I never heard such a talent."

She took the sixpence—whereupon he swiped her
around the head and sent her sprawling.

"But you want to be quicker on your pins than
that," he added. "Cheerio."

She told him what to do and where to go, then
called, *"And* you've missed yer mate. He's just gorn.
She told him you was here. Oo's the slow one now?"—
and, with a cackle of witchlike glee, fled dripping
around the corner of the yard.

Jim cursed and ran into the house. The only light
came from a candle on a rickety table; he seized it and,
shielding the flame, tore up the narrow stairs. The
smells that met him were indescribable, even by the
little girl; how did the fastidious Mackinnon stand it?
And the place was a labyrinth. Faces peered at him
from the gloom—wizened ones like elderly rats, dirty
ones, brutal ones; doors hung crazily open or weren't

there at all; lengths of sacking fell aside to show whole families, six, seven, eight or more people sleeping or eating or slumped in apathy or maybe dead.

But no Mackinnon. The monstrous woman, with a bottle of gin clutched to her like the child's doll, sat on the landing, incapable of movement. He shoved past her into the last room—and found it empty.

She laughed wheezily.

"Where'd he go?" Jim demanded.

"Out," she said, wheezing harder.

He was tempted to take a kick at her. Without a word, he pushed his way past and left the house.

He stood in the darkness of the court—darker now, for he'd snuffed out the candle. The house was quiet behind him, and the little girl had vanished, but his skin crept.

There was someone else in the court.

He was sure of it, though he could see and hear no one. All his senses prickled. He stood still, cursing his stupidity, and reached silently into his pocket for the brass knuckle-duster he always carried.

Then a light hand was laid on his arm, and a woman's voice said, "Wait . . ."

He stood rigid. His heart was thumping wildly. He could see only the dull, wet gleam of a sodden brick wall outside the court; there was nothing but darkness within.

"You're a friend," said the voice. "He's spoken your name. Come with me."

It was like a dream. A shawled, cloaked figure glided past him and beckoned him to follow. And helplessly, as in a dream, he did so.

*   *   *

IN A NEAT, little room not far away, the woman struck
a match and lit a candle. The shawl fell forward over
her face as she bent low to do it, and then she
murmured, "Please . . ."

Jim stood, puzzled, as she lowered the shawl. Then
he understood. A huge, liver-colored birthmark spread
across half her face. Her eyes were warm and fine, but
their expression told him what his expression was, and
he felt ashamed.

"Sorry," he said. "Who are you?"

"Please—sit down. I heard you speak of him to
Mrs. Mooney; I couldn't help . . ."

He sat down at the table, which was spread with a
delicately embroidered linen cloth. Everything he
could see was pretty in a light, old-fashioned way, and
there was a faint smell of lavender in the air. She was
delicate too; her voice wasn't cockney but had a touch
of the Geordie in it, he thought—Newcastle? Dur-
ham?—and it was gentle and musical. She sat across
the table from him, looking down.

"I love him, Mr. Taylor," she said.

"Oh! That's it. I understand now."

"My name is Isabel Meredith," she went on.
"When he came . . . when he left the engagement at
Lady Harborough's the other night, he hardly knew
what he was doing. He came to me because once
we . . . I've helped him in the past. I've given him a
little money. I have very little, as you see. I'm a
needlewoman. That he should have to hide like this,
a man of his talent . . . But he's in great danger, Mr.
Taylor, terrible danger. He . . . What else can he do?"

"He can tell the blooming truth, that's what. He can come to Burton Street—he knows where—and talk to me and my mate Fred Garland. If he's in danger, that's the best thing he can do. But he's got to be straight about it."

She traced a pattern with her fingernail on the cloth. "You see, he's very nervous, very imaginative," she said after a moment. "As an artist, he naturally feels things more than most of us. More acutely."

Jim said nothing. The only artist he knew well was Webster Garland, and he was as tough as a buzzard; what marked *him* out was his single-mindedness and his marvelous eye, not a susceptibility to the vapors.

"Well, look," he said finally. "If it was any other geezer, I wouldn't be bothered. But we're trying to find something out, not about Mackinnon, something else—and he's mixed up at the edge of it. There's fraud, there's financial jiggery-pokery, there's spiritualistic humbug, there's all kinds of wickedness—maybe worse. So what's he done? And how'd you get mixed up with him, anyway?"

"I met him in Newcastle," she said. "He was friendly to me. He was only starting then. He told me he couldn't use his real name on the stage—he's not really called Mackinnon—because his father would find out and have him put away."

"Eh?"

"That's what he said."

"Well, who's his father then?"

"He would never tell me. Someone important. There was a matter of inheritance—a family treasure, or something—and he gave it all up for his art. But his father was afraid it would bring disgrace on the family, you see."

"Hmm," said Jim, profoundly skeptical. "And what about this Bellmann bloke, then? How's he mixed up in it?"

Isabel Meredith looked away. "I think," she whispered, "it might be murder."

"Go on."

"He's never said it directly. But . . . he's given hints and signs. It's something to do with this."

She opened a drawer and took out a pocketbook. From it she withdrew a yellowed newspaper clipping. It was undated.

SENSATIONAL MURDER
PRESERVED IN THE ICE

A sensational discovery was made last month in the forests of Siberia. The body of a man, perfectly preserved in the ice of a frozen river, was found by a hunter. At first it was thought that the victim had fallen into the water and drowned, but upon examination it was seen that he had been stabbed several times in the throat and chest.

There was no clue to his identity, and but for its chance discovery by the hunter, the body would undoubtedly have been carried northward by the spring floods, to be lost forever in the Arctic Ocean.

The case has aroused great interest in Russia, where the disappearance

There the clipping ended. Jim looked up in frustration. "Was there a date on this?" he said.

"I don't know. I found it when . . . it fell out of his coat pocket. When he saw me with it, he went pale. He said it had set off some strange vision in his mind. Why, Mr. Taylor? Does it hold any meaning for you?"

Jim remembered Nellie Budd's voice coming out of the darkness in Streatham: *He's still there, all in a glass coffin.* . . . It *is* all connected, he thought. The body in the ice, the fight in Mackinnon's vision, blood on the snow . . .

"D'you know a woman called Nellie Budd?" he said.

"No," she said, bewildered. "Who is she?"

"She's a whatsit, a medium. Nothing to do with Mackinnon, except that this cutting links up with something she said once. Can I keep it?"

She hesitated. He could tell she didn't want to let anything of Mackinnon's out of her control.

"Well, all right," he went on. "I'll just copy it down. Didn't he say anything more about it?"

She shook her head. Then as he started writing in his notebook she said, "I just don't know what to do, Mr. Taylor. I do love him so much. I'd give anything to help him—anything in the world. . . . Everything about him is so precious to me. I wish I could earn enough to provide for him! To think of him in that horrible place of Mrs. Mooney's, unable to show himself—an artist, a great artist like him! Oh, I'm sorry. I expect this sounds ridiculous, a woman with . . . I could never expect him to want . . . I'm sorry. I shouldn't have said all that. But I speak to no one, and I am so lonely."

Jim finished copying the clipping, glad not to have

to face her. He didn't know what to say; her emotion was so naked and helpless. He ran his finger over the embroidery, his mind racing.

"D'you make this?" he said.

She nodded.

"I can get you a good price for stuff like this. You don't have to live in a poky little room like this, earning pennies. I know what you're thinking—you do it to hide away, don't you? I bet you only come out at night."

"It's true. But—"

"Listen, Miss Meredith. What you've shown me tonight is a big help. I don't know if he's ever going to come back here. I reckon he's done a bunk, meself, out of that stink-hole, and you'll be lucky to see him again. No," he said as she started to protest, "I ain't finished. I'll give you one of our cards, and I'll put another address on the back—it's a young lady. Miss Lockhart. She's one of the firm—she's a good 'un. If you need anyone to go to, you call on her. And if you do see Mackinnon again, make him come and see us. All right? Or let me know yourself. It's for his sake, after all, silly bugg—bloke. If we can clear up this business, he can go back on the stage and do his tricks again, and we can all breathe easy."

As he left Lambeth, he found himself whistling, for he'd made progress; but then he thought of her strange, lonely, passionate life and stopped. Villainy was nothing new to him, and even murder was understandable and clear-cut. But love was a mystery.

WHEN HE got back to Burton Street, he paused in the darkened shop, hearing voices raised in the kitchen.

Sally was there, and she wasn't pleased with Fred, by the sound of it.

Jim turned the handle and walked in. Webster was seated peacefully by the fire, pipe going, whiskey on the arm of the chair, feet on the fender, deep in one of Jim's penny magazines. Chaka lay at his feet, grinding a hambone to splinters and taking up half the floor, while Frederick and Sally were standing face to face across the table, their tempers straining at the leash, voices shaking.

"Evening," said Jim. No one took any notice. He helped himself to a bottle of beer from the larder and came to sit down opposite Webster. "I've found Mackinnon," he said, pouring his beer. "And I know what he's up to. And I found out what Nellie Budd meant. I bet that's more than you silly buggers have done. I'm talking to meself, ain't I? No one's heard a word. Oh, well." He took a long swig from the mug and looked at the cover of the penny dreadful that Webster was reading. "The treasure's under Skeleton Rock," he said, and Webster looked up. "The Clancy Gang put it there after they blew up the bank. Deadwood Dick disguises himself as an outlaw and joins the gang. Ned Buckeye—the new crook—that's Deadwood Dick, only you ain't supposed to know."

Webster tossed the magazine down, exasperated. "What'd you tell me that for?" he said. "You spoiled it."

"I had to wake you up somehow. What's going on with these two, then?"

Webster looked up vaguely at Frederick and Sally. "Don't know," he said. "I wasn't listening. I was

enjoying Deadwood Dick. They quarreling or something?"

Frederick was banging his fist on the table. "If
you'd had the sense—" he was saying.

"Don't you talk to me about sense," Sally came
back, tight-lipped. "I told you not to get in my way,
didn't I? If you want to work together on a case—"

"Shut yer gob-boxes, the pair of you!" said Jim
loudly. "I never heard such a racket. If you want some
news, sit down and listen to this."

They stood for a moment, hostility still crackling
between them; and then Frederick pushed a chair
toward Sally and perched on a stool. She sat down.

"Well?" she said.

Jim told them about Isabel Meredith and read them
the words he'd copied from the newspaper clipping.

"The way I see it," he said, "Mackinnon's blackmailing Bellmann. He got hold of this cutting from
somewhere, put it together with the trance business,
and tried to touch Bellmann for a packet; and naturally
Bellmann won't have it. Simple. What d'you think?"

"What's the connection between Nellie Budd and
Mackinnon?" said Frederick.

"Stone the crows, I don't know," said Jim. "Maybe
they both belong to a Share-Your-Psychic-Secrets
Club. Maybe she's Bellmann's fancy lady?"

"And this business of inheritance," Sally said. "His
father was someone important—was that what she
said?"

"That's right."

"Perhaps that's true. Perhaps he's the heir to something Bellmann wants."

"*If* it's true," said Frederick. "Still, at least we've got a little further. Did this Miss Meredith strike you as being truthful?"

"Oh, yes," said Jim. "I mean, she came up to me in the first place. She needn't have done that at all if she'd wanted to hide anything. She's only got one thing on her mind, and that's keeping him safe. I'm sure she'd lie to do that if she had to, but she wasn't lying to me. I'd swear to it."

"Hmm," said Frederick, rubbing his jaw. "Pax again, Lockhart?"

"All right," she said grudgingly. "But I wish you'd tell me straightaway when you find something out. If I'd known it was Bellmann who was chasing Mr. Mackinnon, I'd have had something else up my sleeve when I saw him."

"It was a damn silly thing to do anyway, if you ask me," said Frederick. "Charging straight in and—"

"Yes, but I don't ask you," Sally snapped. "You've already—"

"Enough!" said Jim. "Who wants some cheese and pickles? Mr. Webster? How's yer bone, Chuckles?"

Chaka thumped his tail on the floor as Jim rubbed his ears. Frederick brought out a loaf of bread and some cheese, and Sally cleared the table, and within a few minutes they were eating. When they finished they put the plates on the bench behind them, and Jim got out his cards and they played whist, Sally partnering Fred against Jim and Webster, and before long they were laughing again, as they had done in the old days, before Sally went to Cambridge, when the partnership was new; before she and Fred had started

quarreling. Looking at them now, thought Jim, you'd
never believe they weren't in love with each other,
and not with a hopeless, doomed obsession like poor
Isabel Meredith's either. This was what love ought to
be like: playful and passionate and teasing, and dangerous, too, with sharp intelligence in it. They were
equals, these two—tigers, at the very least. They
could do anything in the world if they worked together. Why did they have to fight?

10

The Winter Garden

On Monday morning Charles Bertram arrived at the shop with some news. He had a friend at Elliott and Fry's (the smartest photographers in London; they specialized in portraits of wealthy people in fashionable surroundings), and this friend had told him of a commission they'd just received: to take the engagement photograph of Axel Bellmann and Lady Mary Wytham.

Frederick whistled. "When?" he said.

"This afternoon, at Wytham's house in Cavendish Square. I thought you'd be interested. It's a full-scale job—you know what Elliott and Fry are like. There'll be an assistant under-flashlamp holder, a junior lens polisher, a deputy tripod adjuster . . ."

"What's the name of your pal? It's not young Protherough, by any chance?"

"As a matter of fact, it is. D'you know him?"

"Yes—and he owes me a favor too. Well done, Charlie. So Bellmann's getting married, eh? And to that lovely girl . . . Well, I'm damned."

And he seized his coat and hat and ran out.

                    *   *   *

SALLY GAVE a morning a week to Garland and Lockhart's, to keep an eye on the accounts and to discuss
developments with Webster and Mr. Blaine. She'd
come in that morning expecting Frederick to be there
as well, because Mr. Blaine had mentioned the need
for more space and hoped Frederick would back his
arguments.

"You see, Miss Lockhart," Mr. Blaine said as they
stood by the counter, "I think we need some kind of
clerical assistance, but as you are aware, there's very
little room for it to take place in here. I don't know
whether there might be room in a corner of the new
studio. . . ."

"Absolutely not," said Webster firmly. "In fact, I'm
beginning to wonder whether the studio's going to be
big enough anyway."

"How are they getting on with it?" said Sally.

"Come and have a look," said Webster. "Busy,
Charles?"

Charles Bertram joined them in the yard behind the
shop. The new studio building was nearly complete;
the roof was tiled, and two plasterers were working on
the walls, but the windows were still empty. They
picked their way through the planks and the ladders
and the wheelbarrows and stood on the newly laid
floorboards in a patch of thin, wintry sunlight.

"I'm wondering, you see," said Webster, "whether
we're going to have enough room in here for the tracking camera. We'll only manage if we have the rails
going round in a horseshoe shape—and then the light
won't be constant, either. Unless we black the whole

place out and use artificial light. But the emulsion won't be sensitive enough at the speed we'll be using . . ."

Charles saw Sally's expression and said, "There is a solution. This building's quite adaptable—it doesn't have to be a zoetrope studio. There isn't room enough in the shop for everything we do at the moment. Miss Renshaw would be able to take twice the number of bookings if we weren't so pushed for studio space. Why not put a wall across here—just a light partition would do—and divide this into another better studio *and* the office space Mr. Blaine needs? Webster's quite right—we can't get a tracking camera in here, and we were silly to think we could."

"But you must have known . . ." Sally began. "What did you ever have it built for if it's too small?"

The two men looked sheepishly at each other.

"Well, it wasn't when we first designed it," Webster explained. "But we hadn't thought of the tracking camera then. We were thinking in terms of a fixed camera with a rapid plate-changing mechanism. There'd have been room for that in here. And that's where the future lies—with a single camera. So the money's not wasted."

"I suppose you'll want to buy a field next," she said. "You're no better than Fred. Where is he, anyway?"

"Gone to Elliott and Fry's," said Charles. "Your Mr. Bellmann's getting married, and they're taking an engagement portrait."

"Married?" she said, astonished. The idea of marriage seemed so at odds with the Bellmann she'd seen at Baltic House the week before that she could hardly imagine it.

"This field idea . . ." began Webster, not interested in Bellmann. "What d'you think, Charles? We'd have to build a wall and lay the rails perfectly level parallel to it. Facing south. We could make it as long as we liked. Roof it over with glass, perhaps, against the weather . . ."

"Not yet," said Sally. "There's no money for it. Get this studio built and earning as much as you say it will, and we'll see. Mr. Blaine, it looks as though you can have your office space. Do you need a full-time clerk? Or would just mornings be enough?"

The tracking camera that Webster mentioned was an invention of his own, based on an idea from a photographer called Muybridge. It existed only on paper so far, since they hadn't had the space to set it up. It was really a battery of cameras mounted on wheels, which would be drawn on rails past a certain point and exposed in rapid succession in order to capture the movement of a subject there. The idea of photographing movement was in the air at the time; many people were experimenting with different techniques, but no one was close to a breakthrough. Webster believed that he had part of the answer in his tracking camera. Charles Bertram was working on more sensitive emulsions to allow faster exposures. If they could find a way of capturing a negative on paper instead of glass, they might be able to mount a roll of sensitized paper behind one lens and use that instead of the tracking camera—provided they could make a mechanism accurate enough to pull the paper through without tearing it. If they managed that, they could use the new studio for the zoetrope, as Charles called it. There was a lot to be done.

Sally and Mr. Blaine left them discussing it happily, and went back inside to think about what they needed in the way of office help.

EARLY THAT afternoon, Lord Wytham's daughter, Lady Mary, was sitting in the winter garden of his house in Cavendish Square. Too big to be called a conservatory, this glass and iron structure contained palms, rare ferns, orchids, and a pool in which swam slow, dark fish. Lady Mary (in white—a high-necked, ornate dress of silk, with a pearl choker, and everything the color of snow, like a sacrificial victim) sat in a bamboo chair under the fronds of a large fern. There was a book in her hand, but she wasn't reading.

The day was chilly and dry, with a hazy brightness that the glass and greenery diffused into something almost subaqueous. From the middle of the winter garden Lady Mary could see nothing but green and hear nothing but the trickle of water that fed the pool, and the occasional gurgle of steam in the pipes along the wall.

Lady Mary's beauty was not a fashionable sort. The taste of the time ran to women built like sofas, with an air of permanence, comfort, and stuffing, whereas Lady Mary was more like a wild bird or a young animal—slender and light-boned, with her mother's warm coloring and her father's wide gray eyes. She was all delicacy and shy fire; and she had discovered already that her beauty was a curse.

It awed people. Even hardened charmers, eligible young men about town, felt uneasy in her presence, clumsy and dirty and tongue-tied. And quite early on in her teens she had felt an intuition that instead of attracting love, she might even helplessly repel it, by being too beautiful. Already there were shadows of tragedy in her cloud-colored eyes; and her new engagement was only part of it.

After she had been sitting still for some time, she heard voices from the library beyond the glass door. She trembled; the book fell from her hand to the iron grille of the floor.

The door opened, and a footman said, "Mr. Bellmann, my lady."

Axel Bellmann, in a gray morning coat, stepped past and bowed slightly. Lady Mary smiled at the footman.

"Thank you, Edward," she said.

He withdrew, and the door whispered shut. Lady Mary sat quite still at the edge of the pool, her hands folded in her lap, as quiet as the white water lily beside her. Bellmann coughed gently; in the palm-laden air of the winter garden, it sounded like the soft growl a leopard might make before dropping from a branch onto the frail back of a gazelle.

He moved toward her and spoke.

"Am I permitted to wish you a good afternoon?"

"I see no reason to forbid it."

He smiled slightly. He was standing two or three yards away, hands behind his back, a shaft of pale sunlight gilding one side of his heavy blond face.

"You look enchanting," he said.

She didn't reply at once but reached up and broke

off a piece of the glossy palm leaf that hung just over her head and shredded it quietly with her nails.

Then she said, "Thank you." It was little more than a whisper.

He pulled up another chair and sat down close by. "You will be interested, I hope, to hear my plans for our married life," he said. "We shall live at Hyde Park Gate for the time being, though naturally we shall need a place in the country. Do you enjoy the sea, Mary? Do you like sailing?"

"I don't know. I have never been at sea."

"You will enjoy it. I am having a steam yacht built; it will be launched in time for the wedding. We might spend our honeymoon aboard. You could help me choose her name. I hope you will launch her."

She made no reply. Her eyes were cast down sightlessly; the bits of shredded palm leaf lay on her white lap. Her hands were still.

"Look at me," he said. His voice was hard and even.

She looked up at the man she had agreed to marry and tried to keep her expression empty.

"The photographers are coming," he said. "I wish to have a picture that expresses pleasure and satisfaction in our betrothal. As my fiancée, as my wife, as the hostess of my house, you will not use any public occasion to express discontent, whatever you might feel privately. Naturally, I hope you will not be discontented anyway. Do you understand?"

She found herself trembling. "Yes, Mr. Bellmann," she managed to say.

"Oh, not Mr. Bellmann anymore. My name is Axel,

and that is what you will call me. Let me hear you say it."

"Yes, Axel."

"Good. Now tell me about these plants. I know very little about plants. What is this one called?"

Promptly at two thirty, Mr. Protherough of Elliott and Fry's arrived at Lord Wytham's house. His three assistants had an unexpected hour off, with five shillings apiece to keep quiet about it; and in their place were Frederick, Jim, and Charles Bertram.

Jim was wearing his best suit and had his hair slicked down flat. Frederick, with darkened eyebrows and cheek pads to fill his face out, was scarcely recognizable. Mr. Protherough, a sandy-haired young man with spectacles, had entered into the spirit of it, but Frederick knew that his job was at risk if anything went wrong.

The footman who opened the door was disinclined to let them in at first.

"Tradesmen's entrance," he said, sniffing, and made to close the door.

The Honorable Charles, who was dressed with faultless elegance, said, "One moment, my man. Do you know who you're trying to keep out of your master's house?"

The footman opened the door an inch wider. The trace of a sneer appeared on his face.

"Yes," he said. "Photographers. Tradesmen. Tradesmen's entrance round the corner."

"Tell me," said Charles, "when Sir Frederick Leighton was painting Lady Wytham's portrait, did you direct him to the tradesmen's entrance?"

The footman was now looking apprehensive. "No," he said cautiously.

"My card," said Charles, extracting it wearily. "Have the goodness to inform your master that the photographic artists have arrived. Did arrive, in fact, promptly at two thirty, but are now"—he looked at a gold watch—"nearly five minutes late."

The footman looked at the card, gulped, and shrank at least three inches.

"Oh. Ah. I beg your pardon, sir, I'm sure. Please come in. I shall inform his lordship of your prompt arrival, sir. This way, if you please, sir. . . ."

Jim assumed a haughty expression (not easy, after a cheerful wink from Charles) and helped Frederick carry in the equipment. They were shown into the winter garden. While Mr. Protherough organized the setting and checked the light, Frederick and Jim set up the tripod and prepared the plates. They would be wet-collodion pictures; studios preferred the familiar process for large formal photographs—it was fiddly, but it guaranteed a good result. Charles, meanwhile, was talking to Lord Wytham.

It was warm in the winter garden; the sun was thin, but the steam in the pipes kept the air close and moist. Jim, thinking of nothing in particular, mopped his brow as he adjusted the leg of a tripod. He was aware of Bellmann and Lady Mary coming around a corner of the path, and looked up—and then felt as if he'd been struck over the heart with a hammer.

Lady Mary. She was so perfect he could hardly stand. *Lovely* wasn't the word—nor *beautiful*—he felt as if he'd been picked up like a leaf in a hurricane and whirled away—helpless, suddenly and totally and utterly in love. It was quite physical, the effect it had; his knees shook and he had to remember to breathe. He wondered (with the part of his mind that wasn't stunned and could still think) how it was that Bellmann could stand there calmly and talk, while her hand lay on his arm. As if it meant nothing! She was wearing something white and her hair was dark and glossy, and her cheeks were warm, and her eyes wide and misty. . . . He nearly groaned aloud.

In a dream, Jim moved automatically where Mr. Protherough told him, handed a plate to Frederick, held a palm branch out of the way, shifted her bamboo chair near the pool, propped up a white sheet just out of the picture to reflect a little more light on the shadowed side of her face, and all the time talked to her passionately inside his head and listened with awed delight to her imagined responses.

Bellmann didn't matter a bit. He was irrelevant. She marry him? Ridiculous. It was impossible. Look at the way she sat beside him, proud and separate and dreaming; look at how those slender, lovely fingers idly removed a fleck of moss from her skirt and trailed it in the water; look at the warm tenseness of her neck just under the dusky pink ear where the hair curled back waywardly. . . . Jim was lost forever.

Around him the photographic session went on smoothly. Mr. Protherough dived beneath the camera cloth, exposed the plate, emerged again; Frederick handed him a new plate and took the exposed one back; Lord Wytham hovered dimly in the background, then left them alone. Charles watched it all with the proprietorial ease of a landowner watching his gamekeepers at work. They took a dozen pictures altogether, including one of Lady Mary alone, for which Jim gave silent thanks.

When they'd nearly finished, Frederick leaned across and whispered, "Careful, Jim. You're staring."

"Oh, God," Jim groaned, and turned away to hand Mr. Protherough the last plate. This was for a picture of the couple standing beside some classical goddess, but Charles broke in to suggest that Lady Mary should sit. It would improve the balance of the composition, he said, and Mr. Protherough agreed.

"Bring the chair, please, Mr. Sanders," said Charles to Frederick, as Jim helped Mr. Protherough turn the tripod around. Frederick picked up the bamboo chair from beside the pool and carried it to the statue—

And suddenly Jim was aware of a silence.

He looked up to see Bellmann holding Frederick's arm and staring at him intently. Frederick was gazing back in innocent bewilderment.

Oh, keep it up, Fred, thought Jim desperately, he's rumbled you . . .

"Tell me," said Bellmann (and everyone was still now, including Mr. Protherough), "were you at Lady Harborough's house last week?"

"Me, sir?" Frederick inquired in a gentle, studious voice. "No, indeed, sir."

"Posing as a guest?" Bellmann went on, with an edge to his voice.

"A guest at Lady Harborough's? Oh, no, not me, sir. Shall I put the chair this side, or that, sir?"

"Last week," said Bellmann more loudly, "a man—who, if he was not you, was your double—was at Lady

Harborough's house on the evening of her charity concert. That man was prying and watching the other guests in what I thought was a suspicious manner. I ask you again: were you that man?"

But before Frederick could reply, Lady Mary herself spoke.

"You're forgetting," she said to Bellmann, "I was there too. I saw the man you mean, and this isn't him."

"If I may conjecture, sir," Frederick put in diffidently, "you might possibly have seen my cousin Frederick. He's by way of being a private detective, and several ladies and gentlemen have patronized his services where security and the safety of property are concerned."

He blinked innocently.

"Hmm," said Bellmann. "Very well. But it is a remarkably close resemblance." He stood aside for Frederick to put the chair down.

Jim could feel Mr. Protherough relax; if Frederick had been discovered, he'd have lost his job at Elliott and Fry's. They were all taking a risk—and what were they hoping to gain? It was daft.

But if they hadn't come, he'd never have seen her. She sounded so young; she could hardly be more than sixteen. What the hell was going on, that she should marry a man like that?

Jim looked at Bellmann more carefully as he posed, standing beside the chair and gazing down at her. There was danger in that heavy face, Jim felt, but for whom? Lady Mary was toying with a handkerchief, in a sort of sulky boredom, while Bellmann stood, massive, over her. He put his hand on her shoulder and obediently she sighed and composed herself, looking steadily through those wonderful cloud-gray eyes at the lens.

The picture was taken; the plate was put away, and the photographers started to pack up. Charles strolled along the path, talking easily to Bellmann, and then came the moment that Jim had been longing for for twenty minutes—or a lifetime.

She'd stayed by the statue, lost in thought, while Frederick helped Mr. Protherough with the camera and tripod. One hand rested on the back of the chair, the other twisted a curl around her finger; and then she looked up and saw Jim—and her eyes were sparkling.

He took a step toward her. He couldn't help it. She looked over her shoulder swiftly, saw they were alone, and leaned forward so their faces were only inches apart. He felt dizzy, and he put out a hand to her, and—

"*Is* it him?" she said quietly, swiftly. "The man from Lady Harborough's?"

"Yes," said Jim. His voice was hoarse. "My lady, I—"

"Is he a detective? Really?"

"Yes. Something's wrong, isn't it? Can you talk?"

"Please," she whispered. "Please help. I don't know who else to speak to. I'm all alone here, and I must get away. I *can't* marry him—"

"Listen," he said, his heart bursting, "can you remember this? My name's Jim Taylor, of Garland and Lockhart, Burton Street. We're investigating your Mr.

Bellmann. There's something rum going on. But we'll help, I promise. Get in touch as soon as you can and we'll—"

"The chair back here, Taylor, if you please," called Mr. Protherough.

Jim picked up the chair and smiled at her. A little answering smile passed across her face and was gone, like the wind in a cornfield, and then she turned away.

He said nothing to the others as they left. There was nothing he could say; he could hardly believe he was awake, or even alive. He might have felt like singing if he hadn't felt like laughing, and crying bitter tears, all at the same time.

LATER THAT DAY a short, thickset young man stood hammering at the door of a respectable lodging house in Lambeth. Beside him on the step waited another man—a bruiser, to judge by his flattened nose and cauliflower ears. Jim would have recognized them; they were the men he'd rescued Mackinnon from in the Britannia Music Hall.

When the door opened (by an elderly woman in a neat apron), they pushed inside without a word and slammed it shut behind them.

"Listen carefully," said the young man, holding the handle of a stout cane under the woman's chin. "Young lady with a birthmark on her face. Where is she?"

"Oh! Merciful heavens, who are you? What do you want?" gasped the landlady. "Let go of my wrist! What are you doing?"

The bruiser had her arm behind her. The young

man said, "We want to find her. Take us to her—now. And don't shriek out, else my friend here'll break your arm."

"Oh! Oh, please, don't hurt me! Let me go, please—"

The bruiser, at a nod from the other, let go, and the landlady fell against the banister in the narrow hall.

"Upstairs," she gasped. "Second floor."

"Go on, then," said the man with the cane, and she stumbled upstairs ahead of them.

Mr. Harris (for that was his name) prodded the old woman's back with his stick as they climbed.

"Not quick enough," he said. "What's your name, by the way?"

"Mrs. Elphick," she said with difficulty. "Please, my heart isn't strong—"

"Oh, dear," said Mr. Harris. "Mackinnon broke it, has he?"

They were on the first-floor landing. She slumped against the wall, her hand to her breast.

"I don't know what you mean," she said faintly.

"Stop dawdling and get a move on. We need a woman's pure and guiding light, don't we, Sackville?"

The bruiser grunted a simian agreement and prodded Mrs. Elphick into movement. They climbed the next staircase and stopped outside the door of the first room.

"Well, now, Sackville," said Mr. Harris. "This is where we call upon your particular talents. Mrs. Elphick, you are about to witness a scene that may distress you. Bad luck."

"Oh, no, please—" the lady said as Sackville the

bruiser took a step backward and then kicked the door hard with the sole of his foot, just beside the lock. It splintered at once and crashed open, to a startled cry from inside. Sackville shoved the broken door aside and held it back for Mr. Harris, who walked through slowly, tapping his cane in the palm of his hand and looking around curiously.

Isabel Meredith, half her face drained of blood and the other half flaring like a fire by contrast, stood by her table, holding some intricate piece of embroidery.

"What do you want?" she whispered. "Who are you?"

"Mackinnon's what we want. You're looking after him. Does your landlady know?" said Mr. Harris malevolently. He turned to Mrs. Elphick. "Did you know, my good woman, that your tenant's been keeping a man in here? I think he's a man, anyway, except that he keeps running away, which a man don't do usually. Is he here at the moment, Miss Birthmark?"

Isabel gasped. She wouldn't have been pretty even without her disfigurement; she hadn't the vitality. But she wasn't used to outright cruelty, and she didn't know how to respond.

"I said," went on Mr. Harris, "is he here now? Under the bed, for instance? Have a look, Sackville."

Sackville lifted the iron bedstead and tipped it over onto the floor. There was nothing beneath it but a faded china chamber pot. Isabel hid her face.

"Look, Sackville," said Mr. Harris, "A dainty little thunder box. See if he ain't hiding in there."

Sackville aimed a kick at it, and it shattered into a thousand pieces.

"Please—" Isabel began. "He's not here—I promise—"

"Where is he, then?"

"I don't know! I haven't seen him for days! Please—"

"Ah, but you did help him, didn't you? You was seen, you naughty girl. And don't say it wasn't you—you can't hide a dial like that one."

"What do you want?" she cried. "Please, leave me alone! I don't know where he is. I swear it—"

"Well, well. Shame." Mr. Harris looked around. "Now the trouble with me is, I'm a skeptical man. I ain't got a simple faith in human nature—and I think you're lying. So what I'll do is this. I'll ask young Sackville here to tear up and burn all your work in front of your eyes. He could smack you about a bit instead, but you look horrible enough as it is, and no one'd notice. Off you go, Sackville, my boy."

"No! No, please! It's all I've got in the world. Anything but that! It's my livelihood—I beg you—"

She fell on her knees and clutched his coat. Sackville pulled the tablecloth off and started to tear it into small shreds; she wept and shook Mr. Harris's coat, but he took no notice.

"Have a look, Sackville lad. There's bound to be dresses and nightgowns and petticoats and all sorts. Tear 'em up, tear 'em up. Don't feel inhibited by the ladies' presence. These shrieks and cries is a sign, young Sackville, as you're doing your work like a British yeoman."

And though both women tried to restrain him (Mrs. Elphick being flung aside, and Isabel knocked down and nearly rendered insensible), Sackville, within five

minutes, systematically destroyed every specimen of
her work. There were dresses; there were nightgowns;
there were precious christening robes made of lawn,
which needed the finest and most delicate stitching to
repair them; there were items she was making for sale
to her regular customers—pretty lace gloves, shawls,
fine handkerchiefs, embroidered blouses, goffered
widow's caps, filmy muslin petticoats. Everything she
owned was hauled out from its tissue paper wrappings
and ripped to shreds.

Finally Isabel flung herself into a chair and sobbed
passionately. Mrs. Elphick watched, trembling, as
Sackville thrust the large, snowy pile into the fireplace.

Then Mr. Harris opened the one door he hadn't yet
touched, and took out a small japanned tin box. He
shook it, but it was light and didn't rattle.

Instantly Isabel was on her feet.

"No," she said. "I'll—I'll tell you where you can
find him. But don't touch that. Please give it back.
Please."

"Ah!" said Mr. Harris. "This is our little treasure, is
it?" He pried at the lid but found it locked. "Well,
then. Tell me where he is and you can keep it. Else
young Sackville here can find a use for it."

Her hands reached out for it, but he held it back.
She was incapable of taking her eyes from it. Pale and
sickly and trembling with the sense of what she was
doing, she said in a shaking voice, "He's appearing
tomorrow night at the Royal Music Hall in High
Holborn. Please—you won't hurt him?"

He handed her the box, which she clutched at once
to her breast.

"Hurt him? Well, that's out of my hands now. I cannot influence the wheel of fate. The Royal in High Holborn—yes, I know the place. Here y'are, Sackville."

Mr. Harris handed him a box of matches.

"Now," he said, "what you're probably thinking is that as soon as our backs is turned you'll go scuttling off and warn him. I wouldn't if I was you. I wouldn't say a word. I'm keeping Sackville on a leash at the moment, and I wouldn't like to say what he'd do if I let him off it. You just be discreet, that's what I'd do."

"But why? What do you want him for? What's he ever done to you?"

"Oh, me personally? Nothing at all. But my master wants to speak to him somewhat urgent on a matter of family business. See, I'm a lawyer. Did I mention that? Kind of a lawyer, anyway. Now you better stand back, because what'll probably happen in a minute is that the chimney'll catch fire. That could be dangerous, so him and me'll leave in a little while. But I trust you're grateful to us for making the importance of this clear to you. Perhaps you'd care to reimburse me for my time and Sackville's effort? I paid him a sovereign for this job. Course, it comes out of my master's pocket, but think how pleased he'll be if he finds that small expense defrayed already."

There was something in his mock-ingratiating manner that was chilling and horrible; Isabel had no strength left to resist, and with trembling fingers she opened her purse and took out a sovereign. Sackville took it from her.

"Say thank you, Sackville," said Mr. Harris.

"Thank you, miss," he said dutifully.

"And as this is thirsty work, I think half a crown to buy us a drink would be a nice way of showing your appreciation for what we've done."

Another coin changed hands.

"It's all I have," she said faintly. "I have nothing to eat. Please . . ."

"Yes," said Mr. Harris thoughtfully, "I ain't eaten since breakfast neither. A nice chop'd go down a treat. What d'you say, Sackville? But I don't expect you to pay for that," he added to her. "A man's got to eat in the way of nature. I'll pay for that."

"What am I going to do?" she said helplessly.

"I don't know, I must confess. I find that a hard question to answer. Come on, Sackville, strike a match, my boy."

"No!" cried Mrs. Elphick, but she shrank back as Mr. Harris wagged a finger at her. She clutched her mouth as Sackville lit the edge of the cloth crammed into the fireplace. It caught at once with a roar.

Isabel was sobbing like a child, still clutching the tin to herself, and rocking to and fro with misery and guilt. Mr. Harris patted her on the head.

"Never mind," he said. "Put it down to experience, is my advice. Never fall in love with a Scotchman—they can't be trusted. Come, Sackville, let these ladies deal with the fire; we don't want to get in the way, that's bad manners. Good day to you both."

11

~~~

The Demon-Trap

NEXT MORNING, BEFORE THE SUN WAS UP, A HAND THRUST a scribbled note through the mail slot at 45, Burton Street, and a veiled figure slipped away into the gray light.

Jim was the first to find it. He hadn't slept well; images of Lady Mary haunted his pillow, and more than once he'd groaned aloud as he thought of her warm coral cheeks, her cloud-filled eyes, her urgent whisper. . . . Finally he decided there was no more sleep to be had and dragged himself down to the kitchen, yawning and scratching and cursing, and lit the fire to make himself some tea.

As he put the kettle on the hob, he heard the mail slot snap in the empty shop and blinked fully awake. He looked up at the clock on the mantelpiece: it wasn't six yet. Turning up the collar of his dressing gown against the draft, he went into the shop and saw the little scrap of white paper in the dimness. He raised the blind and read:

To Mr. Taylor:

Mr. Mackinnon is in great danger. There are two men going to lie in wait for him tonight at the Royal Music Hall in High Holborn. One of them is called Sackville. I beg you to help by any means possible. There is no one else to ask and I can do nothing for him.

I.M.

I.M.? . . . Isabel Meredith, of course.

Jim grabbed the key from the hook, and, wrenching the door open, ran out to stare up and down the silent street. The gaslights were still glowing, haloed by mist, and the sky was lightening; and though he could hear the quiet clop of hooves and the trundle of wheels from the next street as a trader made his way to market, there was no one in sight, and nothing to show which way she'd gone.

SALLY HADN'T forgotten Axel Bellmann's threat. She was conscious every time she went to her office that there were many workers in the building who watched her go in and out, there was a landlord's chief clerk on the ground floor to whom she paid rent, there was a small import agency (currants, dates, tobacco from Turkey) in the office next-door with whom she shared a coal supply—and that any of them could be working for Bellmann.

She'd wondered briefly whether, to safeguard herself, she ought to employ some respectable woman as a blazon of propriety; but then she'd have to find something for her to do, and teach her to do it, and pay her money she couldn't really afford. In the end she decided to take no notice of the threat and to carry on as normal. But she was glad every time she opened her door to find a woman standing there and not a man, and cross with her own weakness for feeling glad.

As it happened, her first client that morning was a woman. She was a vivacious, bright-eyed Lancastrian girl who'd come to London to study to be a teacher, and she was looking for advice on how best to manage the small amount of money her grandfather had left her. When Sally had described a number of possibilities, and they'd settled on the most useful, the young woman said, "I was ever so surprised to find that S. Lockhart was a lady. I mean, pleased as well, of course. How on earth did you manage to get a job like this?"

Sally told her and then said, "Where do you come from, Miss Lewis?"

"Barrow-in-Furness," she said. "But I don't want to stay in a little corner of Lancashire all my life. I want to go abroad. I'd like to see Canada and South America and Australia. . . . That's why I'm going to train as a teacher, you see. So I'll have something useful to do."

"Barrow," said Sally. "Shipbuilding—is that right?"

"Yes, and docks and railways. Both of my brothers are in the docks. Clerks. They were ever so put out when Grandad left his bit of money to me instead of them—thought they had a right to it, being men. But I was the one who always listened to his tales. He was a sailor, you see. He told me all about Niagara Falls and the Amazon and the Great Barrier Reef and everything, and I got so excited I couldn't wait to be off myself. . . . We used to look at pictures in the old stereoscope, and he'd tell me all about them. He was lovely."

Sally smiled. Then a thought struck her.

"I don't suppose you've heard of a firm called North Star, by any chance?"

"North Star—yes, that's in Barrow. North Star Castings. Something to do with railways? I don't know. There was a bit of trade union trouble, I think. Or perhaps I'm wrong. I tell you who would know. There's a lady who lives in Muswell Hill, wherever that is—is that in London? I thought it was. I'll write down her address. She used to be my Sunday school teacher till she got married and came down here. But her brother used to work for North Star, or the firm that North Star took over, anyway. She'd be able to tell you more about it. Mrs. Seddon, 27 Cromwell Gardens, Muswell Hill. Give her my regards, won't you. Tell her I'll come and see her myself when I've settled in at the college. . . ."

At last, thought Sally. I must be lucky after all.

"Let me know if you need any more advice," she said as Miss Lewis left. "And good luck with your teaching."

AFTER SHE'D finished for the day and locked the office, she stood for a while on the step, deciding whether to go to Muswell Hill there and then or to write a letter, and she was still standing there when Jim found her.

"Sal! Game for a lark? You're not going home, are you?"

"Well . . . What sort of lark?"

"Come to the music hall. Mackinnon's in trouble, and Fred and I are going to keep an eye on things."

They walked along together through the early

evening crowd—the bowler-hatted clerks, the office boys, the news vendors, the crossing-sweepers—and Jim told her about Isabel's note. They waited outside a chophouse for the road to clear so they could cross, and in the fragrant steam and the warm light she caught a glimpse of the Jim she'd first met six years before, a scruffy, inky office boy, tough and bright as a sparrow; and she laughed with happiness.

"Game for a lark?" she said. "I should bloody say so, mate. Lead me to it!"

Chaka caught her expression and wagged his tail.

SALLY WENT HOME and changed her dress, and the three of them met in the queue outside the Royal Music Hall at half past seven. Frederick was in evening dress and carrying a stick, and to his immense surprise she kissed him.

"Worth coming," he said. "What's on the bill, Jim?"

Jim had been studying the poster on the stand outside the doors. He came back to his place in the queue and said quietly, "I reckon Mackinnon's calling himself the Great Mephisto. I don't suppose he's one of Madame Taroczy's Female Hungarian Velocipede Troupe or Señor Ambrosio Chavez, the Boneless Wonder. . . ."

"I wonder what a female velocipede is," said Frederick. "Pit or gallery? I suppose we ought to be close to the stage, in case we need to get up there. What d'you think?"

"There's no quick way down from the gallery here," said Jim. "We want to be as far forward as we can get. The only trouble with that is, we won't be able to watch the audience and look out for this Sackville geezer."

The doors were opened, and the queue moved forward into the gaudy foyer, where flaring gaslights shone on gilt and mahogany and glass. They paid one shilling and sixpence each for seats at the end of the front row and sat down in the smoke-laden atmosphere to watch the orchestra taking their places and tuning up. Jim looked around from time to time at the rest of the audience.

"The trouble is," he grumbled, "we don't know what we're looking for. They're not going to carry placards round their necks, after all."

"What about the fellows you saw when you got Mackinnon out of the Britannia?" said Frederick.

"Well . . . There's a lot of people here, Fred. And they could be backstage, anyway—but I don't think so, somehow. They've got a good stage doorman here. I think they'll come at him from the front, if they do it at all."

Then Sally, looking around herself, glanced up at the boxes on the other side. There were half a dozen of them, and four were dark, but in one of the other two sat three men—and one of them was looking directly at her through opera glasses.

He saw her look, took the glasses away, and smiled and bowed slightly. She saw the glint of light on his gold-rimmed spectacles.

"Mr. Windlesham," she said involuntarily, and looked away.

"What's that?" said Frederick.

"Bellmann's secretary. He's in that box—the second one along—and he's seen me. What do we do now?"

"Well, we're in the same game, that's plain to see," said Frederick, and turned to stare up. "No point in trying to hide now; he can tell we're together. There's another fellow in there, Jim—no, two of them. Can you make them out?"

Jim was craning up as well, but he shook his head. "No," he said. "They're hanging back in the shadow. The shorter one could be the bloke I saw in Mackinnon's dressing room, but I wouldn't like to swear to it. Bloody nuisance. I'd go up and lock 'em in the box, same as I did that night, but they'd see me coming."

Frederick gave them a friendly wave and turned back to the stage. The orchestra was about to begin. He said to the others, "They can watch us, but we can get to the stage more quickly. If it comes to a scrap, Jim, we'll hold 'em off while Sally sticks to Mackinnon. Got your knuckles?"

Jim nodded. "That door behind the master of ceremonies' desk leads straight into the wings," he said. "They picked the wrong place to wait when they chose that box. It's the one advantage we got."

"Unless there are some more of them backstage," said Sally.

They couldn't say any more because the orchestra began, with a crash of cymbals and a thump on the bass drum, and, sitting where they were, they could hear nothing else. Jim, at the end of the row, cast an eye up to the box every few seconds while Frederick gave himself up to enjoying the entertainers.

Madame Taroczsy's Female Hungarian Velocipede Troupe came and went, and so did Miss Ellaline Bagwell (soprano), the Lightning Sketcher, and Mr. Jackson Sinnott (comic and patiotic songs); and still the three men didn't leave their box. Sally looked up once to find Mr. Windlesham's curious and mild expression, complete with glinting spectacles, still fixed on her, and she felt unpleasantly naked. She turned back and tried to ignore it.

Finally the master of ceremonies announced the Great Mephisto. There was a drumroll, the conductor's left hand rumbled at a chord in the bass of the piano while his right hand urged the four string players to a mysterious shimmer, and then with a flourish of cymbals the curtain rose. Frederick and Sally sat up.

There was a slender figure in tail coat and white tie at the center of the stage. He wore a white mask. Sally had never seen Mackinnon, but she knew at once who it was, and not only because Jim sat up alertly on her left and whispered, "That's him, the perisher."

Frederick was as relaxed as ever on her other side. She looked at him, saw an expression of pure, childlike enjoyment on his face, and found herself smiling in response. He turned and winked at her, and then the act began.

Whatever else he was, Mackinnon was an artist. It was clear that the mask was not only a means of concealing his identity but a positive part of the act he was developing—as important as the white-face make-up he'd worn previously. He didn't speak, and the atmosphere he engendered was sinister—emphasized by the number of tricks he performed that featured knives and swords, cutting and piercing and severing. Movement, mime, and above all the expressionless, mesmeric mask, all added to the sense of danger and horror. The audience, which had been rowdy and cheerful until then, fell still—but not with distaste or disapproval: they were awed. So was Sally. He was a phenomenal performer.

They had been watching him for some minutes, unable to take their eyes away, when Jim turned his head briefly to glance up at the box—and shook Sally's arm.

"They've gone!" he whispered.

Alarmed, she turned as well, and saw that the box was empty. Jim swore, and Frederick sat up.

"They had more sense than we did," Frederick said under his breath. "Damn it, they must have got backstage. As soon as he goes off, Jim, we'll make a run for it—"

But then Mackinnon sprang a surprise of his own. The music stopped in mid-bar, the magician stood with arms raised high—then he shook his hands, and two shimmering scarlet cloths rippled downward over his arms and hung to the floor like waterfalls of blood.

Simultaneously all the lights died away except for one narrow spotlight focused on him. There was utter silence in the audience as he walked to the front of the stage.

"Ladies and gentlemen," he said—the first words he'd spoken. His voice was light and melodious, though coming from his masked face it had the mystery of a strange god's voice in an ancient temple.

The orchestra was hushed. No one moved. It was as

if the whole theater was collectively holding its breath.

"Under these silk cloths," he continued, "I am holding two mighty gifts. In one hand I hold a jewel, an emerald of great antiquity and priceless value. In the other I hold—a knife."

A silent shiver ran over the audience.

"Life," he went on quietly, mesmerically, "and death. The emerald will give its possessor, should he wish to sell it, a lifetime of wealth and luxury. The dagger, on the other hand, I shall plunge into his heart—and death will enter with it.

"One of these gifts, but only one, I shall give to the person who is brave enough to answer a simple question. A correct answer wins the emerald—a wrong one wins the knife. But first, the gifts themselves."

He shook his left hand. The cloth rippled silkily to the floor in a blood-colored whisper, and there in his hand was a dark green flame—an emerald the size of a hen's egg, flashing with a sea-deep brilliance. The audience gasped. He set it carefully on the black velvet surface of a small table at his side.

Then he shook the other hand. The cloth fell, revealing the gleaming steel blade of a six-inch dagger. He held it out so the edge was horizontal. With his other hand he plucked at the air—and a white silk handkerchief appeared at his fingertips.

"So sharp is this blade," he said, "that the weight of the handkerchief alone will cut it in two."

He held the handkerchief high and let it fall. It drifted down slowly onto the blade—and without the slightest hitch or pause, fell neatly past it, sliced in half. Another gasp from the audience—more like a sigh this time, with a tremor of fear in it. Sally found herself spellbound too. She shook her head fiercely and pressed her knuckles together. Where were the men from the box? Were they backstage already, waiting in the wings?

"Death," Mackinnon was saying softly, "death by this knife would be as soft and gentle as the falling of the silk. Think of the pain of disease, the misery of old age, the despair of poverty . . . gone in a moment, banished forever! This is as great a gift as the other. Perhaps even greater."

He laid the knife beside the emerald and stepped back a pace.

"I shall do the deed," he said, "here and now, on this stage, in front of six hundred witnesses. And as a consequence, I shall hang. I know this. I am ready.

"Because this is a very solemn choice, I do not expect an answer at once. I shall let two minutes pass, by this clock."

The illuminated dial of a large clock appeared in the darkness behind him, with the hands showing two minutes to twelve.

"I shall set the clock going," he said, "and wait. If no one has offered to answer by the time it strikes, I shall take the gifts and conclude my performance. Tomorrow I shall repeat the offer, and I shall continue until it is taken up.

"Let us see if there is one among you who will dare to do it tonight. It only remains for me to ask the question.

"It is a simple one: What is my name?"

He fell silent. There was not a sound in the theater

except for the constant slight hissing of the gaslights, and the sudden first tick of the clock sounded clearly to every corner of the auditorium.

Seconds passed. No one moved; Mackinnon stood like a statue, his body as still as his masked face. There was silence from the audience, silence from the band, silence from the wings. The clock ticked on. The men from the box must be waiting in the shadows of the wings, held up by Mackinnon's surprise; but they wouldn't stay there forever, and now a minute had gone by.

It was no good waiting, Sally thought. She looked at Frederick and Jim. "We'll have to do it," she whispered, and Frederick nodded. She opened her bag, snatched out the pencil and paper she kept in there, and scribbled hastily. Her hand shook; she could feel the tension of the audience behind her, half convinced that the emerald was real, that he really would use the knife, that life and death really did hang on the outcome.

The hand of the clock was nearly at the twelve. A rustling whisper arose from all around as people breathed in and held their breath. She looked at Frederick and Jim, saw that they were ready, and stood up.

"I can answer it," she called.

A second later the clock struck, but no one heard it in the hubbub that broke out with the release of tension. Every head in the audience craned to look at her: she saw the white of all their eyes in the gloom.

"Good for you!" came a shout, and it was taken up at once with a hoarse and ragged cheer. Sally walked slowly across the front of the auditorium toward the

master of ceremonies, who was standing at the foot of
the steps. Under cover of the applause, she was aware
of Frederick and Jim slipping quietly through the door
that led backstage. But there was no time to think of
that; she needed all her concentration for Mackinnon.

The master of ceremonies offered his hand, and the
applause died away as she climbed up to the stage.
The silence that fell now was even deeper than
before. Sally walked forward. Windlesham is somewhere in the shadows, too, she thought, and he knows
who I am, even if the others don't. . . .

"So," said Mackinnon when she stopped a yard or
two from him. "One has arrived with an answer. She
comes to meet her fate. . . . Now let us hear: What is
my name?"

Sally could see the remarkable blackness of his eyes
through the chalk-white mask. Slowly she held out the
paper. Expecting her to speak, he was a little discon-
certed, but it wasn't visible to the audience: as if he'd
rehearsed the move for weeks, he reached out with
tormenting slowness for the paper, took it, turned to
the audience. Sally could feel their huge, intense
presence on her left.

He unfolded the paper, his eyes commanding silence. Every breath in the building was held—including Sally's. He lowered his eyes and read.

She had written:

BEWARE. BELLMANN'S AGENTS ARE WAITING IN THE WINGS.
I AM A FRIEND.

There had been no time to write more.

Mackinnon didn't blink. Instead he turned to the

audience and said, "On the paper this courageous young lady has written a name—a name that every member of this audience, every man and woman in the kingdom, would recognize. It does me great honor—but it is not my name."

A gasp. He tore the paper into shreds, letting them trickle down through his fingers. Sally found herself held like a small animal mesmerized by a snake. All the resolution she'd felt had drained away completely, and the situation was reversed. A minute ago, he'd been in her power; now she was in his, entirely. She couldn't look at his eyes or the mask or the thin red mouth, only at the moving hands shredding the paper. Beautiful, strong hands. Was the knife real? Would he? No, surely—but then, what?

The only thing she knew now was that his mind must be racing. She hoped it was racing to a solution.

The moment couldn't be prolonged. He reached for the knife, held it in front of him and gazed at it profoundly, and then raised it high. He held it above her, still and cold like an icicle of steel—

And then several things happened at once.

A harsh cry broke out from somewhere in the wings, and something in the same place crashed heavily to the floor as a furious struggle broke out, making the curtains swing and sway.

A trap door beside Mackinnon flew open with a bang. A square platform appeared in the opening.

A woman in the audience screamed, and her scream was taken up by another, and then another.

The orchestra began a frenzied performance in at least two keys of the music from *Faust*.

And then Mackinnon seized Sally by the arm and dragged her to the trap door. She felt his arm around her and marveled at its tense strength.

The lights changed to a flickering, hellish red as the platform, with Mackinnon and Sally on it, began to descend.

The audience was a sea of noise—howling, shrieking, shouting—but Mackinnon's laugh, satanic and powerful, cut through it all as he shook his fist and they sank into the darkness.

The trap closed with a bang over their heads.

The uproar was cut away at once. And Mackinnon drooped. He leaned against Sally and trembled like a child.

"Oh, help me," he moaned.

He'd changed in a moment. In the dim light (a gas mantle some way off in the clutter of beams and ropes and levers was the only illumination) she saw that his mask had slipped sideways. She snatched it off and said:

"Quick—tell me. Why is Bellmann chasing you? I've got to know!"

"No, no, please! He'll kill me! I've got to hide—"

His voice was Scottish now, high and panicky, and he beat his hands together like a distracted child.

"Tell me!" Sally snapped. "If you don't, I'll let them have you. I'm from Garland's. A friend, d'you hear? Fred Garland and Jim Taylor are holding off those men at the moment, but if you don't tell me the truth, I'll give you away. Now tell me why Bellmann's after you, or—"

"All right, all right!"

He glanced around like a trapped animal. They were still standing on the wooden platform, between the iron runners that guided it up to the opening in the stage. It was the kind of thing known as a demon-trap—used in pantomimes to bring the Demon King onstage. Somewhere, Sally thought, there must be a man winding a handle to control it, but there was no one else in sight.

Then there came a clatter of machinery. Sally could see nothing but a tangle of pulleys and chains, but suddenly Mackinnon took fright and dashed away, leaping off the platform and dodging between the hefty wooden pillars that supported the stage.

"Not that way!" called Sally, keeping her voice low.

It worked. He hesitated—and gave her time, in her clumsy enveloping dress, to spring after him and seize him by the arm.

"No! Let me go—"

"Listen, you fool," she hissed. "I'll give you to Bellmann, I swear I will, if you don't tell me what I want to know."

"All right—but not here—"

He looked this way and that. She didn't let go. There was a sputtering gaslight nearby that cast a lurid glare over them, making him look half-crazed and hysterical.

Suddenly she became angry and shook him.

"Listen," she said. "You mean nothing to me. I'd give you up now, but there's something I want to know. There's fraud, there's shipwreck, there's mur-der mixed up in this—and you're involved. Now—why is he chasing you? What does he want?"

He struggled, but she didn't let go; and then he

began to cry. Sally was amazed and a little disgusted. She shook him again, harder.

"Tell me!" she said, her voice low with anger.

"All right! All *right!* But it's not Bellmann, anyway," he said. "It's my father."

"Your father? Well, who is your father?"

"Lord Wytham," said Mackinnon.

Sally was silent, her mind in a whirl.

"Prove it," she said.

"Ask my mother. She'll tell ye. She's not ashamed."

"Who's she?"

"Her name's Nellie Budd. And I don't know where she lives. I don't know who you are either. I'm just trying to earn my living, trying to perfect my art. I'm innocent, I've done nothing to anyone, I tell ye. I'm an artist, I need peace and calmness—I need tae be left alone, not bullied and tormented and hounded without end. It isnae fair, it isnae right!"

Nellie Budd . . .

"But you still haven't told me why he's after you. And what's it got to do with Bellmann? It's no good telling me that it's nothing to do with him—his secretary was here tonight. A man called Windlesham. Why's he involved?"

But before Mackinnon could answer, a trap door banged open somewhere above them, and Mackinnon twisted out of her hands and vanished into the shadows like a rat. She took a step after him but stopped; she wouldn't catch him now.

SHE EXPECTED to find confusion above, with the audience still in an uproar over their disappearance. Instead she found an apologetic stage manager, a stage full of dancers, and the audience in high good humor.

Apparently there should have been a stagehand below to conduct her back to her seat—the trap, the platform, and the red hellfire all being what Mackinnon had devised as a climax to the act. It was the first time they'd played it, and the stage manager was delighted with the effect.

The reason there'd been no one below was that all the available men had been called to deal with a fracas in the wings. Four men had appeared from nowhere, it seemed, and set about each other in fury and, after a huge struggle, had been thrown out. It was probably another angry husband, said the stage manager.

"An angry husband?"

"Well, you see, Mr. Mackinnon's got a way with the ladies. I daresay you noticed. They fly to him like moths. Can't see why, but there you are. It wouldn't be the first time there's been a shindig over that kind of thing where he's concerned. He's a devil for the ladies. Now then, miss, let me find a boy to show you back to your seat. You was in the front row, wasn't you?"

"I think I'll go," she said. "I've had enough entertainment for one evening, thank you very much. Which is the way out?"

ONCE OUTSIDE the theater, she hurried around to the stage entrance, her heart beating hard, and saw Frederick sitting on the step, swinging his stick gently while Jim wandered up and down peering at the ground. Apart from them, the alley was deserted.

She ran up and crouched down beside Frederick.

"Are you all right? What happened?"

He looked up, and she saw his cheek was cut, but he was smiling. She touched it tenderly.

"Ow . . . We sent 'em packing. It was a bit cramped in there—the curtain kept getting in the way—but when they threw us out in the alley here and I could swing the stick, we got on a bit better. Nasty pair they were. Still, I shook some dust out of Sackville and Jim spread the other feller's nose over his face, so we didn't do too badly. At least, I didn't. Found it yet?" he said to Jim.

Jim grunted something. Sally got up and turned his face to the light. His lip was split, and as she saw when he opened his mouth that he'd lost one of his front teeth. She felt a pang: they'd been hurt, and she'd let Mackinnon go.

"Did you find anything out?" said Frederick, getting to his feet.

"Yes, I did. Let's find a cab and get you home—I want to put something on that cut. And Jim's mouth is going to hurt. I hope we've got some brandy."

"Pity they threw us out, really," said Frederick. "I wanted to see Señor Chavez, the Boneless Wonder."

"I seen him before," mumbled Jim. "He's a waste of time. He stands on his hands and sticks his leg in his ear, and that's it. What'd you find out, then, Sal?"

IN A FOUR-WHEELER a few streets away, Messrs. Harris and Sackville were undergoing a painful dressing-down from Mr. Windlesham. But they weren't giving it the attention it deserved; Sackville, having been beaten about the head with Frederick's stick, was even more fuddled than usual, and Mr. Harris, whose nose had felt the impact of Jim's brass knuckles, was preoccupied with diverting the flow of blood away from his shirt front and into a sodden handkerchief.

Mr. Windlesham looked at them with distaste and knocked at the roof. The cab slowed down.

"We ain't there yet," said Sackville thickly.

"Most acutely observed," said Mr. Windlesham. "However, it's a nice sharp night. The walk will do you good. It seems to me that your talents are more suited to terrorizing women than fighting with men. If that is the case, I may have another job for you, and I may not; it depends on how punctual you are in the morning. Seven o'clock in my office, and not a minute later. No blood on the door handle, Mr. Harris, thank you; mop it clean, if you wouldn't mind. No, not with your handkerchief. The tail of your coat will do very well. Good night to you."

Grumbling, muttering, groaning, the two heroes disappeared down Drury Lane. Mr. Windlesham told the driver to take him to Hyde Park Gate; his employer, he thought, would be greatly interested by the evening's events.

12

Phantasms of the Living

"So, what have we got?" said Frederick, helping himself to marmalade. It was the morning after their visit to the music hall, and he and Jim were breakfasting with Sally at the Tavistock Hotel in Covent Garden. "Mackinnon claims to be Nellie Budd's son by Lord Wytham. Well, that's possible."

"That's the yarn he spun to Miss Meredith, too," Jim pointed out. "At least, he didn't name his father and mother, but the story was the same. But that doesn't explain why Bellmann's chasing him. Unless he doesn't fancy him for a brother-in-law. Don't blame him."

"Inheritance," said Sally. "There was something about that, wasn't there? But the illegitimacy might rule that out. What could he inherit from Wytham?"

"Precious little, at a guess. The man's bankrupt, or on the verge of it," said Frederick. "Everything he's got is mortgaged up to the neck. And now he's been pitched out of the Cabinet as well. . . . I don't know. He's a dismal kind of Johnny. I prefer Nellie Budd. No wonder she blinked when I mentioned Mackinnon."

"What about this North Star business?" said Jim.

"North Star Castings," said Sally. "Something to do with iron and steel? It's not listed at the stock exchange. I'll go see this Mrs. Seddon at Muswell Hill tomorrow, but this morning I'm going to see a Mr. Gurney and ask him about psychometry. I've also got a business to run, in the intervals between everything else. . . ."

"Well, I'm off to do some snooping around Whitehall," said Frederick. "I want to see what I can find out about Wytham. And then I'll go and pay another call on Nellie Budd. Talking about business, it's about time I earned some money; I haven't made a penny from this case so far. In fact, I'm down one watch."

"It's all right for you, mate," said Jim bitterly, feeling his bruised mouth. "You can buy another one for thirty bob. Teeth ain't so easily come by. And how you have the cold-hearted cruelty to taunt a feller with kippers and toast when all he can manage is porridge and scrambled eggs, I shall never know. Still, that geezer's going to have trouble with his conk for a while; that's some comfort."

SALLY'S MR. GURNEY was a man she'd met at Cambridge. They'd been introduced by a Mr. Sidgwick, a philosopher who'd done a great deal to further women's education but who was also interested in psychic research. Mr. Gurney was conducting some research of his own in that field, and since he lived in Hampstead, not too far away, Sally thought she'd pay a call on him.

She found him in the study of his pleasant villa,

with music paper on the table and a violin in an open case. He was an intense, wide-eyed man of thirty or so, with a silky beard.

"I'm sorry to interrupt your music," she said. "But I want to find something out, and I don't know anyone else to ask."

"My music? I shall never be a musician, Miss Lockhart. This little sonatina is the height of my ambition—and my ability, too, I fear. I'm taking a new course now; medicine is the field for me. But how can I help you?"

He was a wealthy dilettante, who'd tried scholarship and the law as well as music, and she doubted whether he'd stick to medicine any better. But he had considerable intelligence and a wide knowledge of matters on the fringe of psychology and philosophy, and as she explained the background and what had happened at Nellie Budd's séance in Streatham, he sat up and began to sparkle with interest.

"Telepathy," he said. "That's what your Mrs. Budd's undergoing, by the sound of it."

"Tele—that's Greek. Like telegraph. What's it mean?"

"It's a name for what happens when one person receives impressions from the mind of another. Perceptions, emotions, sense impressions—nothing so connected as conscious thought. Not yet, anyway."

"But does this faculty really exist? Have we all got it?"

"The phenomenon exists. There are records of hundreds of cases. But that's not to say there's a faculty for it. We wouldn't use that word for a man who'd been run over several times by hansom cabs; we wouldn't speak of a faculty for being run over. It might be something that happens to us, rather than something we do."

"I see. She might be receiving impressions without being aware of it. But would the sending out be deliberate? Or wouldn't the sender know he was doing it?"

"The agent, we call it. There seems to be little pattern there, Miss Lockhart. The only generalization I can make is that it usually happens between people who are emotionally close."

"I see. . . . Then there's another puzzling thing, Mr. Gurney. It's connected, but I don't know how at the moment." She told him about Mackinnon's vision of the duel in the snow and how it had been set off, according to his account, by his touching a cigar case.

"Yes," said Mr. Gurney, "that sort of thing's well attested. What sort of man is your percipient? The one who had the vision?"

"Not at all trustworthy. He's a stage magician, a conjurer—a very good one, too—and whether it's got anything to do with that I don't know, but it seems to be impossible to tell when he's speaking the truth. One more thing: If this phenomenon does happen, does it only take place when the percipient handles something that actually belongs to the other person? Or would anything do if it was distantly connected?"

"What sort of thing?"

"Well, a newspaper report. A cutting from a story that might have had something to do with the vision but that didn't mention anyone's name. Could that trigger off a psychometric perception? Or suppose this: Suppose the percipient had had the vision, and later on he came across a newspaper story that didn't overtly mention it but that had a bearing on it. Could he tell that the two things were connected?"

Mr. Gurney jumped up in excitement and plucked a fat volume of notes and cuttings from the shelf above the table.

"Extraordinary thing!" he said. "You've described exactly what happened in the Blackburn case of 1871. If this is a recurrence, it's great news. Look—here it is . . ."

She read through the clippings, all of them dated and annotated with scientific precision. There was a close similarity, though the subject matter of the Blackburn man's vision was nothing more sensational than the escape of his brother from a railway accident.

"How many cases have you got notes on, Mr. Gurney?" she said.

"Thousands. It would be a life's work to sort them out and analyze them."

"Perhaps you should do it instead of medicine. But there's one thing I ought to tell you: This business, whatever it is, seems to be taking place on the edge of a criminal conspiracy. Could you—I know you'll want to write it up—could you please wait to publish it until the danger's passed?"

His eyes opened wide. "A criminal conspiracy?"

She explained a little about the background, and he listened in amazement.

"So this is what they're turning out at Cambridge," he said finally. "Female detectives. I don't think that was quite what the pioneers of university education for women had in mind. . . . Yes, of course I'll do what you say. In any case, our reports always use pseudonyms. My word! Fraud . . . murder . . . Perhaps I should stick to music after all."

It wasn't till the afternoon that Frederick made his way to Streatham. He'd found out one or two things by the simplest means of all—just asking people who were likely to know: office boys, messengers, and the like. The gossip was that while Lord Wytham's political career had passed its zenith, he was all set to flourish in the financial world, having got a seat on the board of an up-and-coming firm called North Something-or-other; and furthermore, he'd been cultivating the new under-secretary at the Foreign Office. All in all, it was worth a morning's work and a succession of weak cups of coffee.

The afternoon was cold and gray, with a thin drizzle just beginning to fall. He was looking forward to seeing Nellie Budd again, he thought, as he turned into the quiet street where she lived.

Except that it wasn't quiet. A crowd of onlookers stood several deep around her doorway, and a four-wheeled ambulance cab waited at the gate. A sergeant and two constables were trying to clear a passage from the door to the cab. Two men carrying a stretcher emerged from the front door, and the crowd parted to let them through.

Frederick started forward. His movement was seen by a uniformed inspector in the doorway, a hard, competent-looking man, and as the stretcher was being put into the cab the Inspector stepped down the path toward him. The onlookers turned in curiosity.

"Can I help you, sir?" the inspector said when he reached the gate. "Were you expecting to see someone here?"

"I came to pay a call on a lady at this address," said Frederick. "A Mrs. Budd."

The inspector glanced over at the cab, nodded to the attendants to close the door and leave, and then turned back to Frederick. "Would you care to step inside a moment?" he said.

Frederick followed him into the narrow hall, where a constable shut the door behind them. A medical-looking man came out of the front room; Frederick could hear a girl sobbing inside it.

"Can she answer questions?" the inspector asked.

"Aye, if you're quick," said the doctor. "I've given her a draught to calm her down, and she'll be feeling sleepy in a few minutes. Better have her put to bed."

The inspector nodded. Opening the door, he beckoned to Frederick to come through. Seated on Mrs. Budd's sofa, her eyes red-rimmed and her chest shaking with sobs, was a housemaid of sixteen or so.

"All right, Sarah," said the inspector. "Stop crying at once and look at me. Your mistress is on her way to hospital; they'll look after her there. Listen to me carefully: Have you seen this man before?"

The girl, still gulping and trembling, looked briefly at Frederick and shook her head.

"No, sir," she whispered.

"He wasn't one of the men who came here today?"

"No, sir."

"You're sure, Sarah? You're quite safe now. Have a good look."

"I never seen him before! Honest!"

She began to cry again. The inspector opened the door and called to the constable: "Here—Davis—take the girl upstairs. Give her a glass of water or something."

The constable took the housemaid out of the room, and then the inspector closed the door again and took out his notebook and pencil.

"Could I have your name, sir?"

"Frederick Garland. 45, Burton Street. Photographer. Now, would you mind telling me why I've been taking part in an impromptu and, for all I know, illegal identity parade? What the hell's going on? And what's happened to Nellie Budd?"

"She was attacked earlier this morning by two men. The housemaid let them in. She said they were . . . marked about the face. Black eyes, swollen nose, that kind of thing. You've got a fine bruise yourself, sir."

"Oh, that's it. I see. Well, I got this when some damn fool opened a railway door in my face. Where have they taken her? And how badly hurt is she?"

"They've taken her to Guy's Hospital. She'd had a fair beating. As a matter of fact, she wasn't conscious, but I think she'll live. She'd better, if those two don't want to hang."

"Will you catch them?"

"Certainly I'll catch 'em," said the inspector. "Sure as my name's Conway. I'm not having that kind of thing going on, I won't stand for it. Now, would you mind telling me your connection with Mrs. Budd, sir? What were you coming to see her for?"

Frederick told him that he'd been photographing a number of well-known mediums for a spiritualist society, and he'd come to see if Nellie Budd would agree to having her portrait taken. The inspector nodded.

"Right you are, sir," he said. "This attack—they didn't make off with anything as far as the girl knows. It wasn't robbery. You've no idea why it might have taken place?"

"None at all," said Frederick.

And that, he thought a few minutes later as he caught an omnibus for Southwark and Guy's Hospital, was nothing less than the truth. He wished he'd plied his stick even harder around the skull of Sackville the night before, and found his fists clenching, for there was no doubt who the two men were. But as for why . . . Bellmann would know. And that little fellow with the glasses: Windlesham.

Very well; they'd pay.

ALL DAY LONG, a woman with a veil had been hesitating outside an office building in the city. She carried a little tin box under her arm, and she kept going to the door, raising her hand, looking around, then lowering it again, and moving off, defeated. It was Isabel Meredith, and the office was Sally's.

Her congenital shyness (for she'd have been shy even without the birthmark) and the misery of the past forty-eight hours had robbed her of the strength of will to climb the stairs and knock. But in the end, desperation overcame timidity, and she did it—to get nothing but silence in reply, for Sally wasn't there.

She left, with her spirits, low as they were, quite

crushed. She wasn't used to good luck; so when she bumped, head down, into a slender figure in a warm tweed coat, she merely murmured, "I beg your pardon" and stood aside—and was astonished to find herself addressed by name.

"Miss Meredith?" said Sally.

"Oh! Yes—yes. Why? I mean—"

"Have you just been to see Miss Lockhart?"

"Yes. But she wasn't in."

"I am Miss Lockhart. I had to be elsewhere this afternoon, making various inquiries, but I've been expecting you. Shall we go inside?"

Isabel Meredith nearly fainted. Sally saw her sway, and caught her arm.

"Oh—I'm so sorry. But I can't . . ."

Sally felt her desperation. This was no time to sit in a chilly office. There was a cab rank across the way; within a minute, the two women were rattling through the crowded streets toward Sally's lodgings.

A WARM FIRE, a comfortable chair, a kettle and a teapot, muffins and butter—and a dog the size of a tiger, black as coal, lying with magnificent abandon on the colorful rug at her feet.

The veil was off. She turned her face full toward Sally and didn't even try to hide the tears. Then hunger overcame her, and she ate while Sally toasted the split muffins on the fire. They didn't speak.

Finally she sat back and closed her eyes.

"I'm so sorry," she said.

"Whatever for?"

"I betrayed him. I'm ashamed, I'm so ashamed . . ."

"He got away. He's quite safe, thanks to your note. You do mean Mr. Mackinnon?"

"Yes. I—I don't know who you are, Miss Lockhart, but I did trust your friend, Jim. Mr. Taylor. I thought you'd be older, somehow. And a financial consultant . . . But your friend said you'd be interested. That's why I came."

She was proud, shy, frightened, ashamed, and angry all at once, Sally thought.

"Never mind," she said. "I am a financial consultant, but that involves a lot of other things. Especially now. And I *am* interested in Mr. Mackinnon. Just tell me everything you can."

Isabel nodded and blew her nose and then sat up straight, as if she'd made a decision.

"I met him in Newcastle," she said. "It was eighteen months ago. I was employed by a theatrical costumer—a small place. I wasn't . . . visible. There was no need to face strangers all day long, and actors and actresses aren't cruel like ordinary folk. They might think things, but they're better at pretending they don't. Besides, they're vain, you know, like children often, and they didn't always notice. I was happy there.

"Then he came to my employer to order a special costume. Conjurers' suits have lots of extra pockets, you see, concealed under the tails and all kinds of places. As soon as I saw him I . . . Have you ever been in love, Miss Lockhart?"

"I . . . You fell in love with him?"

"Completely. Forever. I—tried not to. What could I hope for? But you see, he encouraged me. We saw each other a number of times. He told me I was the only person he could talk to. Even then he was in danger. He had to change his address often—his enemies were relentless. He couldn't stay in one place. . . ."

"Who were these enemies?"

"He didn't ever tell me. He didn't want to put me in danger. I think he did feel something for me, just a little, maybe. He wrote to me every week—I kept all his letters. I've got them with me now."

She indicated the tin box beside her on the floor.

"Did he mention someone called Bellmann? Or Lord Wytham?"

"I don't think so. No."

"What did you think his trouble was?"

"He dropped a hint from time to time that it was a matter of inheritance. I thought he might have been the heir to a great estate, who'd been cheated of his birthright. But all he cares about is his art. He *is* an artist. Such an artist. . . . You've seen him perform? Don't you think he's a great artist?"

Sally nodded. "Yes. Yes, I do. Did he ever talk about his parents, his childhood?"

"Not once. It was as if he'd shut that part of his life away in a tomb. His whole life was his art, every moment, every thought. I knew—I knew that *I* could never be—be his . . ." This was difficult for her; she was twisting her hands and looking down at her lap as she spoke. "But I know that no one else would either. He is a pure genius, Miss Lockhart. If I can be of service to him in some small way I—I'll die happy. But I betrayed him. . . ."

Suddenly a storm of weeping broke over her, and she flung herself sideways in the chair and sobbed in anguish, hiding her face in her hands. Chaka looked up, puzzled, and made a soft keening noise in his throat until Sally stroked his head briefly, and then he lay down again.

Sally knelt by Isabel's chair and put her arm around the other woman's shoulders.

"Tell me how you betrayed him," she said. "Please. We can help him only if we know everything. And I'm sure you didn't mean to. Someone tricked you or forced you, didn't they?"

Slowly, between sobs, the story of Harris and Sackville came out, and how they'd torn up her entire stock in trade. Sally felt a chill of horror; she could imagine only too well what it must be like to have your whole business destroyed around you.

"I didn't tell them. I didn't. They could have tortured me and I'd have said nothing. . . . But they were going to—my letters . . ."

She clutched the little tin box to her breast and hugged it, rocking it back and forth in anguish, like a mother with her dying child. Sally could hardly bear it; and all the time a cold little voice inside her said, *And when have you ever loved like this?*

She thrust it aside, embraced Isabel, and shook her gently.

"Listen," she said. "Those men. I think I know who sent them. It was a man called Windlesham, and he's the private secretary of Axel Bellmann, a financier. He was there—Windlesham, I mean—in the Royal Music Hall with those two. Jim and someone

else, Mr. Garland, fought them off. I spoke to Mr.
Mackinnon, but he wouldn't tell me much. Do you
know where he's living now?"

Isabel shook her head. "He got away safely? He
wasn't hurt?"

"He was quite safe."

"Oh, thank God. Thank God for that. But why are
they doing it, Miss Lockhart? What are they trying
to do?"

"I wish I knew. Now, look, you can't go home.
You've got nothing left to go to. Why not—"

"My landlady asked me to leave, in any case," said
Isabel in a low voice. "I could hardly blame her. I've
got nowhere to go, Miss Lockhart. I slept out last
night. I don't think I . . ."

She closed her eyes and bowed her head.

"There's room for you here. Mrs. Molloy will make
up a bed for you next-door. Now, don't argue," Sally
went on. "I want your help; it isn't charity. We're
about the same size—we'll find you something else to
wear, and Mrs. Molloy's suppers are famous. No,
there's nothing to thank me for. I've still got a home—
and a business. . . ."

And how long would they last? she wondered.
Bellmann's threat had troubled her more than she'd
liked to admit, and it was still there, in the shadows
outside. And here was Isabel: proof that he wouldn't
hesitate to carry it out. As the two of them busied
themselves with plates and teacups and nightgowns
and coal for the fire, the thought retreated; but it came
back later on when Frederick looked in with the news
about Nellie Budd.

Isabel was in bed, which Sally was glad about. Frederick sat by the fire with some coffee and told her that Nellie Budd was still unconscious; she'd been beaten over the head, and the doctors weren't sure if her skull had been fractured. At least she was being well cared for, but it was too soon to tell whether she'd recover. Frederick had brought some flowers to stand beside her bed and had left his name in the absence of any next of kin, since he had no idea where her sister (what was her name? Miss Jessie Saxon?) could be found.

When Sally told him about Isabel's visit from the two men, he nodded as if he'd expected it. Harris and Sackville's joint account was growing; he looked forward to presenting them with the bill.

He sat there for a while in silence, gazing moodily into the fire and occasionally prodding the coals with his stick.

"Sally," he said at last, "will you move into Burton Street?"

She sat up. "We've been through all that, Fred. The answer's no. In any case—"

"That wasn't the question. I've given up asking you to marry me; you can forget about that. I'm thinking about Nellie Budd. If this is the sort of case where they go about beating women unconscious, I want you close at hand, that's all. You'd be a lot safer at Burton Street, and so would—"

"I'm quite safe here, thank you," Sally said. "I've got Chaka and I've got my pistol, and I don't need to be shut up in a fortress and guarded."

She hated herself for that voice—a sort of prickly, priggish complacency. As soon as she opened her mouth she knew what would happen, and she dreaded it; and she had no idea how on earth to prevent it.

"Don't be stupid," he said, and sat up too. "I'm not talking about guarding you like a bloody princess in a fairy tale; I'm talking about keeping you alive. You can work and go about normally, and of course you've got the dog, and we all know you can shoot a cigarette out of a fly's mouth with your hands tied behind your back—"

"I'm not interested in listening to sarcasm. If you've got nothing better to say—"

"All right, then, listen to sense. Those men nearly killed Nellie Budd. For all I know, they *have* killed her. They've destroyed Miss What's-her-name's business. D'you think they'd hesitate—especially after the hiding we gave them—d'you think they'd pause for one moment before setting to work on you? My God, girl, they'd do it with relish. Bellmann's already threatened you with—"

"I can defend myself," she said. "And I certainly don't need your permission to go about normally, as you put it—"

"I didn't put it like that. I don't think that and I didn't say it. If you willfully misunderstand—"

"I'm not misunderstanding anything! I know quite well what you meant—"

"No, you don't, or you wouldn't talk in this asinine way!"

Their rising voices had wakened Chaka. He rolled onto his front, lifted his head to look at Frederick, and growled softly. Sally reached down automatically to stroke his head.

"I don't think you realize what it sounds like when

you speak like that," she went on more quietly, looking not at Frederick but into the fire, and feeling the bitter stubbornness enclose her. "As if I needed protecting and coddling. *I'm not like that.* And when you don't seem to see that, I wonder whether you're seeing me at all."

"You take me for such a fool," he said, and there was real hatred in his voice. "In your heart of hearts you think I'm no different from any other man—no, that's not right. It's not just men. You think I'm no different from anyone, man or woman. There's you and there's the rest of us, and we're all inferior—"

"Not true!"

"It is true."

"Because I take my work seriously, because I'm not flippant and facetious, that means I look down on you, does it?"

"All the time. All the time. Have you any idea of how unlikable you are, Sally? At your best you're magnificent, and I loved you for it. At your worst you're nothing but a smooth, self-righteous, patronizing bitch."

"*Me* patronizing?"

"You should hear yourself. I offer you help, as one equal to another, out of concern and respect, and, yes, affection, and you throw it back in my face. And if you don't think that's being proud—"

"You're not talking about me. You're talking about some stupid fantasy of yours. Grow up, Frederick."

Then she saw his face change. An expression she couldn't read flared in his eyes and then fell back, consumed, so that she thought something had died; and she put out a hand to him, but it was too late.

"We'll finish this case," he said quietly, standing up and taking his stick. "And then I think we'll call it a go."

She got up, too, and took a step toward him. But he left without looking at her, without another word said.

THAT NIGHT, while Sally sat by the ashes of her fire and began one letter after another to Frederick, and found the words as hard to put on paper as they were to say, and finally gave up and put her head on her knees and cried; while Frederick covered page after page with speculations and guesses, and tore them all up, and tinkered with his new American camera before losing his temper and flinging it into the corner; while Webster Garland and Charles Bertram sat and smoked and drank whiskey and talked light and shade, gelatin, collodion, calotypes, shutter mechanisms, and paper negatives; while Jim, alternately scowling with pain and helpless with love, missed cues and pulled wrong ropes and dropped ladders and stood there tamely with lost eyes as the stage manager showered him with abuse; while Nellie Budd lay unconscious in a narrow bed, with Frederick's flowers on a chair beside her; while Lady Mary sat silent and perfect and miserable throughout an interminable dinner; while Chaka dreamed of Sally and hunting and Sally and rabbits and Sally—a man knocked at a door in Soho and waited to be let in.

He was a young man, brisk and smart and vigorous. He wore conventional evening dress, as if he'd just left a dinner or the opera, and he carried a silver-topped cane, with which he tapped the rhythm of a popular tune on the step.

Presently the door opened.

"Ah," said Mr. Windlesham. "Come in, come in."

He stood aside and let the visitor through. This was an office that Mr. Windlesham used for business that he didn't want traced back to Baltic House. He shut the door carefully and followed the young man into a warm, well-lit room, where he had been reading a novel.

"Your cloak and hat, Mr. Brown?"

Mr. Brown gave them up and sat down, looking incuriously at the open book. Mr. Windlesham saw where he was looking.

"The Way We Live Now," he said. "By Anthony Trollope. An amusing book about a financial speculator. Do you enjoy novels, Mr. Brown?"

"No, I don't go much on reading," said Mr. Brown. He had a strange voice, with an accent that Mr. Windlesham couldn't place, since it belonged to no class and no region that he knew. If it belonged anywhere, it belonged to the future: a hundred years from then, voices like Mr. Brown's would be common, though Mr. Windlesham could hardly be expected to know that. "Don't seem to have much time for books," he went on. "Give me a good music hall any day."

"Ah, yes, the music hall. And now to business: You come to me highly recommended, not least for your discretion. But we can talk quite openly to one another, I hope. I understand that you kill people."

"That's correct, Mr. Windlesham."

"Tell me, is it more difficult to kill a woman than a man?"

"No. A woman, in the nature of things, she's not going to be as quick or as strong as a man, is she?"

"That wasn't quite what I meant. . . . Never mind. How many people have you killed, Mr. Brown?"

"Why d'you want to know?"

"I'm trying to establish your credentials."

Mr. Brown shrugged. "Twenty-one," he said.

"Quite an expert. And what is your usual method?"

"It varies. Depends on the circumstances. Given a choice, I'd go for a knife. There's a sort of craftsmanship with a knife."

"And craftsmanship is important to you?"

"I take a pride in my work, same as any professional."

"Quite so. I currently employ two men who are, alas, far from professional in their standards; I could never trust them with a job such as this. Tell me, what are your plans for the future?"

"Well, I'm ambitious, Mr. Windlesham," said the young man. "There's a steady trade in London and on the continent, but nothing big. I think my future lies across the Atlantic. I'm a great admirer of the Americans; I've been over there a couple of times. I like the people, and I like the way they live. I think I'd do well there. I've got a little money saved. My fee for this job'll add to that. Another few jobs and I'll be off. Why d'you ask? Your—er—firm likely to be in the market for a man with my skills in the near future?"

"Oh, I think so. I think so," said Mr. Windlesham, his gold glasses twinkling.

"Who's the client?" said Mr. Brown, taking out a notebook and pencil.

"A young woman," said Mr. Windlesham. "With a large dog."

13

A Great New Work for the Benefit of All Mankind

SALLY WOKE UP OPPRESSED AND UNHAPPY. THE MORNING, just to spite her, was more like April than November: bright and clear and warm, with little fleecy clouds in a broad blue sky. She breakfasted with Isabel on bacon, eggs, and toast, and left her there with Chaka while she went to Muswell Hill.

Mrs. Seddon of Cromwell Gardens was a pleasant lady of forty or so, who invited Sally in to her little parlor and seemed delighted to hear that her pupil Miss Lewis was in London.

"Such a bright little girl she was! I do hope she'll come and see me. . . . Well, what can I do for you, Miss Lockhart?"

Sally sat down. It was just as well she hadn't brought Chaka, because there wouldn't have been room for him. There wasn't room for both women on the sofa because of the profusion of crocheted cushions, so Mrs. Seddon herself sat at the table in the bay window, under a large aspidistra. Every surface in the room was draped—there were three embroidered antimacassars on the sofa; there were two separate cloths on the table; there were doilies on the window sill; there was a tasseled fringe around the mantel-piece; even the birdcage had a little frilly skirt. On the wall hung a sampler with the text STAY, STAY AT HOME, MY HEART, AND REST; HOMEKEEPING HEARTS ARE HAPPIEST.

Sally put down her bag and began to explain.

"I'm trying to find out about a firm called North Star Castings. Someone I know lost some money investing in a company that I think was connected with North Star, and I'm just trying to piece together everything I can. I understand that your brother used to work for them?"

Mrs. Seddon frowned. "Well, in a manner of speak-ing. . . . Is this a matter for lawyers, Miss Lockhart? I mean, are you on your own, or what? Are you repre-senting someone else?"

"I'm representing my client," said Sally, a little taken aback by Mrs. Seddon's suspicion. "I work for myself as a financial consultant."

Mrs. Seddon's expression was troubled. "I don't know, I'm sure," she said. "I've never heard of . . ." She didn't want to finish the sentence, and looked away in confusion.

"Of a woman financial consultant? Nor have most people. But I can assure you it's true. In fact, that's how I met Miss Lewis, your pupil. And the client who lost the money was a woman as well—a teacher like yourself. If you can tell me what you know about North Star Castings, I might be able to help her get it back. Is there something odd about it?"

"Well . . . I don't know how to begin, really. Odd? Yes, I suppose so. My brother Sidney—Mr. Paton, that is—was really quite brought down by it. In fact, he's still out of work. . . . Look, Miss Lockhart, this is going to be hard to explain. I'm not sure I've got it straight in my own mind. Stop me if I'm rambling, won't you."

"Just tell me everything that occurs to you. Don't worry if it's not in order."

"All right. Now, my brother—I think this is important—he's a trade unionist. A socialist. A good man, mind, and my husband, Mr. Seddon, agrees with that, though he's always voted Conservative. But Sidney has that particular point of view, and perhaps it influenced him. I don't know.

"He's a craftsman—a boilermaker. Well, he was. In Walker and Sons Locomotive Works. But the place wasn't doing well—lack of orders, no new investment—that kind of thing. That was—oh, two or three years back. Anyway, about that time the owners sold the works to another firm. And they sent in a new manager—a Swede, he was, Swedish or Dutch or something—and he started laying off the men by the score. It was a funny business. They didn't seem interested in new orders, only in completing what was on the book and then laying off the men."

"Did your brother lose his job?"

"Not at first. He was a fine craftsman—one of the best workers in the firm. He was one of the few they kept on till the end. But he didn't like it, you know. It seemed funny somehow; this young manager had brought in a team of London men, and foreigners, too. They'd go round making notes—notes about everything. Who did this, why he did that, what he did next, how long he took to do it. And not only notes about the job. Private stuff, too—like where the workers lived, what church or chapel they attended, clubs or societies they belonged to, family circumstances—all that.

"Of course, the trade unions didn't like it. But there was nothing they could do about it if the orders weren't there. And yet there was something funny going on, with the manager and his foreign friends coming in every day and making their notes and having their meetings and measuring and drawing and surveying. There was a lot of money at the back of it all, they could tell that. But none of it was coming the way of the men.

"Then one day last May a meeting was held. All the remaining workers were invited to attend—not required, mind: invited. These had been the ones that had been looked at the closest, remember. There wasn't a detail about them—even down to the rent they paid or how many children they had—that hadn't gone into those notebooks.

"So the men, these last hand-picked hundred or so, all trooped into the hall that had been hired. Not a stand-up meeting in the yard: a proper sit-down meeting with refreshments, if you please. They'd never seen anything like it. Can you imagine? My brother couldn't take it in, it was so extraordinary.

"Anyway, when they were all assembled, in came the manager and his friends, and started to talk. I remember Sidney telling me about it, and the impression it made. . . . They said the firm was on the verge of the most exciting and revolutionary development in its history. I can't remember the details, except that Sidney said it made him kind of wild with excitement, and all the other men were feeling the same. It was almost religious, Sidney said—which is odd, coming from him, as I'll tell you in a moment. It was just like one of Sankey and Moody's revival meetings, he said. At the end there wasn't one of those men who wouldn't have been willing to sign his life away for a chance of working there."

Mrs. Seddon paused for a moment. She was looking into the fireplace, frowning. Sally said, "But what were they going to do? Surely they weren't just going to go on building railway engines, after a speech like that? Didn't they explain what their plans were?"

"Not just then, no. It was all stuff about the glorious future and peace and prosperity, about a great new work for the benefit of all mankind, and so on. How they'd be guaranteed a lifetime's work, and a pension, if you please, and new company houses as well, if they'd sign up there and then. Oh, yes—and in exchange for these benefits (and more—there was some kind of health insurance they offered as well) they had to renounce their union membership and sign an agreement not to strike.

"Well, most of the men snapped it up at once and signed. There was a pledge of secrecy in there somewhere—I don't know how legal that would have been, but there was a lawyer there who explained it, Sidney said. It was only afterward that he thought how odd it was.

"There were a few men who were a bit more cautious. Sidney was one. They asked if they could have a day or so to think about it. 'Course you can,' said the manager. 'We don't want to force anyone. Free choice all round. Have a week to think,' he said. 'But you're the best men available, and we'd be sorry to lose you.' Flattery, you see, Miss Lockhart.

"So my brother went home and talked to his wife. There were half a dozen or so like him who were cautious, but the next day they almost all signed up all right. The union tried to argue the case against, but what did they have to offer, compared to the management? And then Sidney heard something from a friend of his at the Workingmen's Literary and Philosophical Institute. There was a story going round that the new management had taken an interest in another business nearby, known as Furness Castings. And they planned to bring the two firms together, and this was to be the great work that would benefit mankind and bring peace and prosperity to the whole world.

"Only my brother Sidney's a pacifist, you see, Miss Lockhart. He doesn't hold with fighting or violence of any kind. He was brought up Chapel, like me, but he took an interest in the Quakers soon after he married. He never actually became a member—what do they call them—a Friend, and I suppose that's why the managers didn't realize, or else they'd have got rid of him before that.

"Because Furness Castings might sound innocent enough, but what they make is guns. Cannons. Armaments, in a word.

"So he said no, thanks, he wouldn't join; and they paid him off, and he hasn't worked since. I send him a little money every now and then, when I can manage it. And that's about all—except that the two firms are amalgamated now, and it isn't Furness Castings or Walker and Sons, it's North Star Castings. And that's all I know."

Sally felt like clapping her hands. This was the first solid indication of what Bellmann was doing—guns, armaments, cannons . . .

"Mrs. Seddon, you've been a great help," she said. "I can't tell you how useful this is. There's one other thing: I don't suppose your brother ever mentioned something called the Hopkinson Self-Regulator?"

She looked doubtful. "If he did, I don't recall," she said. "We never talked much about machinery. . . . What is it?"

"I don't know. It's one of the things I want to find out about. I wonder—could I go and talk to your brother? What's his address?"

"I'll write it down for you. But . . . I don't know, Miss Lockhart, perhaps I shouldn't have told you this. After all, it isn't really my business. . . ."

"No one asked you to sign a pledge of secrecy, Mrs. Seddon. And even if they had, I doubt whether it would have been legal. People do that sort of thing only if they're up to no good. I think your brother's reaction was quite right, and I'd like to go up and talk to him about it."

Mrs. Seddon opened the flap of a little bureau, dipped a pen in ink, and wrote a name and address on a card.

"He's in poor circumstances now," she said, hesitatingly. "I'm well off by comparison. Mr. Seddon's a chief clerk with Howson and Tomkins, the timber

merchants, so we're well provided for. And my brother's an older man. . . . What I'm trying to say, I think,
is that I came from the same background and I haven't
forgotten it. We were poor, but there were always
books in the house—and magazines—*Household Words*
and so on. So there was a pride, you see, a respect for
learning. I've always had that; it was why I did the
Sunday school. And what Sidney'd do without the
institute, I don't know. . . . Oh, I'm just jabbering.
The plain fact is, I don't like it, Miss Lockhart.
Something's wrong up there, and I don't know what it
is. Here's the address."

She gave the card to Sally.

"You will be careful, won't you?" she said. "Oh,
you know your business, of course you do. I'll write to
Sidney and let him know. But I *am* uneasy, there's no
denying it. You won't get him into trouble?"

Sally promised that she wouldn't, and left for
Burton Street.

She was diffident about going in, but she didn't
pause for long. There was an air of bustle and
confusion about the place, where the plasterers were
moving out of the new studio and the glaziers hadn't
arrived, and Webster was angrily dealing with the
foreman from the decorating firm. She found Frederick coming out of the old studio with some exposed
plates in his hand.

"Hello," he said neutrally.

"I've been to see Mrs. Seddon," she said in the
same tone. "I think I know what North Star Castings
does. Are you very busy?"

"Just let me take these to Mr. Potts. Jim's in the kitchen."

She went through the shop and found Jim at the kitchen bench, scowling at an untidy pile of paper and a bottle of ink. He thrust them away when she came in and turned to face her.

"What's up, Sal?" he said.

"I'll tell you in a minute, when Fred comes in. How's your tooth?"

He made a face. "Spoiled me beauty, ain't it?" he said. "It doesn't hurt much, but broken bits keep working their way out. I'd like another crack at that bugger's nose, I don't mind admitting. . . ."

"Right, what's it all about, then?" said Frederick, shutting the door behind him.

She went through what Mrs. Seddon had told her. When she finished, Jim gave a long whistle.

"So that's what he's up to!" he said. "Guns on railway carriages . . ."

"I'm not sure," said Sally. "Walker and Sons made locomotives, not carriages. And this Hopkinson Self-Regulator sounds as if it's got something to do with steam. One of us will have to go up there and find out. I've got Mr. Paton's address." She looked at Frederick. "Could you . . ."

He said nothing for a moment, and then, "Yes, I suppose I could. But why me? I'd have thought you'd be the best person to go, since you made the first contact. Besides, you know a lot more about guns than I do."

She flushed. "I'm not so good at talking to people," she said. "There'd be a lot of . . . well, detecting.

Talking to people and finding things out. You're good at that, and I'm not. You're the best. It's got to be you."

There was another meaning in those words; she hoped her eyes were expressing it too. Her cheeks were hot, but she faced him directly and saw him nod. He looked up at the clock.

"Half past ten," he said. "Jim, could you pass me the Bradshaw?"

Bradshaw's Railway Guide informed him that there would be a train leaving King's Cross in a little over half an hour. While Jim went to call a cab and Frederick threw some things into a bag, Sally scribbled a quick summary of what Mrs. Seddon had told her and added Mr. Paton's address. Then her pencil paused, but before she could add anything else Frederick came back with his cloak and hat. She folded the paper and gave it to him.

"What's today? Thursday? I'll have a scout around, see what else I can find out. Be back on Saturday, I expect. Good-bye."

That was all he said.

"Mr. Blaine's going mad in there," said Jim when he came back. "I think I'll give him a hand with his orders. I got nothing else to do. I was going to see Nellie Budd later on—fancy coming? See whether she's come round, poor old gal?"

"I'm going to the patent library," Sally told him. "I don't know why I didn't think of it before. Whatever this Hopkinson thing is, there'll be a patent for it."

"You really think it's got something to do with North Star? Well, I suppose it cropped up in Nellie

Budd's trance. . . . Here, I've just had a thought. Miss Meredith—I know she's a needlewoman, but she can manage clerical stuff all right. And at a guess she'll be feeling like a useless burden and blaming herself for everything and not wanting to be in the way and generally making everyone miserable—no, all right, I take it back, that ain't fair. But she could do Mr. Blaine's stuff, couldn't she? Kill two birds with one stone. Stop the old boy from going off his nut and help her feel she's doing something useful. What about it?"

For answer she went and kissed him.

"Well, that's better than a whisticaster in the rattlers," he said.

"A *what?*"

"A smack in the gob. Good idea, then, is it? I'll go and see her before I go to the hospital. Take her mind off Mackinnon—maybe."

14

The Steam Gun

THE RAIL CONNECTIONS WERE EXCELLENT; IT WASN'T much past six o'clock when Frederick booked into the Railway Hotel at Barrow, and only a little later when he found the address Sally had written down. He knocked at the door of the little terraced house and looked around at the rest of the street. It was hard to tell what it would be like in daylight; he had the impression of respectability just a shade away from poverty. Every door knocker shone in the gaslight, every doorstep was scrubbed—but in the very next street, sewage flowed down the open gutter.

The door was opened by an anxious-looking woman in her fifties.

"Mrs. Paton?" said Frederick, taking off his hat. "Is Mr. Paton in—Mr. Sidney Paton?"

"Yes, he is," she said. "Is it . . . It's not from the landlord, is it?"

"No, no," said Frederick. "My name's Garland. A colleague of mine was talking to your sister-in-law, Mrs. Seddon, and she happened to mention Mr.

Paton's name. I came up here in the hope that I might be able to talk to him."

She let him in, still anxious, and led him through to the little kitchen, where her husband was mending a pair of boots. He stood up to shake hands—a small, slight man with a heavy mustache and the same anxiety in his eyes as his wife had.

"I'd ask you into the parlor, Mr. Garland," he said, "but there's no fire. And, anyway, most of the furniture's had to go. Some of it we've had since our wedding day. . . . What can I do for you?"

"I won't beat about the bush, Mr. Paton," said Frederick. "I want your help, and I'll pay for it. Here's five pounds to start with."

Mrs. Paton gave a faint exclamation and sat down. Mr. Paton wonderingly took the note Frederick handed him, but put it on the table.

"I don't deny that five pounds would be a blessing," he said slowly, "but I'll need to know the sort of help you want before I accept it, Mr. Garland. Oh, please sit down."

Mrs. Paton, recovered from her surprise, stood up to take Frederick's coat and hat. Frederick sat where Mr. Paton indicated, in the armchair on the other side of the fire. He looked around: plates and cups gleamed on a dresser in the warm lamplight, damp tea towels hung over a line, a stout ginger cat dozed on the hearth, and a pair of spectacles rested on a copy of *Emma* beside the cobbler's last where Mr. Paton's boot was being resoled. Mr. Paton saw where Frederick was looking, and sat down opposite him.

"Plenty of time for reading these days," he said.

"I've worked my way through Dickens and Thackeray and Walter Scott, and I'm on Jane Austen now. Blow me if she's not the best of the lot. Well, Mr. Garland. How can I help?"

Frederick, liking the man at once, decided to tell him everything. The recital took some time, during which Mrs. Paton made some tea and put out a plate of biscuits.

"So what I need to know," he said finally, "is just what's going on at North Star Castings. Now, if you decide you can't tell me, or if you feel you shouldn't because of this secrecy business, I'll understand. But I've told you all the background, so you can see why I want to know and what's at stake. What d'you say?"

Mr. Paton nodded. "That sounds fair to me. And I must say, I've never heard a tale like this before. . . . What do you say, my dear?"

His wife, seated at the table, had listened wide-eyed as Frederick spoke.

"You tell him," she said. "You tell him as much as you like. You don't owe that firm a thing."

"Good," said Mr. Paton. "That's what I think. Right, Mr. Garland. . . ."

During the next twenty minutes Frederick learned all that had happened to the railway works since Bellmann had taken them over. They were now called the Transport Division of North Star Castings, Limited; the other half—the armaments firm that used to be known as Furness Castings—was now called the Research Division, a fact about which Mr. Paton was quietly bitter.

"They're very clever, these men, whoever they are," he said, settling back into his wooden armchair and accepting the attentions of the cat, which had jumped up into his lap. "Research Division. Sounds harmless, doesn't it? Well, research means one thing to you and me, and quite another to North Star Castings, Limited. Murder and bloodshed division, more like. But that wouldn't look so good on the factory gates, would it?"

"Why these two firms, though?" said Frederick. "What have they got in common?"

"I'll tell you what the talk is, Mr. Garland. It's supposed to be a secret, but word gets around. . . . I hear a certain amount at the Institute. I can't really afford the subscription these days, but my sister's been very good. . . .

"Anyway, the word is that North Star Castings is developing a new kind of gun. It's got some polite name, of course—it's called the Hopkinson Self-Regulating Device, or some such—but the name that gets whispered around here is the Steam Gun."

Frederick sat up and took out his pocket book. He found the scrap of paper on which Jim had written down the words that Nellie Budd had spoken in her trance. He smoothed it out and handed it to Mr. Paton, who reached for his glasses and tilted the paper to the lamplight to read it.

"It isn't Hopkinson, but they're not to know. . . . The Regulator . . . North Star! . . . a mist all full of fire—steam, and it's packed with death, packed in pipes—steampipes—under the North Star . . ." he read aloud. Then he put the paper down. "Well, if this isn't the strangest thing I ever heard. . . . Now, look, Mr. Garland, I don't know the first thing about guns, I'm glad to say. And as for this Hopkinson thing, well, I

can't help you at all—but I can take you to a man who could. Whether he will or not I can't promise. But Henry Waterman's a decent sort of feller, and I know for a fact that he's not happy about what he's helping to make. He was one of those who thought hard before signing on. I think he's wishing now he hadn't done it. He's a Unitarian, Henry; a man of conscience, you might say."

TWENTY MINUTES LATER Mr. Paton took Frederick into a plain-fronted house that bore a painted sign proclaiming it to be the Workingmen's Literary and Philosophical Institute.

"We've got a fine library here, Mr. Garland," he said. "We have a debate on the second Tuesday of every month and courses of lectures when we can raise a subscription for them. . . . Look, there's Henry Waterman now. Come along and I'll introduce you."

They went into the library, a small room plainly furnished with a table and half a dozen chairs and lined with shelves containing books on a variety of social and philosophical topics. Mr. Waterman was reading by the light of an oil lamp; he was a heavy, serious-looking man of fifty or so.

"Henry, let me introduce Mr. Garland, from London. He's a detective," said Mr. Paton.

Mr. Waterman stood up to shake hands, and for the second time Frederick went through his story, though this time he shortened it. Mr. Waterman listened attentively. When Frederick finished, he nodded as if he'd just solved a problem.

"Mr. Garland, you've made up my mind for me," he said. "I'm going to break a promise now, but I consider it was a promise they had no right to get. I'll tell you about the Steam Gun.

"It's a weapon on an entirely new principle—new mechanically, new strategically, new in every way. I'm a boilermaker myself; I know nothing about guns, but I can tell you that this one's a horrible thing. I've been working on a system of tubing to feed high-pressure steam into it—the most complicated bit of engineering you ever saw in your life, but lovely drawings, lovely design, really beautifully thought out. I never knew, Mr. Garland, that a piece of machinery could be beautiful and wicked at the same time.

"It's mounted on an ordinary-looking railway carriage, specially reinforced and sprung. The boiler and firebox are at the back of it, fairly small—doesn't have to pull the train along, after all—but very powerful. We can reach four hundred pounds per square inch easy; I'd say there was another hundred in reserve. And she burns coke—smokeless, see. You'd never know she was alight.

"Now, you hear the word *gun* and you think of a long barrel sticking out, don't you? Well, it's not like that. The carriage looks like any ordinary freight carriage, apart from the holes. Tiny little holes—six thousand on each side. Thirty rows, two hundred in a row. And out of each hole come five bullets every second. . . . That's what the steam's for, you see. Can you imagine turning a handle for twelve thousand machine guns at once? It needs every one of those four hundred pounds of steam, Mr. Garland.

"And that's not the end of it. I'm not too familiar with the firing side—getting the steam along the pipes is my job—but from what I've heard, there's a kind of Jacquard mechanism they can bring into play to regulate the firing pattern. I'm sure you've seen the things—a series of cards with holes punched in 'em. They use 'em in weaving, to put patterns in the cloth. Well, with this mechanism the gunner can have one row firing at a time, then the next one down, then the next, and so on; or he can have all the columns firing in turn; or he can fire in blocks, or in short bursts from the whole gun—any way he pleases. Only it doesn't use punched cards, this regulator. It's the same principle, but it's done with electrical connections: lines drawn on a roll of waxed paper using a dense kind of graphite. I tell you, Mr. Garland, the man who designed this is little short of a genius. It's the most stunning piece of machinery I ever saw in my life.

"And it's evil. It's monstrous. Can you imagine the effect on a body of men? Every cubic inch of air within, oh, five hundred, a thousand yards, filled with a red-hot bullet? *Devastation* isn't the word. You'd need something from the Book of Revelations to describe it.

"So that's the Steam Gun. There's one already sent abroad—I don't know where. There's a second nearly ready now; another week or two, and it'll be ready to test. . . . So you see, Mr. Garland, why I'm not happy about it. Sidney here thought harder about this business than I did, and I wish I'd had the courage to say no, like him, at the start. The thought that my skill— and I'm proud of my skill—that my craftsmanship's been perverted into making something like this; the thought that my own countrymen are busy helping it into the world—I tell you, it makes me sick at the heart."

He stopped and ran his hands through his short, iron-gray hair before laying them flat on the table on either side of his book. Sally'd like this man, Frederick thought.

"Mr. Waterman, I'm extremely grateful. I've got a lot of things clear now. But what about the management of the firm? Do you know the name Bellmann?"

"Bellmann?" Mr. Waterman shook his head. "Can't say I've ever heard that name. But it's common knowledge there's foreign money in the firm somewhere. He's a foreigner, is he, this Mr. Bellmann?"

"Swedish. But there's a Russian connection to this as well."

"Russian! Now there's a thing. You remember I mentioned the designer? Said he must be a genius? Well, his name's Hopkinson. That's what we've been told, though no one's seen him. On the drawings we're working from, it's abbreviated to HOP. But it looks odd—almost as though it had been four letters, and they'd scraped off the *K*. And in one place—tucked away, not really visible—I saw this. Here, I'll write it for you." He borrowed Frederick's pencil and wrote:

НОРД

"Now that last letter isn't a *K*, it's a *D*. Are you familiar with the Cyrillic alphabet, Mr. Garland? I take an interest in languages, or I wouldn't have recognized it. And seeing that as a *D* made the other letters sort of change themselves in my mind. It's Russian, you see. In our script it'd be this." He wrote:

NORD

"Nordenfels!" said Frederick. "By heaven, Mr. Waterman, you've cracked it!"

"Nordenfels?" said Mr. Waterman.

"A Swedish engineer. Disappeared in Russia. Very probably murdered. Well, I'm damned. . . . That's wonderful. And you say they're going to test the new gun in a week or two?"

"That's right. They've tested separate systems, such as the boiler, obviously, and the cartridge feed, and the electrical generator, but it's nearly all together now, and then they'll take it up to Thurlby for testing. They test big naval guns up there, on floating targets out at sea sometimes.

"And that's about all I know, Mr. Garland. But now I reckon you can tell me something. What's your interest in this? And what are you going to do about it?"

Frederick nodded. "Fair questions. I'm a detective, Mr. Waterman, and I'm interested in the man behind all this. Steam guns aren't illegal, as far as I know, but I'm beginning to see what he's up to, and as soon as I can pin something on him, I will. But I'll tell you what I'd like to do with the gun, and that's blow it off the face of the earth."

"Hear, hear," said Mr. Paton.

"Well, I could show you—" began Mr. Waterman,

but then the door opened and in came another man, carrying a couple of books.

"Oh, beg your pardon, Henry," he said. "Don't mind me, carry on. Evening, Sidney . . ."

The other two were slightly thrown, but Frederick said, "And what other facilities does your institute provide, Mr. Waterman?"

"Ah—yes, Mr. Garland. Well, it grew out of the Cooperative Society, and the original nucleus was this very library. . . . Some of the books were donated by the Rochdale Corresponding Society. . . ."

It was clear that the other man wasn't going to go. In fact, he joined in to tell the history of the place. Frederick soon became aware of two things: first, that they were all very proud of what they'd built up, and deserved to be; and second, that he was growing thirstier by the minute.

After declining an invitation to look over the rest of the building and inspect the accounts of the Cooperative Society (a pleasure he said he'd reserve for his next visit), he said good-bye to Henry Waterman and left—and found himself staring, for no good reason, at a playbill on the wall of the building opposite.

It was getting close to eight o'clock—dark, with a chilly wind and a spot or two of rain—and the gaslights flared in the changing gusts. Windows were lit up, and a warm glow came from the doorway of a nearby pub. Men trudging home from work, or women hurrying to their kitchens with a couple of herrings or a black pudding, made the street look alive, a place of vivid human activity; but something had caught Frederick's eye, and it wasn't this lame horse or that pretty girl or those two boys squabbling over a cap.

One of the names of the playbill had leaped out at him and then retreated coyly again. The Paramount Music Hall—this week—a list of performers: the Great Goldini and His Performing Doves—Mr. David Fickling, the Lancashire Comedian—Professor Laar, Mesmerist Extraordinary—Miss Jessie Saxon, the Ebullient Songstress—Mr. Graham Chainey, the Cheeky Chappie—

Jessie Saxon.

The old ambrotype—Nellie Budd's sister!

"What's up, Mr. Garland?" said Mr. Paton, seeing Frederick stop, blink, look harder, take off his hat and scratch his head, and finally clap his hat back on and snap his fingers.

"A longing for culture, Mr. Paton. Comes over me in irresistible waves. Care to join me? Where do they keep the Paramount Music Hall?"

MR. PATON declined, and Frederick thanked him for his help and went alone. The Paramount Music Hall was a comfortable, friendly sort of establishment, though with a shabbiness about it that spoke of decline; and most of the acts on the first half of the bill had declined already. It all lacked luster.

Jessie Saxon occupied a spot in the middle of the second half, between a comedian and a juggler. Frederick felt a shiver of surprise when she came on, because she was so like her sister not only in looks but in manner: vulgar, warm, humorous, a little coarse. She knew how to manage the audience, and they enjoyed it; but there was nothing exciting about her act. A few sentimental songs and a joke or two— familiar stuff; no doubt she was an old favorite up there, who'd never managed (or never wanted) to succeed in the south.

Frederick sent his compliments to her dressing room and asked if he might buy her a bottle of champagne—an invitation that was accepted at once. And when he appeared at the door, she blinked and started in astonishment.

"Well!" she said. "A young man! Me admirers these days are usually pushing sixty. Come in, love, sit yourself down and tell me all about yourself. What am I going to call you? Are you a Johnny, or a Charlie, or what?"

It was amazing: she could have been the same woman—but shadowed; and her good humor, her warm flirtatiousness, were the same as her sister's, but strained. Her costumes were shabby and patched; clearly she was going through a bad time.

"To tell you the truth," he said, "I came to see you really because of your sister. Nellie Budd."

Her eyes widened, and she gave a little gasp.

"What's happened?" she said. "Something's happened, hasn't it? I know it has, I know it . . ."

She sat down. Frederick sat, too, and said, "She's in the hospital, I'm afraid. She was attacked by two men yesterday; they knocked her unconscious."

She nodded. She'd gone pale under her make-up.

"I knew it," she said. "I felt it. We were like that— we used to feel everything the other was feeling—and yesterday I had the most horrible shock, I can't tell you, a sort of ghastly falling feeling, and I *knew* something had happened. It were the morning, weren't it? About elevenish?"

"As far as I know, yes, it was," said Frederick.

"Look, it was silly of me to order champagne. Would you rather have a brandy?"

"I'll drink champagne at anything short of a funeral," she said. "I don't suppose there's any likelihood . . ."

"She's holding her own. She's in Guy's Hospital; they're looking after her well. She might have recovered consciousness by now."

"Look, who are you, anyway?" she said. "I don't mean to be rude, but are you a policeman, or what?"

Frederick opened the bottle and explained the background. When he spoke about Nellie Budd's trances, her sister nodded.

"I remember," she said. "I thought there was nothing in it when she took up this spiritualism line. I didn't hold with it—that was one of the reasons we drifted away from each other. We weren't that close recently. Whoever could have done that to her?"

"I think I know who they are, but I don't know why they did it. Look, here's my card. Will you let me know if anything occurs to you?"

"I certainly will. I'll work tomorrow night, and then I'll come down and see her—I must do that. I don't care how far apart we were, a sister's a sister, for all that."

She took the card and tucked it into her bag.

"By the way," he said, "d'you know a chap called Alistair Mackinnon?"

Her reaction was immediate.

"Him!" she said with icy derision. "That little crawling wood louse. Know him? I should say so. And if he was here now, I'd knock his block off. Mackinnon? Macslimey, if you ask me. Ugh! Is he mixed up in this as well?"

"Yes . . . but I don't know how. He seems to arouse strong reactions, anyway. I've lost track of him. He ought to know about his mother."

"His mother?"

"Your sister. Mrs. Budd."

"What?"

She stood up suddenly and faced him, her plump frame quivering with anger and astonishment.

"His *mother*, did you say? You better explain yourself, my lad. You don't go saying things like that to me without a good explanation."

Frederick was as taken aback as she was. He ran his fingers through his hair before he found anything to say.

"I'm extremely sorry," he said. "I was under the impression that he was your sister's son. He said so himself."

"He said that? The little demon. Where is he now? My God, I've a mind to go and tear him limb from limb. How dare he! How *dare* he!"

She sat down again, pale and trembling with anger. Frederick poured her some champagne.

"Here," he said. "Drink this before the bubbles disappear. What *is* the connection between your sister and Mackinnon?"

"Can't you tell?" she said bitterly.

He shook his head.

"Just like a man. They were lovers, of course. Lovers! And I—" She collapsed suddenly into tears. "And I was in love with him too. Like a fool."

Frederick sat, amazed. Jessie Saxon blew her nose,

dabbed her eyes, sipped angrily at the champagne,
coughed, choked, and wailed aloud. Frederick put his
arms around her; it seemed the only sensible thing to
do. She leaned against him and sobbed while he
stroked her hair and gazed around the shabby, narrow
little dressing room, with its cracked mirror and faded
curtains, with the case of make-up on the dressing
table and the oil lamp flaring smokily beside it. . . . It
might be a cozy place if you had someone to share it
with; or an exciting place if you were starting on the
stage. But it must be a terribly lonely place if you were
Jessie Saxon. He held her close and kissed her gently
on the forehead.

When she recovered, she pushed him away softly
and dabbed at her eyes again with little angry movements, before laughing a short rueful laugh.

"Forty-four years old, and sobbing like a girl. . . .
And we *quarreled* over him. Can you imagine it? Oh,
it's so humiliating now. Well, we're all fools when it
comes to love. Wouldn't be human otherwise—we'd
be machines, or horses, or something. I don't know.
What were you asking, love?"

"About Mackinnon in general. He's . . . a client of
mine." He sat up; they were side by side on a hard
little sofa. He leaned across to pour her some more
champagne. "He also claimed that Lord Wytham was
his father. Is that a lie as well?"

"Old Johnny Wytham?" She laughed more genuinely. "He's got a bloody cheek. Mind you—that *could*
be true. He . . . oh, dear, I can't think straight yet."

She looked at herself in the mirror, made a face, and
patted her hair into shape. Frederick prompted her
gently.

"Lord Wytham?" he said.

"Oh, yes. You must think me a fool, carrying on like this. . . . You really want to know about Alistair? Well, he lied to me often enough, but one thing he never altered: he was the illegitimate son of a lord. So it could be true, for what it's worth."

"And you knew Lord Wytham, did you?"

"Used to in the old days. He used to run around with Nellie, but I'm certain she never had a child. Damn it, I'd know, wouldn't I? We were that close. . . . He's a politician now, I'm told. Is he mixed up in this as well?"

"Yes, but I'm damned if I know how. Nor does your sister."

"I wouldn't bet on it," she said, and helped herself to another glass.

"I beg your pardon?"

"You'd probably find out if you went up and asked around in Carlisle," she said. "That's where I last saw her and where we quarreled. . . . Last year. Only last year."

"What was she doing there?"

"Oh, this silly spiritualism lark. There was a circle, or a league, of the idiots in Carlisle, you see, and she was asked up there and I was playing nearby and that insect Mackinnon was playing a little town near Dumfries—I found out that Nellie was keeping him. Can you imagine! He hadn't perfected his art—his *art*, he calls it—and he kept breaking engagements. Well, theater managers won't stand for that, and rightly. So he was on his uppers, and Nellie stepped in and . . . That's it, really. A little place called Netherbrigg— just over the border."

"Isn't that where Wytham's estate is?"

"Yes, it is. But I hadn't seen him for years, and nor had Nellie. He married, you see, and stopped gadding about the music halls. What was her name now? . . . Lady Louisa Something . . . Big landowners. Graphite mines."

"Graphite?" Frederick sat up.

"Something like that. What *is* graphite?"

"They make pencils with it. . . ." And Steam Guns, he thought, but he didn't mention that. Instead he let her talk as she liked: she was a garrulous soul, and was obviously glad of his company. He learned little more of interest to his inquiry. But about her own life she was eloquent: funny and vivid and scandalous, and when he'd finished laughing, he said, "Jessie, you ought to write your memoirs."

"There's a thought," she said. "But would they print 'em?"

They agreed about the unlikelihood of that and parted fast friends. And before Frederick got into his cold bed at the Railway Hotel, he got out a map and looked for Dumfries and Carlisle and Thurlby, where the firing range was. Not far away, really. A morning's train ride, perhaps; and where was Wytham's estate? Not marked. Or was that it? And as for graphite . . . Lady Wytham's family . . . Bellmann . . . Poor old Nellie. Poor Jessie, too. Both in love with Mackinnon. What the devil had he got to make all these women starry-eyed? Extraordinary. Quite extraordinary. But Sally hadn't taken to him. Sensible girl. Thurlby . . . go there in the morning.

15

Scots Law

SALLY SPENT THE REST OF THURSDAY IN HER OFFICE, dealing with business; and first thing on Friday morning, she went to the patent library.

It was in the Great Seal Patent Office, just off Chancery Lane: a large building like a museum, with a high glass roof and cast-iron galleries all the way around. Sally had been there before, in connection with a client who'd wanted to invest all his money in an invention for making a new kind of sardine tin; she'd been able to show him that it wasn't as new as he'd thought, and persuaded him to buy government stocks instead.

She began her search by looking in the alphabetical index of patentees for anything under the name of Hopkinson. She started with the volume for 1870, feeling that there was unlikely to be anything relevant earlier. She found nothing there, but in the 1871 volume there was listed a patent for steam engines under the name J. Hopkinson.

Was that it, then? Surely she wouldn't find it as quickly as that? After all, Hopkinson wasn't an uncommon name, and there were patents dealing with steam engines on every page of the index, as she saw from glancing through it.

She made a note and turned to the next volume. There was nothing in 1872, but in 1873 and 1874 J. or J. A. Hopkinson had registered two more patents for steam boilers. There was nothing else up to the present. Out of interest she looked up Nordenfels but found nothing.

She went to the desk and filled out a slip requesting the Hopkinson specifications and, while she was waiting, looked up *Garland* in the alphabetical index for 1873. There he was: *Garland, F.D.W., 1385, May 20, Photographic lens*. She had made him patent it when she first began to look after the finances of the firm. It hadn't brought him in any money yet, but the patent would run for another nine years; there'd be time to get it into production, if she could find someone with an interest in manufacturing it. She found herself looking forward to it, to dealing with businessmen and managers and investors again. Something enterprising, something clean and open and honest after all this murk and cruelty! Fred could deal with the technical side that he was so good at, and she'd look after the finance, the planning, the marketing . . .

But he might not want to. *Finish this case, and then we'll call it a go*, he'd said. He meant their friendship as well as anything deeper; his expression had told her that. Would he feel like taking up a new kind of partnership? She doubted it somehow.

She looked around at the men—lawyers' clerks, most of them, she guessed, and one or two private inventors—busily leafing through bound volumes or scratching away with steel pens at the rows of library desks. She was the only woman in the building, and that had brought her some curious looks, but she was used to that. They were careful men, competent and steady and reliable, and she had no doubt of their ability and their usefulness—but Frederick outshone them like the sun. There was no comparison, any more than there was with that flimsy wraith Mackinnon. Fred was incomparable. She had no doubt now about how she felt: she loved him. She always would.

And he'd said she was unlikable . . .

"Miss Lockhart?" It was the man from the desk. "The specifications you requested are ready, miss."

She took the blue booklets and sat at a desk to read them. Each contained a set of folded drawings and a description of the invention. The first was headed:

LETTERS PATENT to John Addy Hopkinson of Huddersfield, in the County of York, Engineer, for the Invention of "IMPROVEMENTS IN STEAM BOILERS AND IN APPARATUS TO BE USED THEREWITH," sealed 5 June 1874, and dated 24 December 1873.

She began to read, but it was soon clear that this wasn't the machine Bellmann was making in the North Star works. Nor were the others: a new kind of moving grate for conveying fuel to the firebox of a steam engine, a new design of boiler . . . Innocuous. This was the wrong Hopkinson.

She took the booklets back to the desk and asked,

"Is there an index classified by subject? Suppose I wanted to look up all the patents concerned with firearms manufacture, for instance—how would I do that?"

"There is a subject index, yes, miss. But the printed index for those years is away at the binder's. If you wanted to look something up you'd have to search through the written slips. Was there something in particular you were looking for?"

"Yes, there was, but . . ." Another thought occurred to her. "You keep foreign patents here, don't you?"

"Yes, indeed, miss."

"Russian ones?"

"Certainly. In the section over there, under the gallery."

"Is there a translation service, by any chance?"

"I'll see if Mr. Tolhausen is free. Could you wait a moment?"

He went into the office behind, and she thought through what she wanted to find out. If Nordenfels had patented an invention in Russia, there'd be a record of it here. But there was nothing to prevent anyone exploiting a foreign invention in Britain if there wasn't a British patent for it; so even if Bellmann were doing that, he'd be breaking no law. On the other hand, if she could prove that Bellmann had stolen the idea . . .

"Mr. Tolhausen, Miss Lockhart."

The translator was a dignified gentleman in his forties who betrayed not the slightest surprise at finding a young woman making technical inquiries.

She warmed to him at once and explained her quest. He listened courteously.

"We shall start with the alphabetical index," he said. "Nordenfels . . . Arne Nordenfels. Here is a patent, dated 1872, for a safety valve for steam boilers. Another here in the same year for improvements in circulating high-pressure steam. In 1873 we have . . ."

He stopped. He was turning the page back and forth, frowning.

"There is a page missing," he said. "Look. It has been carefully cut out."

Sally felt her heart beating fast. "It's the page with Nordenfels on it?"

Her eyes could make nothing of the unfamiliar script, but she could see the neatly trimmed edge where the leaf had been cut.

"Could you look in the following year?" she said.

He did so. Again there was a page missing at the place where *Nordenfels* would have appeared. Mr. Tolhausen came as close as his dignity would allow him to being outraged.

"I shall report this at once. I have never known such a breach of regulations. It is most distressing."

"Before you do, could you check the next couple of years for me? And the subject index?"

He checked the subject index for each year under both *steam engines* and *armaments,* which took some time, since both subjects had long entries. Altogether they found seven patents for steam engines in the name of Nordenfels, but in the armaments section for 1872 and 1873 Mr. Tolhausen found more pages missing.

"Yes, they are the pages for Nordenfels,"he said. "But the index is cross-referenced. One moment . . ."

He turned back to the steam engines section and nodded. "Aha," he said. "Here is a patent for the application of steam power to machine guns. And here is one for a steam-powered gun to be mounted on a railway carriage. But the number of the patent is on the armaments page, which is missing. This is outrageous. I must apologize to you, Miss Lockhart, for the failure of supervision—clearly someone has managed to cut these pages out without being noticed. It is extremely annoying. I must thank you for bringing the matter to my attention."

Sally thanked him for his help, noted the dates and numbers of those patents there was a record of, and turned to go. Before she left a thought struck her, and she took out the alphabetical index of British patents again. If Bellmann were going to make any money from this thing, wouldn't the patent have to be registered in his name?

And there it was. In the 1876 volume she found: *Bellmann, A., 4524, Steam-powered Gun drawn on Railway Carriage.*

As simple as that!

She closed the book, feeling more satisfied than she'd felt for months. Miss Walsh, she thought, you'll get your money back now. . . . As she left the building and turned down into Chancery Lane she found herself smiling.

She didn't notice the young man in the bowler hat who'd been sitting at the desk nearest the door and who folded his papers quietly as she passed. She didn't notice him get up and follow her out; didn't notice as he wandered down Fleet Street behind her and into the Strand; didn't notice as he came into the tea shop at the corner of Villiers Street, where she had lunch. He sat in the window and had a cup of tea and a bun and read his newspaper, and then he followed her out, but still she didn't notice.

He took care that she wouldn't. He was dressed inconspicuously, and he was good at his job. One bowler hat is very like another; and in any case, she was thinking of Frederick.

AT THAT MOMENT, Frederick was in Thurlby, where the firing range was. It stood on the Solway Firth, and as far as he was concerned, the Solway Firth could keep it. It was a grim, flat, desolate place, with nothing but a dreary village and a railway line leading along the shore for miles before vanishing behind a tall fence and a locked gate. Notices warned of extreme danger, and the wind came off the sand dunes laden with gritty salt. There was nothing to be seen there.

He decided to travel on to Netherbrigg, the little town over the Scottish border where Jessie Saxon had said Mackinnon had been staying. Lord Wytham's estate was only a few miles away, on the English side, but there wasn't, he thought, much chance of finding anything out there. He took a room at the King's Head in High Street at Netherbrigg and asked the landlord where visiting theatrical folk usually put up. Did they stay at the King's Head?

"Not here," said the proprietor firmly. "I wouldnae take their money. Godless mummers."

However, he gave Frederick a list of lodging houses, and after lunch Frederick set out to visit them. The sun had come out, though a cold wind was blowing, and the place looked like any little market town. The music hall itself wasn't open at the moment; Frederick was surprised that the place was big enough to support one at all.

A dozen addresses and no map make for a good deal of walking, even in a small town, and it was late in the afternoon when he found what he was looking for. It was his ninth call: a house in Dornock Street, a shabby place with a grim gray chapel in the middle of it. The landlady's name was Mrs. Geary, and yes, she did take boarders.

"Theatrical people, Mrs. Geary?"

"Sometimes, aye. I'm no' fussy."

"Do you remember a man called Alistair Mackinnon?"

A flicker of recognition, and a smile. She wasn't a bad sort. "Aye," she said. "The wizard."

"That's the feller. I'm a friend of his, you see, and—may I come in for a minute?"

She stepped aside and let him into the hall. It was a neat place, smelling of polish, with half a dozen theatrical photographs on the walls.

"Very kind of you," he said. "This is an awkward business. Mackinnon's in a spot of trouble, and I've come up here to see if I can help him."

"Doesn't surprise me," she said dryly.

"Oh? Has he been in trouble before?"

"If ye could call it that."

"What sort of trouble?" Frederick said.

"Ah, well, that'd be telling, wouldn't it?"

He took a deep breath.

"Mrs. Geary, Mackinnon's in danger. I'm a detective, and I've got to find out what's threatening him, so I can help—but I can't ask him directly, because he's vanished. Let's take one thing at a time. Do you know a Mrs. Budd?"

Her eyes narrowed slightly. "Aye," she said.

"Did she ever stay here?"

She nodded.

"With Mackinnon?"

"Aye."

"Were they—forgive me, but I must ask—were they lovers?"

A flicker of grim amusement crossed her face. "Not in this house," she said decisively.

"A man called Axel Bellmann—have you come across that name?"

She shook her head.

"Or Lord Wytham? Do you know of any connection with him?"

"Ah," she said. "So that's it."

"What? You *do* know something, then. Mrs. Geary, this is a serious business. Nellie Budd was attacked the other day and left unconscious; there might be murder involved. You must tell me what you know. What's the connection between Lord Wytham and Alistair Mackinnon? Is he Lord Wytham's son, as he claims to be?"

Now she smiled. "His son? There's a thought. All right, Mr. Whatever, I'll tell ye. And it couldn't happen in England, either. Come in the parlor."

She led him into a pretty little room with more theatrical portraits and a tall piano. Despite her dry manner, she seemed to be a popular landlady, to judge by the number of affectionate inscriptions on the photographs. He had time to examine them while she went to get some tea, and looked in vain for a picture of Mackinnon.

"Well, then," she said when she came back, nudging the door shut with her heel. "I thought it would come out eventually. I didn't imagine there'd be murder mixed up in it—that's a nasty shock. Ye'll have tea?"

"Thank you," he said. She was going to tell it her own way, he thought, and he might as well let her. And then she surprised him.

"Ye'll know about the other fellow?" she said.

"Which other fellow?"

"He came up here a while back; oh, some time now. Asking the same questions. A wee man with gold spectacles."

"Not Windlesham?"

"That was his name," she said.

Bellmann's man. . . . So whatever he'd found out might be the reason for Bellmann's pursuit of Mackinnon.

"And did you tell him what he wanted to know?"

"I am not in the habit of concealing the truth," she said austerely, handing him a cup of tea. "If I havenae mentioned him before, it's because I havenae been asked. I spread no tales, either, mister."

"No, of course not. I didn't mean to imply that you did," he said, trying to keep his patience. "But this man's connected with the people who are after Mackinnon—and who attacked Nellie Budd. I've got to find out why."

"Well, now," she said. "The beginning of it all was with poor Nellie Budd. I hope she's not badly hurt?"

"Well, she is badly hurt, as a matter of fact; they might have fractured her skull. Please, Mrs. Geary. What happened?"

"Nellie asked me to find lodgings for Mackinnon and sign a statement for a lawyer, saying which date he'd come to stay here. And I had to certify that he'd spent each night in the house. Nellie paid his rent, ye know. He had no engagement at the time. Three weeks he stayed here and never strayed once. Twenty-one days, ye see. That's the law."

She was enjoying this, but Frederick was not.

"Twenty-one days?" he said as patiently as he could.

"Twenty-one days' proven residence in Scotland. It never used to be necessary in the old days. But they changed the law twenty years ago, and the hotel trade's prospered this side of the border, so I can't complain."

"Please, Mrs. Geary—what are you talking about? Why should he have to prove he'd spent twenty-one days in Scotland?"

"Ooh, it's quite simple. If ye've done that, ye can get married by simple declaration in front of two witnesses. So that's what he did, ye see."

"I don't see—quite. Whom did he marry? Not Nellie Budd?"

She laughed.

"Don't be daft," she said. "Wytham's girl, that's who. Lady Mary. He married her."

16

Craftsmanship

MR. BROWN, THE BOWLER-HATTED CRAFTSMAN, WAS USED to waiting. He had waited all Thursday and all Friday morning, and he was prepared to wait all week if necessary. His visit to the patent library in Sally's wake was interesting, because it showed him that she did occasionally go out without that dog.

But there was precious little opportunity for his sort of craftsmanship on the crowded pavements of Fleet Street or the Strand. He watched her from behind his newspaper as they sat in the little tea shop in Villier's Street, and wondered if his chance would come when she was alone or if he'd have to take on the dog as well.

She was pretty, he thought. Pretty in a strange way, half English—the blond hair, the trim figure, the neat, practical clothes—and half not: the dark brown eyes, the air of decision and intelligence and boldness. The Americans had girls like this. It wasn't a type the English produced naturally. All the more reason for him to go to America. All the more reason to kill her and earn the money.

Pity, though.

For the rest of the day he stayed with her, taking a cab to follow the omnibus she took to Islington, waiting till she came out of her house with the dog, wandering at a discreet distance behind her as she roamed. When the chance arose, he slipped into the shop doorway and changed his bowler hat for the flat cap he carried in his leather bag or reversed his cloak to show a different-colored tweed. She didn't notice. She seemed to be drifting along at random, with that great patient brute padding happily at her side.

She'd led him to the new Embankment, where he'd had to watch her watching them erect that preposterous obelisk just brought over from Egypt. She was happily calculating angles and heights and breaking points, and admiring the capable, unfussy way the engineers were working; Mr. Brown was watching the dog.

Then she'd wandered up toward Chancery Lane again and spent half an hour in a tea shop—too small to follow her into, this time; he had to drift up and down the pavement across the lane, watching the reflection in the shop windows. A waitress brought tea for Sally and a saucer of water for the dog. Sally seemed to be writing something: a letter? In fact, she was listing all the implications and consequences she could imagine of Bellmann's taking out a patent for someone else's invention, and realizing that she needed to talk to Mr. Temple again. And that she wanted to talk to Frederick.

When she came out, she didn't see the anonymous figure in the gray tweed cloak, though she passed within two feet of him. He went on following her—along Holborn, and up through Bloomsbury, past the British Museum, into a street where she lingered for a few minutes across the road from a photographer's shop, looking at the window display, perhaps; and then, as darkness was falling, he'd walked behind her through the quiet streets to her home in Islington.

THE DOG.

He was afraid of it, no question about that. A colossal brute, with a mouth that could enclose your head and a tongue that would lap up your entrails. . . .

Being a professional, he accepted fear as a warning and weighed his chances all the more carefully. It was no good just being quick and accurate—he'd have to be damn near invulnerable. And as for craftsmanship, it was wasted on animals. The knife for the girl—but for the dog, a gun.

He didn't carry a gun, but he knew where to get one quickly. An hour after Sally had returned, Mr. Brown was stationed in the dark little garden beneath the plane trees in the center of the square. She'd be out later. Dogs need what is politely called exercise before being shut in for the night.

It would be an interesting technical problem, managing the knife and the gun so quickly one after the other. But there was a skill he'd find a ready market for in America. . . .

He settled down to wait.

AT HALF PAST ELEVEN the sound of a door opening broke the silence of the square. A light rain had fallen earlier, but it hadn't lasted long. Everything was wet and cold and still.

The warm yellow of the doorway against the darkness of the housefront showed him the silhouette of the girl and the dog and, for a moment, another female figure behind them; and then the door was shut, and her light footsteps came out onto the pavement.

They came, as he guessed, toward the little garden at the center of the square—but turned away at the railing, despite the open gate, and walked slowly around the edge. A cab turned into the square at the same time and crawled to a halt outside a house on the opposite site. Mr. Brown kept still and never let her out of his sight while he listened to the cabdriver and his passenger arguing over the fare.

The girl and the dog wandered along slowly, she apparently lost in thought, he casting this way and that, sniffing, lifting his head and shaking it so that the chain jingled.

Finally, and not without audible curses, the cab-driver gathered his reins once more, and his horse moved on. The quiet one-two-three-four clatter of its hooves and the iron trundle of the wheels lasted a long time before they were lost in the general blur of sound from the busier streets beyond the square.

And still the girl walked on. . . . She'd almost completed the circuit of the square. Earlier in the evening, and unobtrusively, Mr. Brown had explored the house around the edge and the streets between them, in order to be sure of a way out. He knew that opposite her now there was a narrow close—an alley, almost—between two of the tall, severely handsome, old brick houses.

He saw her look across at it and step into the road. Surely she wouldn't go down there—it was perfect, even better than the darkness under the trees. . . .

But she did, hesitating a moment and then letting the great dog pad ahead of her into the alley. And now Mr. Brown moved. He took the pistol in his left hand, the knife in his right, concealing them under the thickness of his cloak, and came silently out of the trees and crossed the road. Without a glance to either side, he slipped into the alley and listened.

Silence. They hadn't heard him.

He could see them ahead, against the dim light coming from the other end. The alley was narrow and the dog was ahead of her: very well.

Knife first.

He pushed the cloak back, freeing both his arms. Then he sprang forward, thumb on the blade, and was on them before they had time to turn.

She heard him at the last moment and twisted aside. But he struck and hit home, and she gasped as if all the air had been punched out of her lungs and fell at once.

Change hands. Quick! The knife was stuck!

He slapped the gun into his right hand and tugged the knife free from her with his left, and then the dog—an explosion of snarling—jaws, teeth, whirling movement—

It slammed into him as he fired. They fell together, and he jammed the barrel into its hot black side and fired again, the shots like cannon fire in the tiny alley.

It had him by the left arm, and its teeth crushed flesh and bone. He fired again, twice more, but he hadn't bargained for the weight of it, the way it shook him against the wall like a rat—two more shots, right into it! Into its very heart—and he *heard* his arm snap. It could kill a horse, a bull, this terrible strength, it was awesome—

He dropped the gun and snatched the knife from the nerveless fingers of his left hand.

Where was he, for God's sake? Upside down?

Banged from side to side—it was like a hurricane. He'd fired into its body time and time again and still it came on—

He drove the knife up into it, again, again, again, grating on bone and slippery with blood and it made no difference; the dog wasn't feeling it—it still had its teeth in his arm—it felt as if they'd met in the center of it! The pain—the fear. He drove the knife up again, again, again, again, driving, thrusting, hacking—no craftsmanship now, this was panic—and the snarling and the thrashing worsened. He felt dizzy with weakness and still he stabbed, driving the knife into throat, belly, back, chest, head—and then it let go.

Blood—so much blood.

His arm screamed. It hung down uselessly beside him.

And then with a surge like a wave of the sea the dog was at his throat, tearing—

Something spilled. A terrible gush, spilling out.

And a weakness came over the dog. Its jaws loosened and it trembled, and the snarling diminished to a sigh, and it stood away and shook itself, almost in puzzlement. Drops flew from it. And it sank to a sitting position and then slumped clumsily forward.

Mr. Brown dropped the knife and dragged the cloak, sopping, up to his throat. He was lying against the wall with his legs under the body of the dog, and the life was gushing out of him. The sound it made appalled him.

But he'd done it. He might not survive the dog, but the girl was dead. He reached out dimly and his hand met her hair, wet on the stone beside him.

Then a voice spoke from the entrance of the alley. "Chaka?" it said.

He TWISTED and knelt up in a moment of final terror. She was there, holding a lantern. Bareheaded—blond—that face, that lovely horrified face, those eyes!

It wasn't possible—

He looked down and snatched aside the cloak that hid the dead girl's face.

A huge birthmark spread across it from jaw to forehead.

The wrong girl—and he—his craftsmanship—

He bowed his head and fell forward into everlasting horror.

SALLY RUSHED in and flung herself down in the narrow space beside the girl, setting the lantern on the cobblestones by her head.

"Isabel—" she said. "Isabel—"

She laid her hands on the other girl's cheek and saw her eyelids shake, and then open wide. She looked crazed, like someone waking from a nightmare.

"Sally," she whispered.

"Did he—" Sally began.

"He stabbed me—but it didn't—the knife caught in—in my stays. Oh, how silly—I fainted—but Chaka—"

And Sally felt as if some god had struck her a great blow over the heart.

She caught up the lantern again. Its quivering light danced over the body of the man, over the streams of blood on the stones, and lit the dark head and dim eyes of the dog.

"Chaka," she said aloud, with all her love in the shaking of her voice.

And the dog heard, at the edge of death, and lifted his head to her and thumped his tail on the ground, once, twice, thrice, before his great strength left him. She threw herself full length and held his head and kissed it again and again, sobbing, her tears mingled with his blood as she cried his name.

He tried to answer, but his throat was mute. Darkness was everywhere. Sally was with him. It was safe. He died.

17

~~~

The Removal Van

THE ORDINARY KIND OF TIME STOPPED THEN, AND FOR HALF the night another kind took over: a phantasmagoric shadow show filled with police and onlookers and a doctor for Isabel (cut along her ribs) and then a grumbling man with a cart summoned to take Chaka away. But Sally wouldn't allow that; she paid him to take the body into her landlord's garden instead, and gave him half a crown for a tarpaulin to cover it with. Chaka would be buried where she chose.

Isabel went to bed as soon as the doctor had left— dazed and trembling now, and beginning to hurt. Sally answered questions: yes, the dog was hers; no, she didn't know why Miss Meredith had been attacked; no, she didn't recognize the man; yes, Miss Meredith lived here; yes, she usually walked the dog at that time; no, neither she nor Miss Meredith had received any threats. . . .

In the end the police seemed to accept that it had been a chance attack by an opportunist, though she could tell that they were puzzled. He was too well armed for an ordinary street robber, and to take on anyone accompanied by a dog like that when there were plenty of easier targets—well, it was odd. They left, shaking their heads. It was after three o'clock when she got to bed, and no matter how many blankets she piled on, she couldn't stop shivering.

FIRST THING next morning she went to her office—and found it empty.

It had been ransacked.

Her files, her carefully arranged correspondence, the folders on all her clients, the details of their shareholdings and savings—it was all gone. The shelves were empty; the drawers of the cabinet hung open.

She felt lightheaded, crazy, as if she'd walked into the wrong office. But, no—there were her table and chairs, there was the sagging divan. . . .

She ran down to the office of her landlord's chief clerk, who managed her rental.

"Where are my files? What's happened?"

For an instant, pure shock passed over his face—as if he'd seen a ghost. Then it closed into tight-lipped coldness.

"I'm afraid I cannot say. And I must point out that I have received information about your use of this office that is most disturbing. When the police came this morning, they—"

"The police? Who called the police? What did they want?"

"I did not think it proper to inquire. They removed certain documents, and—"

"You let them take my property from my office? And did you get a receipt?"

"I am not going to stand between a police officer and his duty. And do not take that tone with me, young lady."

"Did they have a warrant? On whose authority did they enter my office?"

"On the authority of the Crown!"

"In that case they will have had a warrant. Did you see it?"

"Of course not. It was none of my business."

"Which police station did they come from?"

"I have no idea. And I must—"

"You allowed police officers into my room to take away my property—you didn't ask for a receipt—you didn't see a warrant. This is England, did you know that? You have heard of a search warrant, I suppose? How do you know that these men were really police officers?"

He banged the desk and stood up, shouting, "I will not be spoken to like that by a common prostitute!"

The word hung in the sudden silence.

He was staring fixedly at the wall behind Sally, unable to look her in the face.

She looked him up and down, from the red spots in his thin cheeks to the papery knuckles clutching the desk.

"I'm ashamed of you," she said. "I thought you were a businessman. I thought you could see straight and deal fairly. Once, I'd have been angry with you—but now I'm just ashamed."

He said nothing as she turned and left.

*　　*　　*

THE SERGEANT on duty at the nearest police station was an elderly, avuncular soul, who frowned and tut-tutted in a concerned away as Sally began the story.

"Your office?" he said. "You've got an office, have you, miss? That's nice."

She looked at him carefully, but he seemed to be listening. She went on. "Did the policemen come from this station?"

"I don't really know, miss. We've got a lot of policemen here."

"But surely you'd know what was going on? They took some documents. They must have brought them back here. Has no one come in with paper or files or letters brought from an office in King Street?"

"Oooh, hard to say. There's a lot of paper comes in and out of here. You'd better give me the details."

He licked his pencil—and then she saw him wink at the constable behind the desk nearby, and saw the young man turn away to hide a smirk.

She didn't answer.

She had suddenly realized something about people like this—whether they were businessmen, police-men, civil servants, hotel proprietors, landlords, or what: it was that they didn't mean what they said. They never told the truth. What they seemed to be doing—catching criminals, buying and selling, bank-ing, administering, making things—wasn't the real business of their lives at all. It was a cover. They were only playing at it, and they didn't even do it well, because they didn't believe in it. The real, secret business of their lives lay in keeping power for people like themselves. That was all they really cared about, and they were desperately serious about it, because the thought of losing the little power they had was terrifying to them; and they didn't mind what damage they did to truth or honesty or justice in the struggle to hang on to it.

"On second thought," she said, "don't bother."

She put her hand out for Chaka and looked down for the warmth of his love and his goodness, but there was nothing there, because they'd killed him.

The tears spilled over her cheeks and she left.

SHE REACHED Burton Street only ten minutes after Frederick got back from the north. He was tired and disheveled and unshaven, having spent the night on a slow train, and he'd eaten nothing since lunch the previous day, but he pushed aside his coffee and toast, listened intently to what she told him, and then called Jim.

"Job for Turner and Luckett," he said. "Sally— finish my coffee for me. . . ."

AN HOUR LATER a removal van drawn by a lean gray horse pulled up outside Baltic House. Two men with green baize aprons got off, put a nosebag over the horse's head, and walked in past the stout commissionaire.

"Load o' files," said the taller man (a lugubrious fellow with a large mustache) to the porter. "They come in earlier, or something. They got to be moved to Hyde Park Gate."

"That's probably where Mr. Bellmann's gone, then," said the porter. "I dunno where they put 'em. I better ask the chief clerk—I think he was handling 'em."

An office boy was sent to find out, and five minutes later the removal men were carrying the first load down and stowing them in the back of their van. As they came in for a second load, the porter said, "You got a letter, have you? I better have a look. And I'll need a receipt."

"Oh, yus—here you are," said the removal man. "You go on up, Bert—start on the next load."

The more slightly mustached removal man went ahead while the porter scrutinized the letter authorizing the removal. When the files were all in the van, the first removal man wrote out a receipt on his firm's stationery and gave it to the porter before climbing up onto the box. The younger man removed the horse's nosebag. The commissionaire saluted as they drove away.

When they were around the corner and out of sight of Baltic House, the younger man spoke for the first time.

"Well, Fred," he said.

"Well, Jim," was the reply.

Jim pulled at his mustache, wincing as the spirit gum clung to his lip.

"Don't pluck at it nervously," said Frederick. "A good manly tug's all it needs."

He reached across and yanked it free with a sharp tearing sound. A fusillade of oaths followed from Jim—enough, as Frederick said, to make the horse blush.

"Tell you what," he said when the tirade had abated. "I'll turn in here and you jump down and turn the sign round. And we'll take off these aprons—just in case anyone wakes up and gives chase. . . ."

Two minutes later, with their flat caps changed for

bowler hats and the sign on the van reversed to read
WILSON BROS., WHOLESALE GROCERIES, they were on their
way back to Burton Street.

"OH, FRED,—I don't believe it!"
Sally stood in the yard behind the shop and looked
into the back of the van. She ran her hand over the
nearest pile of cardboard folders and then turned and
flung her arms around Frederick.

He responded in kind, and the embrace only came
to an end when a round of applause broke out from
somewhere above them. Frederick looked up to see
the broad grins on the faces of the glaziers who were
putting the windows into the new studio.

"What the devil are you grinning at?" he roared.

But then he saw the funny side of it and grinned
himself; Sally smiled too. They went into the
kitchen.

"D'you want to check them?" he said. "See if
they're all there?"

"In a minute. . . . Oh, Fred, thank you, thank
you!"

She spread her hands, helpless, and sat down in
tears. Jim opened a bottle of beer and poured it out for
them. Frederick drank deeply.

"How did you *do* it?" she said. "It's unbeliev-
able. . . . I really thought I'd lost everything."

"I wrote a letter," he explained, "on the firm's
stationery—not this firm, Turner and Luckett's—
authorizing the removal of certain files to number
forty-seven, Hyde Park Gate. That's all."

Turner and Luckett didn't exist. Frederick had had
various items of stationery printed in that name, which

had earned their keep several times already. Sally nodded, beginning to smile.

"I guessed they were at Baltic House," Frederick went on. "Obviously they weren't in the police station; Bellmann's men might have worn police uniforms to impress your landlord's clerk, or they might even have been real police—I bet he's got enough influence to swing that—but he's the only one who'd be interested in them. No, we waited till we saw Bellmann leave the building, and then we just walked in. I guessed they wouldn't question it if they thought the files were being moved to Bellmann's house."

"We've done it before," said Jim. "It's funny, ain't it, Fred? Amazing what you can get away with. You could walk in anywhere with a bit of paper in your hand—you could get away with murder, almost."

"Oh, if I'd lost these . . ." Sally felt cold at the thought. If her files were out of her hands, she couldn't look after her clients' money—and if the stock market moved in the wrong direction, it could be disastrous. She'd made some surprising profits for some of her clients, but she'd had some narrow escapes, too. Everything depended on having the information close at hand and being able to move quickly; when she thought what she might have lost . . .

"Could you take them to Mr. Temple's for me?" she said. "There isn't room for them here, and since they know where I live, that's not safe either."

"I'm going to have a bath," said Frederick, "and then I'll have something to eat, and then I'll take 'em wherever you want. And while I'm eating, I'll tell you what I found out up north. But not a word of that till

I've got some food inside me—though I tell you what, Jim: we've got to find Mackinnon."

Sally was different, Frederick thought as he shaved. More than just shaking her, Chaka's death had altered something deep inside her. Was it in her eyes? Her mouth? It was hard to say where the expression showed, but it moved him unbearably. And when she'd arrived, dark-eyed and paper-white—it was the first time he'd ever seen her helpless in that way, frightened, needing him. And the way she'd clung to him . . . Everything was changing.

Over lunch he told them about Henry Waterman and the Steam Gun, and Sally added her findings from the patent library. Webster came in from the studio, heard what they were talking about, and sat down to listen.

"What d'you think happened, then?" he said. "Summarize."

"Bellmann and Nordenfels went to Russia," Sally began. "Nordenfels designed this gun and patented it there, only they couldn't build it in Russia because they haven't got the factories, or the techniques, for that matter. They needed somewhere with a lot of locomotive-building experience."

"Then they had a fight," went on Frederick. "They quarreled over something—don't know what—doesn't matter, really. Bellmann killed Nordenfels and stole the plans for his gun and came to this country—and invented a designer called Hopkinson."

"And patented the invention in his own name. He must have had Russian money," said Sally.

"Why?" said Webster.

"Well, when his match business collapsed he was left with nothing. But when he arrived in this country in '73 he had no end of money. This is just a guess, but I think he was subsidized by the Russian government. They wanted the Steam Gun built, and they funded him to get it done. The rest of his activities—the shipping, the buying up of companies and selling off their assets—all that's just spare-time stuff. The Steam Gun's the main thing. . . . But, you know, I can't see who'd use a gun like that."

"I should think any general would give his right arm for it," said Webster.

She shook her head, and Frederick smiled, recognizing Sally the military tactician.

"In the first place, you could use it only where there's a railway line," she explained. "And you couldn't expect an enemy to wait politely until your engineers had laid down a line in the right place. Besides, it only fires broadside, doesn't it?"

"That's what I understood from Mr. Waterman," said Frederick.

"In that case the line would have to go right through the middle of the enemy position. Otherwise you'd have to have it parallel to their lines—and even then half your fire power would be aiming back at your own troops."

"I see what you mean," said Webster. "But that's ridiculous."

"Only if it's designed as a battlefield weapon. But perhaps it isn't."

"If it's not for fighting battles with," said Frederick, "what the devil *is* it for?"

"Well . . ." Sally began. "Suppose you were the ruler of a country, and you didn't trust your people. You thought there was a danger of revolution. As long as you had railway lines to the main cities and ports, and a number of Steam Guns, you'd be perfectly safe. It's an ideal weapon for that sort of thing. It's not to use against your enemies—it's to use against your own population. It really *is* evil."

They were silent for a moment or two.

"I reckon you've cracked it, Sal," said Jim. "But, look—are you going to move in here or not? For one thing, they know you're still alive. And once they twig we've snitched your files back, they'll go barmy. I would. And *she* ought to move in as well—Miss Meredith. We've got the room, after all."

"Yes," said Sally. "I think it would be best if I did." She didn't look at Frederick.

Jim went on: "And what's this about Mackinnon, Fred? You found out why Bellmann's chasing him, then? What's it all about?"

Frederick told them.

As he spoke Sally could see Jim's face getting redder and redder. Eventually he turned away and began elaborately to trace a design with his fingernail in the scrubbed wood of the kitchen table.

"So there you have it," Frederick said when he'd finished. "Scots law. You can get married at sixteen there, without any consent at all. I should have spotted it before I got to Netherbrigg: Gretna Green's the first village over the border. I guess Nellie Budd arranged it out of some kind of sentimental sympathy—she can't have been in love with him. That was just Jessie's jealousy. But where does that leave Wytham? Where does it leave the girl, for heaven's sake? We have to assume that Bellmann knows about it, since Windlesham got the facts out of Mrs. Geary some time ago. Obviously Mackinnon's in danger, but . . ."

"He's in danger while no one knows about the marriage," Webster pointed out. "As soon as it's public knowledge, he's as safe as houses. Not even Bellmann would dare to bump him off then; the whole world would know why. Come to that, d'you suppose her papa knows?"

"Mrs. Geary said he did," said Frederick. "He came to her, apparently, and tried to pay her to keep silent about it. She sent him away with a Calvinist flea in his ear. I liked her, you know. Dry as dust, but she had a sense of humor—and completely honest. She said she'd say nothing until she was asked, and then she'd tell the truth, and no one could make her do less or more than that."

"So Wytham knew about it all the time he was arranging the engagement photograph and announcing it in *The Times*," said Webster. "He's in trouble, isn't he?"

Sally said nothing. She was thinking about Isabel Meredith.

Suddenly Jim stood up.

"Think I'll go out for a breath of air," he said; and without looking at anyone, he left.

"What's the matter with him?" said Webster.

Frederick groaned. "The boy's in love," he said. "And I forgot all about it. Look, Sally—we'll take your stuff to Mr. Temple's, and then go to Islington and pick up Miss Meredith and whatever you want to bring here. Then I'll find Jim and we'll go and look for Mackinnon. What a case. What a case . . ."

18

Hyde Park

IT WAS A DRY, MILD AFTERNOON, WITH A FITFUL SUNSHINE breaking through filmy clouds. Jim made his way to Hyde Park, fists thrust into pockets and a scowl on his face, and it was well for Alistair Mackinnon that he didn't bump into him.

But by the time he'd reached the park he'd calmed down. He made his way to the carriage drive and sat on the grass under a tree, running his fingers through the dry leaves beside him and watching the carriages pass to and fro.

It was the wrong season to drive in the park. The proper time to be seen here was the summer; the drive was so crowded then that the traffic hardly moved at all, but that wasn't the point. The point was to come here and be seen with your groom and your landau or your victoria, your grays or your bays—to be acknowledged by Lady This, to cut Miss That. In the winter all that social jostling took place indoors, and the carriage drive was left to the few people who wanted to breathe some fresh air and exercise their horses.

But Jim had come there to see Lady Mary.

Ever since that dreamlike day when he'd seen her in the winter garden, his mind had been fixed on her like a compass needle on the north. He'd haunted Cavendish Square, watched her leave and come back, seen her in the drawing room window. . . .

He admitted to himself that he was besotted. He'd known girls, dozens of them, barmaids and housemaids and dancers, bold ones and shy ones and provocative ones and prim ones; known them to talk to and flirt with, to take to the music hall or on the river. He'd never had much trouble attracting girls. There was nothing special about his looks, but he was maturing into a sort of rough handsomeness, most of which was due to his vitality and confidence. He was easy with girls, too, liking their company as well as their kisses: hasty kisses by area steps, or longer ones in the darkness behind the scenes in a theater or in the seclusion of a bower in the old Cremorne Gardens before they closed.

But that was nothing like this. Never mind the social gulf between them: she the daughter of an earl, he the son of a cabdriver and a laundrywoman; even if they'd been able to meet in a social way, he'd still have wanted to treat her differently, because *she* was utterly different. Every little movement she'd made that day in the winter garden, every curl of her rich hair, every shade of warm color in her cheek, the memory of her sweet breath on his face as she leaned close to whisper—it was all infinitely precious; and he didn't know what in the world he could do about it.

Except watch. And in his watching he'd learned that she was in the habit of driving out in the afternoon; and at a guess, she came to the park. But it was a good guess. It was the obvious place to go. And as a carriage came past Jim's tree he looked up from the leaf he was shredding and found himself gazing into her face.

She was driving past in a pretty little victoria. The top-hatted coachman stared straight ahead as he held the whip at the correct arrogant angle. She was leaning back listlessly, but when she saw Jim she sat up at once and made as if to speak, putting out her hand—and then the carriage swept past and she was hidden from sight by the hood.

Jim was on his feet at once and running a step or two after it, helplessly. But then he saw the coachman incline his head and lean back a little, as if to hear something, and the carriage slowed down.

He closed his eyes. It was thirty yards away; he heard the clop of hooves come to a stop, and a sentence or two in her voice to the coachman, and then the carriage moved away.

She was waiting for him under the trees. She had on an astrakhan coat and was carrying a muff of the same material; a hat trimmed with dark green ribbon sat high on the crown of her head. She was perfect. Jim found himself moving toward her without knowing how or why or what was happening; and he found his hands reaching out, and saw hers responding, all without thinking; and then in a confusion of recollection and awakening they remembered who they were and stood in an awkward silence.

Jim took off his cap. That's what you did, he thought, to ladies.

"I told the coachman I wanted to walk," she said. She was as nervous as he was.

"Neat little carriage," he said.

She nodded. "You've hurt your mouth," she began, and then looked away and blushed.

As if they'd agreed on it, they began walking slowly along under the trees.

"D'you always come out alone?" he said.

"You mean without a chaperon? I used to have a governess, but she was dismissed. My father hasn't very much money. Or used not to have. Oh, I don't know what to do. . . ."

She sounded like a young child—shy and trusting and wary—and her extraordinary beauty had something unformed about it too. It was as if she didn't know what to do with it, as if she'd just been put into the world.

"How old are you?"

"Seventeen."

"Look," he said gently, "we found out about Mackinnon."

She stopped and closed her eyes. "Does *he* know?" she whispered.

"Bellmann? Yes. He's hunting him down. He nearly got him the other night—that's where I lost my tooth. You can't have expected to keep it secret, after all. Your father knows, doesn't he?"

She nodded. They walked on slowly.

"What can I do?" she said. "I feel like a prisoner. Like someone sentenced to . . . to death, almost. There's nothing I can do to escape. It's like a nightmare."

"Tell me about Mackinnon," Jim said.

"We met at a charity performance he gave at Netherbrigg. At our house. We managed to meet later and . . . Well, I must have fallen in love. It was so sudden. We were going to get married and go to America. A woman called Mrs. Budd helped to arrange it and saw to the lawyer and everything. But then when it came to going away, somehow Alistair couldn't decide, and it turned out that I couldn't get at my money, either, so we had nothing. My father tried to have the marriage declared invalid. But there were no grounds for that because we'd . . . we'd spent the night at the boardinghouse where he was staying. So the marriage was legal in every way. I suppose it still is. And now . . ."

Her voice broke, and she started to cry softly. He couldn't help it; he put his arms around her and pressed her face gently into his shoulder. She was so light—her warm, clean hair was so soft—and it was so strange, that moment, like something in a dream. Before he knew what he was doing, he kissed her.

Nothing happened. The moment passed; she leaned away slightly, and the two of them were separate again.

"But your father," Jim began haltingly. "If he knows . . ."

"It's money," she said. "Mr. Bellmann is going to pay him lots of money when we're married. He doesn't know I know that, but it's obvious. And he's so deeply in debt that he daren't refuse it. He's looking for Alistair, too, now. If they don't find him before long . . ."

Her voice broke again with sheer misery. He tried to put his arm around her, but she gently evaded him, shaking her head.

"If I marry Mr. Bellmann I'll be a criminal," she said. "A bigamist or something. And if I don't, then Papa will go to prison. I can't tell *anyone* about it. But if they do find Alistair they'll do something terrible. I know they will. . . ."

They walked on. Somewhere a bird was singing. The sun on her face, with its clear midwinter light, only showed how perfect the soft bloom of her skin was, how delicate the bones under her cheeks and temples. Jim felt dizzy and weak, like someone recovering from a serious illness, and he knew that this moment couldn't last long; the coachman would soon complete the circuit and come up behind them.

She said, "It's like our winter garden here, as if nothing else exists. I'm with you, but I feel alone. I wish the old pleasure gardens were still there. Like Vauxhall or Cremorne. Then I could go there in disguise and see the lights in the trees, and the fireworks, and watch the dancing."

"You wouldn't have liked Cremorne. It was cheap and shoddy and dirty at the end, before they closed it. Still, it was all right at night when the dirt didn't show. You don't like *doing* things, do you? Only watching them. Aren't I right?"

She nodded. "Yes," she said. "Quite right. I don't think I've ever done anything that was good." She wasn't pitying herself, just telling him a fact.

"You stopped the carriage, though."

"Yes. I'm glad I did. I don't know what he'll say.

He'll probably tell my father—well, he certainly will. I'll say I just wanted to walk." They moved on a little way, and then she said, *"You* do things. You're a detective. And a photographer."

"Not a photographer, really. I . . . I write plays."

"Do you?"

"All the time. But no one's put one on yet."

"Are you going to make a fortune?"

"Bound to."

"And be famous? Like Shakespeare?"

"Course I am."

"What are your plays about?"

"Murder. Same as Shakespeare." But not real murder, he thought; he'd never written about a real person, really getting killed, and the sickening shock you felt when it happened. It would be too horrible; worse than vampires by a long way.

They drifted on a little farther. He'd never known such happiness, or such apprehension.

"You know," he said, "you're . . . lovely. Beautiful. I can't find the words for it, but I've never seen anyone like you. Never, anywhere. You're the most— perfect . . ."

To his surprise her eyes filled with tears.

"I just *wish* . . ." she said indistinctly, and sniffed. "I just wish there was something else to say. I'd rather be in disguise. Or in a mask. It all comes back to that, to being *beautiful.*"

She made the word sound loathsome.

"You're just the opposite of someone I met the other day," he said. "Well, she's not ugly, but she's got a birthmark right across her face, and she hates anyone to see it. And she's in love with . . ." With your husband, he thought. "With a bloke, and she knows he'll never love her, and that's the only thing in her life."

"Oh, the poor girl," she said. "What's her name?"

"Isabel. But, look, we're going to have to stop old Bellmann. You know what he's up to? You know what he's making up there in Barrow? You can't marry a monster like him. Any halfway-decent lawyer would be able to prove they were forcing you into it against your will. You won't get done for bigamy, don't worry about that. The safest thing all round would be to come out with it, make it public. Damn your father's debts; he got himself into the mess, and now he's putting you through this hell to buy himself out of it. But until it's out in the open, no one's safe—especially Mackinnon."

"I'm not going to give him away," she said.

"What?"

"I shan't tell them where he is. Oh—"

She was looking over his shoulder, and despair suddenly flooded her lovely features like the shadow of a cloud racing over a sunlit garden. He turned, and saw the victoria returning. The coachman hadn't seen them yet.

Jim turned back urgently. "D'you mean you know where he is? Mackinnon, I mean?"

"Yes. But—"

"Tell me! Quick, before the carriage gets here! We've got to know—can't you see that?"

She bit her lip and then nodded quickly. "Hampstead," she said. "Fifteen Kenton Gardens. Under—under the name of Stone—Mr. Stone."

Jim brought her hand up to his mouth and kissed it. It was all ending so fast.

"Can you come here again?" he said.

She shook her head helplessly, eyes on the carriage.

"Write to me, then," he said, scrabbling in a pocket for one of Fred's cards. "Jim Taylor. That address. Promise."

"I promise," she said, and with a last troubled look took his hand. Their hands clung as their bodies moved apart, and then they were touching no longer, and she stepped out of the trees. Jim stayed where he was as the coachman pulled the little carriage up. He saw her look back once, timidly and swiftly, and he didn't see any more, for something strange had happened to his eyes, and he wiped them angrily with the back of his hand as the carriage moved away and vanished in the traffic near Hyde Park Corner.

ISABEL HAD SAT without a word as Sally told her of Mackinnon's marriage, and she'd merely nodded and followed silently as they went out to the cab. She got in beside Sally, still silent, and covered her face with the veil.

"How's your wound?" Sally said after the cab had moved out of the square. "Is it very painful?"

"I hardly feel it," Isabel said. "It's nothing."

Sally knew she meant *In comparison with what you've just told me.* Isabel was nursing the little tin box as if not even death would part her from it. They'd thrown some clothes into a large carpetbag and left at once for Burton Street; there would be a lot of rearranging of rooms to do, and Sally was anxious to get Isabel busy as soon as possible in order to take her mind off Mackinnon.

When they arrived, they found confusion in the yard. The glaziers were leaving the studio, and the decorators were bringing their materials over to make ready for an early start on Monday, and the two groups of men were passing back and forth and getting in each other's way, and Webster's temper was beginning to fray.

Sally showed Isabel to the room she was to have: a neat little place on the top floor, with a dormer window overlooking the street. Isabel sat on the bed, still clutching her box, and said, "Sally?"

Sally sat down beside her. "What is it?" she said.

"I mustn't stay here. No—listen—you must let me go away. I bring bad luck to people."

Sally laughed, but Isabel shook her head passionately and gripped her hand.

"No! Don't laugh! Look what I've done already—to my landlady, to you, to your dog. It's *me*, Sally, I swear it! There's no good luck where I am. I was born cursed. You must let me go away and be on my own. I'll find some little place out in the country somewhere—I'll work on the land. But I mustn't be with you and your friends. I'm no good to you. . . ."

"I don't believe that for one minute. Look, at the very least you're a godsend to the shop. They're desperate downstairs for someone who can deal with the clerical work, and I know that's not what you're best at, but if you could help us with it for a while you'd be worth your weight in gold. Honestly, Isabel, I'm not just inventing a job for you out of charity—the work needs doing. I know the news about Mr. Mackinnon hurt you. But the hurt will go in time, and meanwhile we need you here."

Finally Isabel gave in; she hadn't much strength to argue, in any case. She asked to be shown the work she was to do, and then sat down, silent and pale like a prisoner, to do it. Sally was troubled.

But she didn't have time to tell Frederick about it, because no sooner had he come back from Mr. Temple's than Jim arrived.

"I've found Mackinnon," he said. "He's in Hampstead. We'll have to fetch him, Fred. You better bring your stick. . . ."

NUMBER FIFTEEN Kenton Gardens was a trim little villa on a tree-lined road. The door was opened by a middle-aged woman, presumably the landlady, who seemed surprised to see them.

"I'm not sure . . ." she said. "Yes, Mr. Stone is in, but the other gentlemen said they weren't to be disturbed."

"Other gentlemen?" said Frederick.

"Two more gentlemen. They arrived about fifteen minutes ago. Perhaps I'd better go up and ask—"

"It's really quite urgent," Frederick told her. "If we could see Mr. Stone ourselves, we could explain."

"Well . . ."

She let them in and directed them to the front room on the first floor. They saw her back downstairs before they stepped quietly up to the door and listened.

They heard a voice—a thick voice, a voice that sounded as if its owner was having trouble breathing.

It was saying "Ah, but you're such a sly bugger that we can't trust you. What we'll have to do, I think, is break one of your fingers. . . ."

Frederick leaned closer.

They heard Mackinnon say instantly, "If you do that, I'll *scream*. The police will come. I warn you—"

"Oh, you're warning us?" said the first voice. "That's interesting. I thought we were warning you. I see your point about the scream, though. That's just what you would do. What we'll do is stuff this towel in your gob, then you won't be able to. That's a good plan, isn't it? Go on, then, Sackville. Thrust it firmly home. . . ."

Jim and Frederick turned to each other, eyes shining. Over the gagging and struggling sounds behind the door, Frederick said, "Sackville and Harris! Our lucky day, Jim. Got your knuckles?"

Jim nodded gleefully. This was exactly what he wanted.

"In we go," he said.

Frederick turned the handle quietly, and they walked in.

Mackinnon was seated on a rush-bottomed chair with his hands tied behind him, his mouth filled with one end of a towel (the rest of it emerging like ectoplasm), his eyes bulging.

Over him stood Sackville, a frown of puzzlement on his grisly face. Harris, whose face looked as if a horse had kicked it, gaped and swallowed and took a step backward.

Frederick shut the door.

"Oooh, you are greedy," he said. "You don't know

when to stop, do you? Look at your poor nose. I thought you'd have learned by now. As for you, Mackinnon," he went on, "you stay there. I want a word with you about my watch."

Suddenly Harris took a step forward and lashed at Frederick with the rubber blackjack he was holding. Frederick stepped aside and cracked him over the wrist with his stick, and then Jim was on him like a terrier, in an explosion of knuckles, knees, head, feet, and elbows.

Sackville flung Mackinnon's chair aside. The pinioned wizard crashed into the washstand with a muffled howl and then slid down sideways to face the wall, still gagged and bound to the broken chair, while Sackville seized another chair and swung it at Frederick. Before it could connect, Frederick jabbed his stick forward and into Sackville's ribs, throwing him off balance—and then they were fighting in earnest, hand to hand, face to face.

Sackville was a big man, but Frederick was fast and fit, and he had the advantage of not having learned to box. He had no inhibitions about not using his feet or not hitting below the belt; and as far as Jim was concerned, anything you did in a fight was fair, because if you didn't do it, the other bugger would, so you might as well do it first. And since the obvious target was Harris's nose, Jim went for it at once, and cracked his forehead smartly onto the bridge of it before Harris swept his legs away from under him and kicked him in the ribs.

The room wasn't large: bed, dressing table, washstand, chest of drawers, a couple of chairs, and a wardrobe comprised the whole of the contents and left little room to move about in. Harris and Sackville were made desperate by fear; Jim by frustration and anger; Frederick by the memory of Nellie Budd's battered face, silent on a pillow in the hospital ward. None of them was in any mood to mind the furniture. Before long, most of it was lying in splinters on the floor, or crashing against the walls, or breaking over shoulders, arms, heads, and backs.

Mackinnon had dragged the towel out of his mouth and was squealing and wriggling in fear, still tied to his chair. Sackville fell over him, kicking him on the leg, and he yelled, but the breath was knocked out of him as Jim crashed down under a blow from Harris and struggled out of the way before he could follow it up.

Frederick had gone down under a blow from Sackville, come up dazed, and found the leg of a chair at hand; he'd just swung it against Sackville's head and seen the man fall when he felt a stillness in the room.

He shook his head and looked.

Jim was standing, balanced, wary, holding a hand to his cheek. Blood was trickling thickly through his fingers. Facing him was Harris—and he was holding a knife.

"Watch him, Fred," Jim said quietly.

Harris pushed aside the wreckage of the wardrobe with his foot, giving himself room, and then lunged forward, stabbing upward, aiming for the stomach. Frederick tried to leap across the gap but found his leg caught in Sackville's grip, and lashed out with his other foot, losing sight of Jim as he fell. He swung his fist at Sackville, and twisted around desperately to see

Mackinnon, of all things, free of the rope, reaching up
to grab Harris's knife hand.

Harris snarled, snatching his hand away, and Mackinnon cried out—but it gave Jim his chance. As
Harris looked back Jim swung his fist full into the
center of the other man's face. It was the hardest
punch he'd ever landed in his life. Harris went down
like a log.

"Well done, mate," Jim said to Mackinnon, and
winced as the blood fell more freely from his cheek.
Harris had slashed at his eyes and missed by half an
inch.

"Tie 'em up before they come round," said Frederick. "Mackinnon, got some money? Give your landlady a tenner for the furniture and help us downstairs
with these apes. Oh—tell the cabby he's got some
passengers coming."

While Mackinnon scuttled off to see to the terrified
landlady, Jim and Frederick removed braces, belts,
and bootlaces from the other two and secured them as
tight as parcels. It wasn't easy; though Harris and
Sackville were too far gone to struggle, Frederick was
dizzy from blows to the head, and Jim's fists were
swollen.

They finally got the pair downstairs and into the
cab, and Frederick borrowed a length of rope from the
cabbie and tied it round them as an extra precaution.
The cabbie watched with interest.

"Where to, guvnor?" he asked Frederick. "Smithfield?"

Smithfield was the main meat market for London.
Frederick laughed painfully.

"Streatham police station," he said. "Care of Inspector Conway."

He took out a card, scribbled MRS. NELLIE BUDD: ACCOUNT RENDERED on it, and pinned it to Sackville's coat before shutting the door.

Jim watched, satisfied, as the cab drove away.

"If that bastard wants to use his nose again," he said, "he'll have to dig it out of his face with a spoon."

"You paid the landlady for the frolic?" Frederick asked Mackinnon. "Get a bag packed. You're coming to stay in Burton Street for the weekend—and no arguing. Oh—and bring my watch."

19

Siege

IT WAS HALF PAST THREE WHEN THEY GOT BACK TO Burton Street. Sally called a doctor to see to Jim's cut cheek, made Frederick sit down and drink some brandy, and arranged a camp bed for Mackinnon in Jim's bedroom; then she went to the shop to tell Isabel that Mackinnon was there and watched as Isabel turned pale, nodded, and bent over her work again without a word.

The doctor's attentions didn't improve Jim's temper. As soon as the wound had been dressed, he slammed out to the new studio to exchange insults with the painters, whom he remembered from their previous visits. Mackinnon sat, pale, in the kitchen while Frederick rummaged in the biscuit barrel.

"Did they hurt you?" Frederick said.

"A few bruises, thank you. Nothing grand."

"You did well to grab his wrist like that. He'd have done for Jim otherwise. . . ."

The back door opened, and Jim came in no less disgruntled than when he'd gone out. He helped himself to a biscuit and sprawled on the sofa.

"Different lot of painters," he said. "All they want to do is get on with the job. They got no conversation at all. Remember the last lot, when we had the shop done? They sent Herbert out one day for the loan of a left-handed screwdriver. Then when he couldn't find one they said sorry, what they really wanted was a pound of small holes. They gave him tuppence to go round to Murphy's and buy 'em. Poor little bugger. What are we going to do now, then?"

"Shut the shop," said Sally, coming in. "I've told Mr. Blaine and the others to go home early. We'll lock up and have some tea—that's what we'll do now. I thought Jim would finish the biscuits, so I've bought some crumpets. I hope you like crumpets, Mr. Mackinnon. Have those painters gone yet?"

MUCH LATER that evening (Isabel having gone straight to her room without seeing Mackinnon, Jim having gone to bed sore and tired, Webster and Mackinnon having simply gone to bed) Frederick and Sally found themselves alone in the kitchen.

She was curled up in a corner of the old sofa; he was lying back in the armchair on the other side of the fire, with his feet on the coal scuttle. The oil lamp on the table shed a warm glow on the checkered tablecloth, and on the cards Mackinnon had been amusing them with, and on the golden whiskey in the decanter, and on Sally's blond hair. Frederick leaned down and put his glass on the floor beside the chair.

"You know, he actually joined in," he said. "Mackinnon, I mean. He grabbed for the knife Harris was about to stick in Jim. What are the options, Lockhart?

First of all, get this wedding business in the papers, that's what I think."

"You're right," she said. "We'll go to the *Pall Mall Gazette* in the morning. After that . . . well, I'll ask Mr. Temple's advice about the patents. I think we've almost got him, but I'm not sure he's completely hooked yet. The Russian patents being missing—that's circumstantial. Not quite incriminating, I think. We need to know—"

"We need to know how far up his influence goes. The police who raided your office—were they real police? If they were, he's got a lot of pull. Which means that we've got to go extra carefully. It's a question of timing."

"Waiting for the right moment. . . . Who were those people Lord Wytham was seeing at the Foreign Office? If we can find out the departments they're responsible for, we'll have a better idea of what to do next."

"That's easy enough. They're a gossipy lot over there. I'll go and hang about in Whitehall on Monday, see what I can pick up . . ."

"You know," she said after a few moments, "I still don't know how I'm going to get my client's money back. Unless there's a reward. Actually, now I think of it, there is. For information about the loss of the *Ingrid Linde*. The one thing we haven't explored . . ."

She leaned forward and poked the fire. Ash fell through the grate, and a little volley of sparks crackled upward.

"Fred?" she said.

"Mmm?"

"I want to say sorry. For the other night. It was hateful of me and I've felt miserable ever since. Because I love it so much when we work together. And we *are* a good team. If you still want to—"

She broke off then, finding it hard to continue. Frederick sat up, reached across, and turned her face to his.

And then the doorbell rang in the empty shop.

He swore and sat back.

"Now who the devil can that be?" he said.

They looked at each other and then at the clock. It was half past ten.

"I'll go and see," he said, standing up. "I won't be long."

"Be careful, Fred," she said.

He made his way through the darkened shop and unlocked the front door. There, blinking mildly in the drizzle, stood a slight figure in a bowler hat and topcoat.

"Mr. Garland, I believe?" he said.

It was the man from the box in the music hall— Bellmann's secretary. Taken by the man's nerve, Frederick laughed.

"Good evening," he said. "Mr. Windlesham, isn't it? You'd better come in."

Frederick stood aside and took Windlesham's coat and hat.

"Sally," he said as they entered the kitchen, "I think you know this gentleman."

She blinked with surprise and sat up.

"Forgive me for calling at this late hour," said the little man. "We met before, Miss Lockhart, under

unfortunate circumstances. I was hoping that you—
and Mr. Garland—might do me the honor of listening
to a proposition I would like to put before you."

Sally looked at Frederick and then back at Windlesham. Her eyes were wide.

"I might add that I am speaking entirely for
myself," he went on. "Mr. Bellmann doesn't know
I'm here."

The two men were still standing. In the silence that
followed the last remark, Frederick pulled out a chair
at the table and offered the place to Windlesham.
They sat down, and Sally left the sofa to join them.
She turned up the light and tidied the playing cards
out of the way.

"I fully understand your hesitation," said Windlesham. "May I explain why I've come?"

"Please do," said Frederick. "But let's be clear
about this. You're not working for Bellmann?"

"Technically, I am still in his employment. But I
think it would now be to the greatest advantage of the
greatest number if I changed my allegiance, so to
speak. I cannot approve of Mr. Bellmann's North Star
venture. Try as I will, I cannot do it, Miss Lockhart.
To my mind the Hopkinson Self-Regulator is a monstrous thing and should not be let loose upon the
world. I've come to you because I've watched your
activities with increasing admiration—yours and Mr.
Garland's—and I've come to place what I know at
your disposal." He took off his glasses, which had
steamed up in the warm room. "I am assuming you've
found out about the Hopkinson Self-Regulator? I've
no proof that you have, but I'd be surprised if . . ."

"The Steam Gun," said Frederick. "Yes, we know about that. And about Hopkinson."

"Or Nordenfels, hmmm?" Mr. Windlesham replaced his glasses, beaming gently.

"What do you want in return?" Sally said. She was still numb with surprise at his appearance—and not in the least inclined to trust him.

"Simply—how shall I put it?—protective corroboration," he replied. "When Mr. Bellmann's enterprise collapses, as it will before long, I want someone to vouch for the fact that I have been, as it were, spying on him and not working for him. I had hoped you would supply that assurance."

"Why not go to the police now?" said Frederick.

"The time's not ripe just yet. Mr. Bellmann's influence reaches high up in the police—yes, and in the judiciary—and any attempt at this stage would misfire. Believe me, I am certain of that. We would find ourselves embroiled in suits for libel and slander, and we would lose, and it would only serve to warn the wrongdoers. No, the time to go to the police is not now but when the organization is about to collapse."

"Why should it collapse?" said Frederick.

"It's overextended," said Mr. Windlesham. "I can let you have the details of loans, share issues, dividends, and so on; the gist of it is that the money is sunk in the Self-Regulator, all of it, and they're not being produced fast enough. There are unforeseen shortages of materials, difficulties with testing—it's an extraordinarily complicated machine, you know. Again, I can let you have the details. Mr. Bellmann has, I estimate, three weeks before catastrophe.

Things could occur to put it off—if he could acquire a supply of graphite, for instance, it would help him—but the end is not far off."

"Who's the customer?" said Sally. "Who's buying these Steam Guns, or Self-Regulators?"

"Russia. The czar is increasingly concerned about the growth of anarchist movements among his people. And with the Russian expansion into Siberia—you've heard of the proposed railway?—you can understand how useful the weapon would be. But North Star is actively seeking other customers. The Prussian government is interested. The Mexican ambassador has sent an observer up to the firing range. It's at a point of balance, you see, Mr. Garland, a critical time. If we can tilt it the right way . . ."

"Tell us about the *Ingrid Linde*," said Sally.

"Ah! The missing ship. That—er—belongs to a phase of Mr. Bellmann's career that took place before I joined him. But I believe that the passenger list contained the name of a man who had witnessed Mr. Bellmann's quarrel with Arne Nordenfels. The collapse of the Anglo-Baltic line, of course, meant that Mr. Bellmann's shipping activities could expand without hindrance."

"I'd like some written evidence of his involvement," said Sally.

"That would be difficult. I shall make a search—I shall have to be extremely discreet, but I shall do my best."

"You mentioned influence," said Frederick. "How far does it reach into the government? Or into the civil service?"

"Oh, quite some way. Mr. Bellmann's money has already helped in the matter of the various export licenses and regulations connected with the export of arms. Your inquiries, if I may say so, have been remarkably astute. They would soon have embarrassed some very highly placed people."

"Well, who?" said Frederick. "You've told us nothing we didn't know already. Names, Mr. Windlesham, names."

"Sir James Nash, the Inspector General of Artillery at the War Office. Sir William Halloway-Clark, undersecretary at the foreign office. The ambassador to Russia. There are several others less highly placed."

"Has this been discussed in Cabinet?" Sally asked. "Is it government policy to allow this gun to be made and sold?"

"Oh, no. Most certainly not. The officials I mention are acting quite improperly. There would be the most appalling scandal if it came out."

"Lord Wytham," said Frederick. "What's he up to?"

"Ah!" Mr. Windlesham twinkled. "The father of the bride! A romantic little episode, the Scottish adventure, don't you think? And have you had any more success than our agents in the search for that elusive young man?"

"Since you ask, yes," said Frederick. "We've got him safe. He's in London, being looked after by a good friend of mine. He won't get away—and you won't find him. What's Lord Wytham going to do?"

"Yes," said Mr. Windlesham sadly, "it's difficult for him. He was given a directorship on the strength of his many connections in government. There he might have been useful, but the—er—Scottish affair will come out soon; Mr. Bellmann is aware that it can hardly remain quiet for much longer. It's one of the embarrassments that are hanging over him. More embarrassing for Lord Wytham, of course. Perhaps fatally so."

"I wonder what you mean by that," said Frederick. "No, don't bother to explain. Were you responsible for hiring Sackville and Harris, by the way? And the man who attacked Miss Lockhart last night?"

"As to that," said Mr. Windlesham earnestly, "I must plead guilty. I did it with repugnance, believe me, with shame and regret, and ever since it happened I have been consumed with remorse and anxiety. I have never felt such relief as when this morning I heard that you were alive. And as for Mrs. Budd—I have arranged for her hospital bills to be paid in full. A private matter, with my own money—naturally it is not something I could charge to the firm's account without giving rise to suspicion."

"Why attack her, anyway?" said Frederick.

"As a warning to Miss Lockhart," said Mr. Windlesham simply. "Had we been more aware of Miss Lockhart's qualities, we would have taken a different line. I argued against it from the start; violence of any sort is anathema to me. But Mr. Bellmann overruled me."

Frederick looked at Sally. Her face was expressionless.

"Well, this has been most interesting, Mr. Windlesham," he said. "Thank you for coming. There's a cab rank at the end of the street."

"Er—my proposal? You understand, I took a risk in coming here. . . ."

"Yes," said Sally. "I suppose you did. We shall have to think about it. Where can we reach you?"

He took a card from his waistcoat pocket.

"This is an office where I can be contacted. I'm not always there, but a letter to that address will reach me in twenty-four hours. . . . Miss Lockhart, Mr. Garland, may I press you for an indication? However slight? I am beginning, you see, to be afraid."

His face was flushed, his spectacles gleaming.

Frederick said, "Quite so. Well, if it comes to action, you skip over this way and at least you won't have one of our bullets in you. In the meantime you'd better stay where you are, don't you think?"

"Oh, thank you, Mr. Garland. Thank you, Miss Lockhart. I have a positive terror of any kind of violence. Mr. Bellmann is an intemperate man—easily aroused—violent passions . . ."

"Quite. Here's your coat and hat," said Frederick, helping him through the darkened shop. "We'll write to you, I've no doubt. Good night. Good night!"

He locked the door and went back to the kitchen.

"What d'you make of that, then?" he said.

"I don't believe a word of it," she said.

"Good. Nor do I. Positive terror of violence? He's the coolest customer I ever saw. He'd arrange a murder with no more fuss than ordering a fish dinner."

"That's right, Fred! I remember now—when he called on me and Chaka growled at him, he didn't turn a hair. He's lying—he must be. What's he up to?"

"I don't know. Buying time? But it shows we're on the right track, doesn't it?"

He sat down opposite her and moved the lamp so he could see her. Her dark eyes looked at him gravely.

"Yes," she said. "Fred, when he came—"

"I was just going to tell you something. Something to the effect that whatever I said the other day about not liking you and about putting an end to what we do together—whatever I said, it was moonshine. I couldn't give you up, Sally. We belong together, and we will till we die, and I wouldn't have you any other way."

Then she smiled—such a clear, open, happy smile that he felt his heart leap.

"Sally," he began—but she stopped him.

"Don't say a *word*," she said.

And she stood up, her eyes bright. She leaned down and blew out the lamp, and they stood for a moment in the dim glow from the fire. Then she made a little involuntary movement toward him, and within a second they were clinging tightly together, pressing their faces clumsily toward each other in the darkness.

"Sally—" he said.

"Shhh!" she whispered. "I don't want you to speak. I've got a reason."

So he kissed her instead, on the eyes, the cheeks, the throat, the fierce mouth, and again he tried to speak. She clamped her hand over his lips.

"Don't speak!" she said warmly into his ear. "If you say another word I'll—I won't—oh, Fred, Fred . . ."

She pulled at his hand, commanding, nervous, urgent. She opened the staircase door, and within a minute they were in her bedroom. The fire in there had burned low, but there was a glow still in the embers, and the room was warm. He nudged the door shut and kissed her again, and they clung like children, trembling, and pressed their mouths together as if they were drinking each other.

She stood back then and lit a candle. As the soft yellow light spread into the room, she pulled the pins from her hair so that it fell loose around her shoulders, and unfastened her dress and stepped out of it. There was a moment when he said, "Sally—" but it was involuntary, like a gasp of shock at how lovely she was without clothes. And then they were both naked.

"Now," she said, "not a word, not a word . . ."

She touched him slowly all over, and they lay down.

MR. WINDLESHAM didn't go to the cab rank at the end of the street. There was a carriage waiting for him around the corner, but when he got in, it didn't move off at once; the driver waited while Mr. Windlesham lit a lamp and wrote a page or two of notes in a little book. And even then they didn't move. After another minute or so, a man in workman's clothes came out of the alley behind Burton Street and tapped at the window. The horse, catching some odd scent from the man's clothes—paint? turpentine?—tossed its head in the shafts.

Mr. Windlesham lowered the window and looked out.

"All clear, guvnor," said the man quietly.

Mr. Windlesham fished in his pocket and handed him a sovereign.

"Good," he said. "Thank you very much. Good night to you."

The man touched his cap and made off. The driver released the brake and flicked his whip, and the carriage moved away toward the west.

A LITTLE LATER Frederick looked down at Sally. Her eyes were sleepy now, but very bright, and her mouth was soft.

"Sally," he said. "Will you marry me?"

"Of course," she said.

"Why wouldn't you let me speak?"

"In case you said that before we . . . before we did this, and you wouldn't have seen that I brought you up here because I wanted to, and not because we were going to get married. D'you see? I wanted to do it. I wanted us to be like this. Naked, together, like this. Oh, Fred, I do love you. It's taken so long. I'm so sorry about it. . . . I thought I wouldn't be able to do my work if I was married. Or if I admitted I loved you. I know it's silly, now. But since last night, since Chaka was killed, I've seen that my work's part of me, I'm not part of it. And I've seen how much I need you. D'you know where I realized that? It was in the patent library . . ."

He laughed. She bit his nose.

"Don't laugh," she said. "It's true. There's no one like you, no one in the world. . . . Oh, I'm different now, Fred. I'm not good at thinking about things like this and getting them right, not yet. But I'll try. And I will be good at it, I promise."

The embers settled in the grate with an ashy whisper.

"Did I mention that I loved you?" he said. "I've

loved you ever since you came along that horrible road on the Kent coast, with Mrs. Holland after you. Sally, my sweet . . . Did it hurt?"

"Only a bit. It's so *strange*, isn't it? But I wanted to so much. . . . Oh, Fred, it's been so long."

He kissed her again, gently this time, and pinched the candle out.

"We're lucky," he said.

"We deserve it," she whispered, and lay close in his arms.

MR. WINDLESHAM'S carriage drew up at 47, Hyde Park Gate, let him out, then trundled around into the stable behind.

He gave his coat and hat to the footman, and a minute later he was shown into a large study.

"Well?" said Axel Bellmann from behind the desk.

"He's there. There were some playing cards on the kitchen table. They might have been playing a game, of course, but they were laid out as if someone had been doing tricks with them. As soon as I came in she tidied them away. And when I brought up the subject of Scotland, the young man glanced involuntarily toward the stairs."

"And everything else is ready?"

"Everything is prepared, Mr. Bellmann."

The financier's heavy face moved slightly, and the likeness of a smile appeared.

"Very good, Windlesham. Will you have a glass of brandy with me?"

"That is very kind of you, Mr. Bellmann."

It was poured and handed, and Mr. Windlesham sat down, arranging his coattails carefully.

"Were they taken in by your proposition?" said Bellmann.

"Oh, no. Not for a moment. But it held their attention for the necessary time." He sipped his brandy. "You know, Mr. Bellmann," he went on, "I am really quite favorably impressed by those two. It's a great pity there's no prospect of making terms with them."

"Oh, it's too late for that, Windlesham," said Axel Bellmann, sitting again and smiling. "Far too late for that."

20

Sleeplessness

JIM COULDN'T SLEEP.

Mackinnon, in the camp bed by the door, snored gently—an infuriating noise; Jim felt like throwing a boot at him. The complacency of the man! All right, he'd done his bit in the fight—but there was no need to snore about it. Jim lay awake and cursed.

It was partly, of course, Lady Mary. That kiss . . . And to know that a moment like that, so strange and out of time, would never come his way again. He was tormented with love for her. How could she have married . . . Oh, don't think of that; it was hopeless.

And it was partly the pain of the cut on his cheek. What the doctor had done to it he couldn't imagine, but it blazed and throbbed and ached till he felt like crying out. The only thing that relieved *that* was the thought of the blow that had felled Harris.

And it was partly something else. Something was wrong. After fretting about it all evening, he'd finally worked out where this uneasiness came from. It was the painters. It wasn't just that he didn't know them— it was that they didn't seem like painters somehow.

They had the right gear and the right clothes, but all they seemed to be doing was shifting things about and waiting for him to leave.

Things weren't right.

Damn silly case this had been all around. Who was going to pay them? Who was going to thank them for clearing it all up? Was a grateful government going to come forward and press expenses on them? Rot and blast and shrivel Bellmann, Wytham, Mackinnon, the whole bloody lot of them.

He was wider awake than ever—and on edge with nerves, as if he'd learned that there was a bomb in the room with a fuse burning low, and he couldn't find it. All his senses were preternaturally sharp: Mackinnon's breathing rasped at his nerves, the bedclothes were too hot, the pillow too hard for his cheek. . . . It was no good. He'd never sleep now.

He swung his legs over the side of the bed and felt for his slippers. He'd go downstairs, sit in the kitchen, do a bit of writing, have a cup of tea. Mackinnon stirred on his camp bed as Jim stepped over him, so Jim told him *sotto voce* what he thought of him, and magicians, and Scotchmen in general. He unhooked his dressing gown from the door and went out onto the landing.

He closed the door quietly behind him—and sniffed.

There *was* something wrong. He ran to the landing window overlooking the yard and pulled back the curtain.

The yard was ablaze.

Unbelieving, he stood still and rubbed his eyes.

The new studio wasn't there anymore; instead a wall of flame billowed upward, roaring softly. And the lumber in the yard—the planks, the barrows, the ladders—they were on fire too. As he peered down, horrified, he saw the back door fall open, and flames gush out from inside the building. . . .

Three steps took him to Frederick's door. He flung it open, yelling, "Fire! Fire!"

The room was empty. He called up the narrow stairs to the top floor: "Fire! Wake up! Fire!"

Then he ran down to Webster and Sally on the first floor.

FREDERICK HEARD his first shout and sat up at once. Sally, beside him in the narrow bed, woke with a start.

"What is it?" she said.

"Jim—" he said, and pulled on his shirt and trousers. "Sounds like a fire. Get up, love—quick."

He opened the door as Jim came hurtling down the stairs. Jim blinked with surprise to see him coming out of Sally's room, but didn't pause.

"It's bad," he said, hammering on Webster's door. "Fire, Mr. Webster! Get up—now!" he shouted into the room. "The new building's ablaze, and I think the kitchen is too!"

"Right," said Frederick. "Run up to the top and make sure Ellie and the cook get down as quick as they can—oh, and Miss Meredith, too. Is Mackinnon awake? Bring 'em down here to the landing."

There was only the one staircase, which led through a door at the bottom into the kitchen. Frederick looked down and then turned back to Sally. She was at her door now, tousled, sleepy, beautiful. . . . He seized her in the doorway and crushed her to him, and she came without hesitation, and they kissed more passionately now than they'd done earlier; but it could only last a second or two.

"Bring your sheets into the other room," he said. "I'll run down and see if we can get out through the shop."

But as he reached the bottom of the stairs and felt in the darkness for the door, he knew it would be impossible. There was a fierce roaring from the kitchen, and the heat, even through the door, was appalling. He opened it, just to be sure—and knew at once that he shouldn't have done so, for the flames leaped at him like a tiger, knocking him backward and seizing his whole body. He slipped and fell, rolling blindly through the open door, and felt as he crashed to the floor something fall heavily across his neck and shatter. He groped for the door, pulled himself up, and stumbled back through before slamming it shut. He was ablaze. He beat at himself—his shirt was gone, his hair was crackling—he tore off the burning sleeves and hit at his head to extinguish the flaring hair before stumbling back to the landing.

"Fred! You all right?"

It was Jim, with Ellie the maid and Mrs. Griffiths the old cook, both of them wide-eyed and trembling. Frederick didn't know if he was all right. He tried to speak, but there was something wrong, as if he'd swallowed some smoke. Sally came out of Webster's room and ran to him with a cry of fear. He held her gently away and mimed the tying of sheets together.

"Yes—we've done that," she said, and he thrust Ellie at her, and then the cook, and she understood at once, bless her, and took charge.

Webster's room was over the old studio, overlooking the street. Frederick didn't know whether the fire had reached there yet, but Sally's room was over the kitchen and didn't seem as safe. As Mackinnon came down, shaking, Frederick shoved him after the others and fought for breath.

"Help the women out—climb through window—stairs no good—"

"I'm no' climbing! I cannae stand heights—"

"Burn, then," said Jim, and turned to Webster. "Chuck your mattress out," he told him, "and sling him out after it. Here, Fred—" he pulled Frederick aside. "Trouble up there," he said quietly. "Miss Wotsit. She's locked herself in. Says she wants to stay, if you please. Here—you all right?"

Frederick nodded. "I was a bit dizzy," he said hoarsely.

"Where you been?"

"Down the bottom. Smoke. Can't get through. Come on, then. I suppose Bellmann's responsible for this."

"Them painters," Jim said as they hurried up the first flight of stairs. "I thought they were wrong from the start. I should've got up earlier—I knew there was something wrong. Here—you've got a hell of a cut on your neck, mate, d'you know that?"

"Something fell on me," Frederick mumbled. And then came a cry from below, and a rending crash, as the floor of Sally's room collapsed into the kitchen.

"Wait there," said Jim, and darted down.

Mackinnon had gotten out, and Mrs. Griffiths had clambered bravely down the flimsy sheets, but they were having trouble with Ellie. She'd gotten halfway out and couldn't go any farther.

"Go on, you silly great girl!" Sally was urging her, but she just gasped and blinked and clung in terror to the knotted sheets.

"You'll have to go down with her, Jim," Sally said.

"All right. But you go first—show her how it's done."

He hauled Ellie in again and let her fall to the floor, sobbing, and then helped Sally out.

"Give Fred a yell. Tell him to carry on," he said to Webster.

Webster called up and heard an answer. "I hope he can manage," he said. "The building won't last long. I'll go and give him a hand."

"You stay here," Jim said. "I'll take Ellie down, then come back up meself. You make sure the knots don't slip."

Webster nodded, and Jim sprang to the window sill, as agile as a monkey.

"All right, Sal?" he called down.

The houses opposite were lit like a stage set, and a crowd was already beginning to gather. Sally reached the bottom and called out that she was safe, and Jim turned back.

"Come on, Ellie," he said. "Let's get you down."

She clambered up hastily beside him.

"Now, then—get hold of the rope like this—that's it. I'll go down a bit, see, and give you room. Good linen, this is, it won't break—I nicked it from a good hotel. That's it—good gal—"

His voice receded. Webster waited at the top.

AT THE FOOT of the top flight of stairs Frederick had to stop, because the floor was sloping. Or at least it seemed to be sloping. The building sounded like a ship at sea, it was creaking so much. A muffled explosion came from the direction of the studio, and Frederick thought, Chemicals—hope Sally's out—

But he pushed himself up the narrow stairs, dark and hot and swaying. Or was it him? This was a dream. When he reached the top, it was a lot quieter, as if the fire were a hundred miles away.

It was hard to breathe. His strength was draining away by the minute; he could feel it leaking, like blood. Perhaps it *was* the blood. He raised his hand and banged at Isabel's door.

"No!" came the muffled response. "Please leave me."

"Open the door at least," he said. "I'm hurt. I can't struggle with you."

He heard a key turn in the lock and a chair being pulled aside. The gentle glow of a candle as she opened the door, and her loose hair and nightgown, made it seem like another sort of scene altogether, and only made him feel further lost, deeper in a dream.

"Oh! You're—what have you done?" she cried, standing aside to let him in.

"Isabel, you must come—there isn't much time," he said.

"I know," she said. "It won't be long now. I won't

come, you know. You've been so kind to me here. What have I got to escape for?"

She sat down on the bed. Spread out all around her were a score or more sheets of paper—letters, from the look of them, covered in dark bold writing. She saw him looking.

"Yes," she said, "his letters. Reading them . . . it's always made me happier than anything else in my whole life. I'll never have anything better if I live to be a hundred. And if I *do* live—what have I got to look forward to? Loneliness and bitterness and regret. . . . No, no, go, please, you must. Leave me. *Please.* You must go . . . for Sally. . . ."

Her eyes were bright, her whole expression sparkled. His head was swimming; he had to cling to the chest of drawers in order to remain upright, and he heard her words distantly but very clearly, like a daguerreotype in sound.

"Isabel, you silly bitch, come downstairs and help me out, if you won't come yourself," he made himself say. "Everyone else has left, and the building's going to collapse any minute. You know I won't go till you—"

"Oh, you're so stubborn—it's mad. Has *he* gone?"

"Yes. I told you, everyone. Come on, for God's sake."

She looked so excited, though, like a girl going to her first ball, flushed and pretty and young; or like a bride. . . . He was almost afraid he'd died already, and this was some dream state of the soul. She said something else, but he couldn't hear it. There was a roaring in his ears, like the fire—well, it might have *been* the fire—and this floor was creaking now too.

He tore the curtain aside and pushed open the window. This room faced the street, like the landing window below; if they jumped, maybe—

He turned to the bed. She was lying on it, face down, her arms spread wide. She was facing him, and her hair had fallen softly over her cheek and jaw so that only her eyes and her clear forehead were visible; but he could see that she was smiling. She looked transcendently happy.

Suddenly he felt angry at the stupid waste of it and stumbled across the floor, meaning to drag her to the window. But she clung to the bed, and he found himself dragging that, too, until, sick with pain and exhaustion, he fell across her. It would be so easy to give up.

Oh, God, what a waste.

The heat was intense now. The door was outlined in flames, and the floor was sagging and creaking like a ship in a gale. The air was full of sound—roaring, flailing sheets of sound, like audible flames. All kinds of sounds were mixed up in it. Music, even . . . bells . . .

She moved. Her hand found his and clung.

"Sally?" he said.

It might have been Sally. She'd lain beside him like this, but they'd been naked then. Sally was strong and fearless, and lovely, incomparable. . . . Lady Mary was beautiful, but Sally . . . Where was she?

Oddly enough it felt like drowning. There was an area of terrible pain around him—he could feel it there—but it didn't quite touch him. Instead he lay inside it, trying to breathe, and the air came into his wounded lungs like water.

He was going to die, then.

He turned his head to Sally to kiss her for one last time, but she whimpered. No, that was wrong. Sally wouldn't do that. Sally was somewhere else. This girl couldn't help it. Get her out, and—

He reached for the window, and the floor collapsed.

21

Into the Shadow

IT WAS STILL DARK WHEN THEY BROUGHT HIS BODY OUT. Sally had waited with the others in the shop across the road while the firemen fought the blaze, and wrapped herself in a borrowed cloak and held Webster's hand and said not a word.

They'd watched every movement the firemen made. Sometime in the early morning it had begun to rain, which helped the pumps; the fire had blazed so swiftly and completely that it hadn't been able to sustain itself for long, and the firemen were able to move into the smoldering, sodden ruins and look for Frederick and Isabel.

Then there was a shout. One man looked up and back at the shop across the road for a moment, and others clambered up to help him.

Sally stood up and smoothed down her cloak.

"Sure you want to?" said Webster.

"Yes," she said.

She gently unclasped his hand and gathered the cloak around her and went into the road, into the drizzle, the cold, the smell of ashes.

They were bringing him down so carefully that at first she thought he was still alive, except that there was no urgency in their movements. They laid him on a stretcher in the light of a flickering lantern and, seeing her, stood aside. One man took off his helmet.

She knelt down beside him. He looked asleep. She laid her cheek beside his and thought how warm he felt. She put her hand on his bare chest, where only a few hours before she had felt his heart beating, and thought how still it was now. Where had he gone? He was so warm. . . . It was a mystery. She felt like stone; she felt dead, and he felt alive.

She kissed his lips and stood up. The fireman who'd removed his helmet bent over and covered Frederick with a blanket.

"Thank you," she said to him, and turned to go.

She felt a hand on her arm and looked around to see Webster.

"I've got to go," she said.

He was looking older than he'd ever seemed before. She would have embraced him, but she couldn't stay, or everything would collapse. There was something she had to do. She gently disengaged his hand, shaking her head, and left.

FOR THE NEXT forty-eight hours or so Sally moved about in a trance. One idea possessed her, and she was numb to all else—except for one or two moments when feeling broke through and nearly swamped her. But there was something she had to do, and she had to do it for Fred. And that was reason not to feel for the moment.

She remembered nothing of the journey north, though she must have gone to her lodgings, for she had a bag with her and she had changed her clothes. She arrived in Barrow late on Sunday night and became sufficiently aware of things to notice the hotel keeper's raised eyebrows at a young lady traveling alone—but not sufficiently aware to mind it.

She went to bed at once. She slept badly, waking often to find the pillow wet and herself bewildered, as if she could feel things in her sleep but not know what they were. She breakfasted early, paid her bill, and as the sun broke uneasily through watery clouds and gilded the dingy streets she set out toward her destination. Not knowing the way, she had to stop and ask, and she found that she couldn't keep directions in her head for long, so she had to ask again; but little by little she made her way to the edge of the town, and then she turned a corner and found herself looking down at the birthplace of the Steam Gun, the empire of Axel Bellmann, the North Star works.

It was a narrow valley filled with fire and steel, with the glint of railway lines in the strengthening sun, with the drift of steam and the clang of mighty hammers. A rail line led into it from the south and out of it to the north, and a dozen sidings were laid out between the buildings, with shunting engines moving lines of trucks to unload coal or iron or to shift items of machinery. The buildings themselves were light, glassy structures for the most part, iron-framed and delicate to look at, and despite the presence of the chimneys and locomotives, everything in sight was clean and glittering and new.

It looked like a mighty machine itself—a knowing one, with a mind and a will. And all the men she saw, and the hundred or more she couldn't, seemed not like individuals but like cogs or wheels or connecting rods, and the mind that moved them all was housed, she could tell, in the three-story brick building in the very center of the valley.

The building was like a cross between a comfortable modern villa and a private railway station. The front door, complete with Gothic porch, opened directly onto a platform by a siding and looked out over the heart of the valley. There were flower beds along the platform, bare now but neatly weeded and raked. On the other side of the house a carriage drive curved up to a similar though smaller door and around the corner to a stable, where a boy was raking gravel. On top of the building stood a bare flagpole.

As Sally stood looking down at this busy, prosperous, flourishing scene she felt a strange sensation: as if waves of pure evil were coming from it, shimmering like a heat haze. Somewhere down there they made a weapon more horrible than anything the world had seen, and the power that made the weapon had reached into her life, wrenched out the dearest part of it, and dropped it dead at her feet, all because she had dared to question what was going on. Whatever could do that must be evil, and the intensity of it was almost visible in the shimmer and glint of the sunlight on the glass, the steel rails, the quivering air above the chimneys.

It was so intense that for a moment she quailed. She was very frightened, in a way she'd never been frightened before—more than a physical way, in the way that evil was more than physical. But she'd come here to face that. She closed her eyes and breathed deeply, and the moment passed.

She was standing beside a grassy bank overlooking the valley. She found herself scrambling down a little way to the cover of a group of trees, where she sat on a fallen trunk and looked over the valley more carefully.

As the morning went by she noticed more and more details, and began to see a pattern in the work. None of the shunting enginers, or the chimneys on the buildings, produced any smoke; they were probably burning coke, which accounted for the cleanliness of the valley. The three cranes she saw lifting lengths of steel pipe or sheet iron off the railway trucks seemed to have a different sort of engine, however: it might have been hydraulic or even electrical. Electricity certainly powered whatever went on in the most isolated of the buildings. Wires led to it from a little brick structure nearby, and whenever a shunting engine took a line of trucks to it, it didn't go up close, as it did elsewhere, but stopped in a siding a little way off, where the trucks were collected by a different kind of engine altogether—one that looked as if it drew its power from an overhead wire in some way. At one point this engine broke down, and instead of allowing the steam engine to bring the trucks in, they harnessed a team of horses to them.

So that building, which was set off from the rest, and where they didn't want to bring live fire, must have been where they kept explosives.

She watched it all, immobile, free of feeling, as if she were just an eye.

Toward late afternoon she saw signs of new activity in the building with the flagpole. Upstairs windows opened, flashing in the sunlight, and a housemaid appeared at one of them, apparently dusting or cleaning. A tradesman's cart drove up, and something was unloaded; smoke appeared at two of the chimneys; another housemaid, or perhaps the same one, came out to polish the brass on the door at the platform side. And finally, toward sunset, Sally saw what she'd been waiting for: a signal changed beside the main rail line from the south, a locomotive whistle echoed through the valley, and an engine pulling a single carriage rolled in and through the maze of sidings toward the building.

The locomotive was one of the Great Northern Company's, but the carriage was a private one, painted a handsome dark blue with a silver emblem on the doors. As it came to a halt beside the platform a servant—a butler or a steward of some kind—came out of the house to open the carriage door. A moment later Axel Bellmann got out. His heavy build, the metallic sheen of his blond hair under the silk hat, were unmistakable even at a distance. He went into the house, and behind him a valet and another servant from the house unloaded luggage.

Meanwhile the locomotive, uncoupled from the car, steamed off and out of the valley. A minute or two later a maid with cleaning equipment—broom, dustpan, duster—came out of the house by a side door and went into the carriage; and shortly afterward, a flag fluttered up the flagpole, with the same emblem that was painted on the carriage door. She could see it clearly now in the rays of the setting sun: it was a single silver star.

Luggage, servants, a house . . . He'd come to stay, then. Sally hadn't expected it to be as simple as that.

She was feeling stiff. She was hungry, too, and thirsty, but that wouldn't matter for long. Being stiff would matter. She got up and walked about under the trees, watching as the shadows lengthened, as the glow in the windows below seemed to get brighter, as the working pattern changed. When the valley was full of shadow, a whistle sounded, and a few minutes later she saw the first of a stream of men making their way out of the gates and homeward. Those parts of the works where a continuous process of manufacture was going on were still busy, staffed by a new shift, but the rest were closed down with a night watchman outside each building. The area around the explosives building was lit as brightly as a stage, perhaps by electricity; the lights glared on the white gravel, and the place had an unreal air, like something on a magic-lantern slide.

It was getting damp. The grass Sally was walking on was already wet with dew. She picked up her bag and without thinking found herself clutching it to her breast like a child, and sobbing.

His quiet face in the rain, among the ashes . . .

She nearly broke down altogether as a wave of pity and sorrow and love and longing crashed through the barrier around her, and she cried his name aloud in the surging grief that nearly drowned her; but she clung in her extremity to the idea that had brought her here, like a drowning sailor to a spar, and the wave washed over her and receded again.

She had to move. She picked her way through the trees, concentrating on her movements—left foot around those roots, lift your skirt to avoid those brambles . . . Then she was on the road again, with a measure of control.

She brushed her skirt down, adjusted her cape, and set off down toward the valley, into the darkness.

As she'd expected, there was a man on guard. What she hadn't expected was the sheer size of the place, which was apparent now that she was close to it. And the massiveness of the iron gates, and the solidity of the spiked fencing, and the brightness of the lights that illuminated the gravel inside the gate. And the guard's uniform, with the North Star emblem on his breast and cap. And his arrogant manner, strolling slowly to the gate, swinging a short stick, eyeing her narrowly from under the peak of his cap. It all struck a chill, even in her remote heart.

"I want to see Mr. Bellmann," she said through the bars.

"You'll have to wait till I have instructions to let you in," he replied.

"Will you please let Mr. Bellmann know that Miss Lockhart has arrived to see him?"

"I'm not allowed to leave this gate. I've had no instructions to admit anyone."

"Send a message, then."

"Don't tell me my business—"

"It's about time someone did. Send a message to Mr. Bellmann at once, or he'll make sure you're sorry for it."

"Suppose he ain't here?"

"I saw him arrive. Miss Lockhart is here to see him. Let him know at once."

She stared him down. After a few seconds he turned and went into his hut, and she heard a bell ring in the distance. He waited inside. Soon she saw a light approaching from the house, which became a servant carrying a lantern. When he got to the gate, he looked curiously at Sally before going to confer with the guard.

After a minute they came out. The guard unlocked the gate and Sally went inside.

"I have come to see Mr. Bellmann," she said to the servant. "Could you take me to him, please?"

"If you'll follow me, miss, I'll see whether Mr. Bellmann can see you," he said.

The guard locked the door behind them as Sally followed the servant along the path between the engine sheds and the main sidings toward the house. As they went along, feet crunching on the gravel, Sally heard a noise from the sheds on her left as of gigantic metal drums being rolled along, and somewhere farther off there was a continual throbbing, like a giant's pulse, with occasional flurries of hammering or the grinding whine of metal on stone; and from one building set back from the path, where the doors—great metal sheets hung on rollers—were open, came a hellish glare and showers of flying sparks as white-hot steel was poured.

Each of the sounds hurt her and frightened her. She couldn't help but feel them as inhuman and monstrous, the noises made by instruments of hideous torture. The deeper they moved into this world of metal and fire and death, the smaller and frailer she felt; and she grew more and more conscious of how hungry she was, and how thirsty, and how tired, and how her head ached and her feet were drenched, and of how untidy she must look, how weak, how inconsequential.

She'd stood once at the foot of the Schaffhausen Falls in Switzerland and felt overwhelmed by their sheer power. If she fell in, she'd be swept away in a moment as if she didn't exist. She felt the same way now. This enormous enterprise—millions of pounds, vast intricacies of organization and supply and economy, the secret connivance of great governments, with hundreds, if not thousands, of lives directly involved in it—and all of it moving with a momentum infinitely greater than anything she could bring against it—

That didn't matter.

For the first time she allowed herself to think of Fred directly. What would he do, faced with something so much stronger than himself? She knew at once; he'd measure himself coolly against it, and if it was stronger, well, he'd know, that was all. He wouldn't hesitate—he'd laugh happily and attack it all the same. Oh, how she loved that bright-eyed courage! Never foolhardiness: he was always *aware*—as if he were more conscious than anyone else in the world. He always knew. So to do what he did in the burning house needed, oh, so much courage—

She stumbled and found herself helplessly sobbing on the dark path, clutching her bag, weeping with racking, choking spasms while the servant stood a little way off, holding the lantern. After a minute—two minutes? three?—she brought herself under control, mopped her eyes with her shredded handkerchief, and nodded to the servant to move on.

Yes, she thought, that was what he'd do: measure the odds and attack all the same, and do so joyfully. So she would do that, too, because she loved him, dear Fred; she'd do it to be worthy of him, she'd face up to Bellmann though she was horribly afraid. She'd be like Fred and show no fear, though now that she was closer the fear of Bellmann gnawed at her entrails like a fox. She could hardly put one foot in front of the other.

But she managed. And, head high, tears still glistening on her cheeks, she climbed the steps behind the servant and entered the house of Axel Bellmann.

LATE ON Sunday morning, Jim Taylor had awakened to find himself with a sick headache and a crippling pain in his leg—which, he saw when he dragged himself to a sitting position, was in plaster to the knee.

He didn't recognize where he was. For a minute, in fact, he had trouble remembering anything. Then it came back—or some of it did—and he sank back into the comfortable pillows and closed his eyes, but only for a moment. He remembered Frederick going back up to that crazy bitch Isabel Meredith, and he remembered pulling himself free of Webster or Mackinnon or someone and trying to climb back up after him. But that was all.

He pulled himself upright again. He was in a

comfortable, even luxurious, room he'd never seen before, and he could hear traffic outside the window, and there was a tree—where the bloody hell was he?

"Hey!" he yelled.

He found a bellpull beside the bed and yanked it hard. Then he tried to swing his legs over the side, but the pain defeated him, and he yelled again.

"Hey! Fred! Mr. Webster!"

The door opened, and a stately figure in black came in. Jim recognized him: it was Lucas, Charles Bertram's manservant.

"Good morning, Mr. Taylor," he said.

"Lucas!" said Jim. "Is this Mr. Bertram's place, then?"

"It is, sir."

"What's the time? How long have I been here?"

"It is nearly eleven o'clock, Mr. Taylor. They brought you here toward five in the morning. You were unconscious, I understand. You'll notice the doctor has seen to your leg."

"Is Mr. Bertram here? Or Mr. Garland? And Mr. Mackinnon—where's he?"

"Mr. Bertram is helping at Burton Street, sir. I could not say were Mr. Mackinnon is."

"What about Miss Lockhart? And Frederick? Young Mr. Garland, that is? Is he all right?"

A flicker of compassion crossed the man's calm features, and Jim felt something like a cold iron hand clutch at his heart.

"I'm very sorry, Mr. Taylor. Mr. Frederick Garland died in the attempt to bring a young lady out of the building. . . ."

Suddenly the room dissolved into a watery blur. Jim sank back and heard the door close quietly as Lucas left, and then found himself crying as he hadn't done since he was a kid—great shaking sobs of overwhelming grief and, mixed in with them, cries of anger and denial; denial that he, Jim, was crying, denial that Frederick was dead, denial that Bellmann should be allowed to get away with this—for he knew how it had happened. Bellmann had killed Frederick as surely as if he'd thrust a knife into his heart. And he'd pay, by God. How could that happen to Fred—the fights they'd survived together, the way they'd ragged each other and teased and laughed?

Another storm of weeping. Men didn't cry in the fiction Jim read and wrote, but they did in real life, all right. Jim's father had cried when consumption had carried off his wife, Jim's mother, when Jim was ten; and the neighbor, Mr. Solomons, he'd cried when the landlord had evicted his family and left them in the street—cried with storms of curses; and Dick Mayhew, the lightweight champion, had wept when he lost his title to Battling Bob Gorman. There was no shame in it. There was honesty.

He let it wash over him and subside a little, and then pulled himself upright again and tugged on the bellpull. Ignoring the pain in his leg, he swung himself sideways and put his feet on the floor. A moment later Lucas came in with a tray.

"Miss Lockhart," Jim said. "Where's she, d'you know?"

Lucas put the tray on the bedside table and pulled it around in front of Jim, who noticed for the first time

that he was wearing a nightshirt of Charles's. There
was tea on the tray, and toast, and a boiled egg.

"I understood Mr. Bertram to say that she left
Burton Street not long after the firemen brought Mr.
Garland's body out of the building, sir. I couldn't say
where she might have gone."

"And Mackinnon? Sorry if I've asked you before,
Lucas. I'm more than a bit dazed. What d'you know
about what happened?"

Lucas stood by while Jim drank the tea and buttered
some toast, and retailed what he had heard. At five
that morning, Webster had sent a message asking for
Charles's help. Charles had gone at once to Burton
Street, to find Jim in need of medical attention after
falling from the knotted sheets while trying to climb
up after Frederick. Charles had sent Jim back to Lucas
at once and had arranged for a doctor to set Jim's leg.
Charles was still in Burton Street with Webster, where
he was likely to remain for some time. Sally had
vanished, and so had Mackinnon. Jim closed his eyes.

"I'll have to find him," he said. "Has Mr. Bertram
told you anything about this business, Lucas?"

"No, sir. Though of course I was aware, in a general
way, of something unusual. I must advise you, Mr.
Taylor, that the doctor who set your leg was particularly
insistent that you should not move. Mr. Bertram told
me to prepare the room for you and make you comfortable for a long stay, sir. I really would advise—"

"That's good of him, and I'll tell him so when I see
him. But I can't sit around—this is urgent. Would you
call a cab for me? And clothes—I suppose mine are
burned, or something. Damn it, I was in me nightshirt,

I remember now. Can you find me something to wear?"

FIFTEEN MINUTES later, wearing an ill-fitting tweed suit of Charles's, Jim was in a cab bound for Islington. When the cab stopped outside Sally's door, Jim called up to the driver to wait, and hauled himself (with the aid of a stick he'd borrowed from Lucas) up the steps and rang the bell.

Only a moment later Sally's landlord opened the door. He was an old friend; he'd worked for Frederick in the old days, before Sally had arrived, and he knew them all well. He was looking worried.

"Is Sally here?" said Jim.

"No, she left earlier on," said Mr. Molloy. "She come in, I dunno, about five in the morning, I suppose, changed her clothes and left. She was looking terrible. What's going on, Jim? What's happened to your leg?"

"Listen, old boy: there's been a fire at Burton Street. Fred's been killed. Sorry to spring it on you like this. But I've got to find Sally, 'cause she's going to put herself in trouble. She didn't say anything about where she was going?"

The little man had gone pale. He shook his head helplessly. "Mr. Fred—" he said. "I don't believe it."

"I'm sorry, mate. It's true. Is your missis here?"

"Yes. But—"

"Tell her to wait here for Sally, in case she comes back. And if you want to help, you couldn't do better than cut along to Burton Street. I reckon they could do with a few spare hands right now. Oh—" A thought had struck him, and he looked around the neat hall. "Got anything of Sally's? Here, this'll do."

Mr. Molloy looked up, blinking, as Jim reached up and took a bonnet that Sally often wore off a hook near the door.

"But where are you going?" said the little man. "What's going on, Jim?"

"I've got to find her," Jim said, hobbling down the steps as best he could. "Go and help Mr. Webster; that's the best thing to do."

He swung himself into the cab, gritting his teeth against the pain, and called up, "Hampstead, mate. Kenton Gardens—number fifteen."

MACKINNON'S LANDLADY shrank back when she opened the door, recognizing Jim from the day before.

"It's all right, missis," he said. "No trouble today. Is Mr. Mackinnon in?"

She nodded. "But—"

"All right, then. I'll come in, if I may. Stay there!" he called to the cabby, and limped inside, sweating now as the pain took hold, and sat down on the stairs to pull himself up backward. The landlady watched, open-mouthed.

At the door of Mackinnon's room he pulled himself upright again and banged hard with the stick.

"Mackinnon!" he called. "Let me in, will you?"

Silence from inside. Jim banged again.

"Come on, open up! For God's sake, Mackinnon, this is Jim Taylor. I'm not going to hurt you—I need your help."

There was a shuffling, and a key turned in the lock.

Mackinnon looked out, pale and suspicious and sleepy, and all Jim's anger nearly boiled over. So much to do, and this miserable worm had crawled back here to go to sleep! With an effort he controlled himself.

"Let me through, will you?" he said. "I've got to sit down. . . ."

He hobbled to a chair. The landlady had wasted no time getting fresh furniture in; the room still bore the scars of yesterday's fight, but the bed and the wardrobe at least were brand-new.

"Sally," Jim said. "Where'd she go? Any idea?"

"No," said Mackinnon.

"Well, we've got to find her. Now there's a trick you do, I don't know what it's called—not a trick, I mean, some kind of psychic thing—I've read about it. I think you're a genuine psychic, aren't you, at least part of the time? Take this."

He handed Sally's bonnet to Mackinnon, who took it and sat limply on the bed.

"I've read that what they do is they take something that belonged to the person and concentrate on it, and they get an impression of where that person is. Is that right? Can you do that?"

Mackinnon nodded. "Aye," he said, licking dry lips. "Sometimes. But—"

"Go on, then. That's hers. She used to wear it a lot. You've got to find out where she is, and you've got to do it now. Go on—I won't interrupt. Tell you what, though—if you've got a drop of brandy in here, I wouldn't say no. . . ."

Mackinnon glanced at Jim's leg and produced a silver flask from the bedside table. Jim took a deep swig and caught his breath as the fiery liquid ran down his throat. Mackinnon picked up the bonnet.

"Very well," he said. "But I guarantee nothing. If I see nothing. I can tell nothing. And this is hardly the time to . . . I know, I know. Let me concentrate."

He sat down on the bed, holding the bonnet in both hands, and closed his eyes.

Jim's leg was throbbing vilely. His head was aching too. He took another mouthful of the spirit from the flask and let it trickle down slowly this time and closed his eyes like Mackinnon. One more mouthful, and then he screwed the top back on the flask and put it in his pocket.

"North," said Mackinnon after a minute. "She's going to the north. I think she's in a train. I have the impression of a silver emblem. A star, maybe? Aye, that's what it is. It could be her destination, I suppose."

"North Star," said Jim. "That makes sense. She's going north, you reckon?"

"No doubt about it."

"Where?"

"Well, she's still traveling. This is not an exact science, you know."

"I'm aware of that. But can you tell, northeast or northwest? Or how far north she is now?"

"It's fading. You mustn't question so much," Mackinnon said severely. "Now it's gone altogether."

He dropped the bonnet on the bed and stood up. Jim pushed himself up on the stick.

"All right," he said. "Get dressed, then. I don't know when you left Burton Street. Perhaps you don't

know that Fred's dead. He was the best pal I ever had,
and I'm never likely to find a better. And now Sally's
gone and put herself in danger, and we're going to find
her, you and me. I don't know what I'd do if she went
as well, 'cause I love her, you know that, Mackinnon?
You know what that means, love? I love her like I
loved Fred, like a pal. Wherever she goes, I go, and
you got to come with me, 'cause it's on account of you
that they got into this mess in the first place. So get
dressed, and hand me that Bradshaw."

Speechless, Mackinnon passed over the railway
guide and began to put on his clothes as Jim turned
the pages with a trembling hand and looked for the
Sunday connections to the north.

22

Power and Service

BELLMANN'S HOUSE WAS OPPRESSIVELY WARM AND RICHLY, almost densely, furnished. The servant asked Sally to wait in the hall and offered a chair, but it was too close to a radiator, and she preferred to stand next to the window. There was a coldness inside her that she didn't want to dissipate.

After a minute or two the man came back and said, "Mr. Bellmann will see you now, Miss Lockhart. Follow me, please."

As they left the hall a clock struck nine, and she was surprised at how much time had passed. Was she losing her memory? She felt more and more remote from the world. Her hands were shaking badly, and her head was throbbing.

She walked after the servant down a carpeted corridor and stopped while he knocked at a door.

"Miss Lockhart, sir," he said, and moved aside to let her in.

Axel Bellmann was in evening dress. It looked as if he had just dined alone, for there was a decanter of brandy and a single glass with the scatter of papers on the desk. He got up and came toward her, hand outstretched. She heard the door close, but only dimly, because there was a roaring in her ears, and she dropped her bag. It fell heavily to the rich carpet. He bent at once to pick it up for her and helped her to a chair.

She realized with a blush at her own stupidity that she had been going to slap him. To slap him—as if that would make the slightest difference!

"May I offer you some brandy, Miss Lockhart?" he said.

She shook her head.

"Something warm, then? You have come in from the cold. Shall I ring for coffee?"

"Nothing, thank you," she managed to say.

He sat down opposite her and crossed his legs. Sally looked away. The room they were in was even warmer than the hall, if possible, because not only was there a large iron radiator under the window, but a fierce fire burned in the grate—coke, she noticed. All the furniture was new. There were prints on the walls— shooting scenes, fox hunting—and above the mantelpiece and between the windows hung various sporting trophies: antlers, the head of a stag, a fox's mask. One wall was entirely covered in bookshelves, but not one of the books looked as if it had ever been opened. The room had the air of having been ordered complete from a catalog, with all the conventional accessories for a wealthy gentleman's study, without his having the trouble of assembling them himself.

Then she looked back at Bellmann and saw his eyes.

They were alive with compassion.

She felt as if she'd been suddenly stripped naked and plunged into a snowdrift. She had to catch her breath and look away, but then she felt her eyes drawn back again, and she hadn't been wrong: there was compassion and understanding and tenderness in his face, or she couldn't read human expression at all. And strength—such a strength as she hadn't seen since her childhood, when she woke from a nightmare to cling to her father and saw from the love in his eyes that she was safe, everything was secure, there were no bad things in the world.

"You killed Frederick Garland," she said in a shaky whisper.

"You loved him?" Bellmann said.

She nodded. She didn't trust her voice.

"Then he must have deserved your love. I knew when you came to see me the first time that you were a remarkable young woman. That you should come again at this time means that I was right. Miss Lockhart, you shall have the truth now. Ask me what you will—I promise I shall give you the truth. All of it, if you want."

"Did you kill Nordenfels?" she said. It was the first thing that came to mind.

"Yes."

"Why?"

"We disagreed over the future of the Self-Regulator. He came to think of it as disgusting, and wanted to destroy all records of it so it would never be built; I saw it as a device to promote human happiness. We quarreled and fought a duel like gentlemen, and he lost."

His voice was quiet, his tone frank and sincere, but it was out of joint with his words. She couldn't take in what he was saying.

"Human happiness?" she said.

"Would you like me to explain?"

She nodded.

"It is simply that the Self-Regulator is too appalling to be used. Once enough of them have been built, wars will come to an end, and civilization will develop in peace and harmony for the first time in the history of the world."

She tried to understand how that might be true. Then she said, "Did you arrange for the *Ingrid Linde* to disappear?"

"The steamship? Yes, I did. Would you like to know how I arranged it?"

Sally nodded. She felt unable to speak.

"She carried a gasification plant in her engine room, like most coal-burning ships. A *Capitaine* Marine Gas Plant, to be precise. It burned some of the coal to produce gas for lighting and so on, and the gas was stored in a large, expandable metal tank. Very safe, you know. Now, also in the engine room, on the main shaft that turns the screw, there was an automatic counter. It clicked on one turn every revolution, and told the engineer when to grease the bearings. Well, inside that counter I soldered a series of metal pins that would line up when a certain number was reached—a number that would mean the ship was somewhere in the middle of the sea. When that happened, the pins would complete an electrical circuit and fire a spark plug that I had put in the main gas tank. Naturally I was not there to see it take place, but judging by the result, it must have worked, don't you think?"

Sally felt sick. "But why did you do it?"

"First, because it hastened the decline of the Anglo-Baltic company, which I needed to accomplish for financial reasons. You had spotted that when you came to Baltic House; it was astute of you, but you could not have known the second reason, which was that on board the ship was an agent of the Mexican government bound for Moscow, with documents that would have induced my Russian backers to withdraw their support. That would have been disastrous. As things stand now, I am on the point of signing a contract with that same Mexican government, so everyone has benefited—workers and their families and children, whole communities, both in this country and in Mexico. There are poor children in Barrow who will eat and go to school because of what I have done. There are families in Mexico who will have medical supplies, clean drinking water, transport for the produce of their farms, security, education—all because I sank the *Ingrid Linde*. It was a completely humane act, and if I had to do it again, I would do it without the slightest hesitation."

"What about the innocent people who died?"

"I cannot pretend to regret the deaths of people I never knew. No one can do that. If they say they do, they are lying. Humbug, I believe you call it. No, I promised you the truth, and this is the truth: I do not regret killing those people. If I had not sunk the ship, a much greater number would have died—of starvation and poverty and ignorance and war. It was an act of the highest charity."

Sally was feeling dizzy, seated though she was. She closed her eyes and tried to control the sickness, tried to bring Fred back to mind, tried to remember what she was doing and why.

Eventually she said, "What about your connections with the British government? When Mr. Windlesham came to Burton Street on Saturday night he told us the names of some officials who were in your pocket. Why do you need to work like that? And why did Mr. Windlesham come to us, anyway? We didn't believe him when he said North Star was on the point of collapsing. I think you sent him."

"Of course I did. I sent him to spy. But you ask about the government—it's a very interesting, very delicate matter. . . . Of course, you know that the real business of government is carried on far out of the public eye. You may not be aware that much of it is unknown even to ministers, sometimes even to ministers of the departments that might be expected to be concerned. It is so with all states, of course, but particularly so with Britain, for some reason. Thanks to the contacts I made through Lord Wytham (though their purpose was quite unknown to him) I have my hands now on the levers of real power in Great Britain. But, you know something, Miss Lockhart: in nine hundred and ninety-nine cases out of a thousand, this secret power, this invisible authority which no one has voted for, works for good. For the benefit of the ordinary citizen. In hundreds of ways that they would never understand, ordinary lives are better for this benevolent oversight, this hidden, fatherly hand that guides and protects. Among all men who are truly powerful—and, as I've explained, that is not always

the men the world thinks are powerful—there is a
kind of comradeship, an ideal, almost a freemasonry of
service. Has the life of the employees of North Star
improved? Is it better than when they were making
locomotives? Of course it is. Go and look into their
houses. Visit the schools. Inspect the hospital that we
have just built. Watch a football match on the sports
ground we have laid out. They are prosperous and
healthy and happy. They don't know why, but you
and I know. When wars have finally ceased, when
peace reigns all over the world, they won't know why
either; they'll put it down to improvements in education, or an evolution in the human brain, or the
sophistication of the economic system, or an increase
in churchgoing, or better drains. We shall know
better. We shall know that the real reason is that gun
which is too horrible to be used. But it doesn't matter
that they won't know; let them feel the benefits—that
is all that matters."

Sally sat quietly, her head bowed. It was all slipping
away from her.

"What do you *want*?" she said.

"Oh, power," he said. "Power is very interesting.
Shall I tell you why? Because it is infinitely changeable. You take money, which is financial power, and
with it you employ men—muscle power—to build you
a factory, and in the factory you burn coal, which is the
power of heat, and you change water into steam, and
you lead the power of the steam into the cylinders of
an engine and turn it into a mechanical power, and
with that mechanical power you build more engines,
and sell them, and turn them back into financial power

again; or you take your steam engines and make a dam to hold back vast quantities of water, and construct pipes and valves and let the water run through with great force and turn a dynamo, so that the power of money changes into water power, which changes into electrical power, and so the changes go on, infinitely. Another word for it is energy, of course. An English poet—so Windlesham tells me, I have not enough time to enjoy the poets—an English poet wrote 'Energy is eternal delight.' I could not express it better. Perhaps that is why we have poets."

Sally could think of no answer. She knew with some distant part of her that he was utterly wrong, that there were arguments to refute everything he said, but she knew she'd never find them now. He was so strong, and she was so tired. She swayed, pulled herself upright, and forced herself to raise her head to look at him.

"You're wrong," she said, and her voice was hardly audible. "About the people. I know what they say. They hate the Steam Gun, your workers. They know what it means, and they loathe it. You keep it secret because you're afraid of what people would think if they knew—that's the only reason. You know the British people wouldn't stand for it if they saw it clearly for what it is—a tyrant's weapon, a coward's weapon. You misjudge us, Mr. Bellmann. You misjudge your workers and you misjudged me."

"Oh, I didn't misjudge you," he said, "I admired you from the start. You have true courage, but you are innocent. These British people you mention: shall I tell you the truth? If they knew, they wouldn't mind.

They'd have no scruples about making the most horrible weapon ever invented—none whatever—they wouldn't give it a thought. They'd take their wages and enjoy their sports field and be proud of their children and, in fact, you know, they'd be proud of the weapon as well, and want one with a British flag on it, and sing about it in the music halls. Oh, there are a few idealists, pacifists—harmless people. There is room for them. But the majority are as I describe, not as you describe. Reality is with me. I promised you the truth: there it is."

And she knew that he was right.

She looked across at him again. He was still sitting calmly, relaxed, powerful, one leg over the other, hands resting along the arms of the chair. His hair shone gold in the lamplight; his face was unlined, she noticed now, and full of a strange, luminous wisdom, yet with an undertow of rippling humor, as if to say *Pain and suffering and sadness—yes, they exist, but they are not the whole, and they pass. The world is delightful, like the play of sunlight on water. Energy is eternal delight. . . .*

"You know," he said after they'd been silent for almost a minute, "I made a mistake in seeking the hand of Lady Mary Wytham. She is very beautiful, and the connections she brought—her graphite mines, for instance—would have been most useful, but it was still a mistake. It involved me in the ridiculous pursuit of that comical Scotsman Mackinnon—well, you know all about that. Too late to do anything about it now, of course; the engagement is over. Wytham himself will suffer most, but it is his own fault. I wonder. . . . An idea occurs to me, Miss Lockhart. You may treat it as pure fancy, but there is more to it than that. Here it is: *You* are the sort of young woman I should marry. You are strong, brave, intelligent, and resourceful. Lady Mary's beauty would fade. Yours is not as dazzling, but it is a beauty of mind and character, and it will grow stronger. You are a match for me. And I am a match for you. We have been fighting each other; we each know the other's measure. May I ask you a question now? I know you will answer it truthfully. Out of the enmity you once felt for me, has there come respect?"

"Yes," she whispered. Her eyes were held by his; she dared not move.

"We disagree on many things," he went on. "That is good. You have an independent mind. Perhaps you will change my opinion on some matters; perhaps I shall convince you of the merits of my viewpoint on others. One thing is certain: You would not be passive and decorative, which would have been Lady Mary's limit. Even if she had been free to marry me, I do not think she would have been happy. You, Miss Lockhart, I judge to be a woman for whom happiness is secondary anyway. What you want most is activity and purpose. I can promise you that—all that you want. You understand what I am doing? I am proposing marriage to you—marriage, and more than marriage: partnership. Together, you and I, we would be magnificent—and who knows? In the rare intervals in all that vital work, when you have a moment to catch your breath, you may find yourself with a sensation that is hard to put a name to, until you remember that is it a by-product of work, called happiness. Miss Lockhart"—he sat forward now and reached out to take her hands in his—"will you marry me?"

Sally felt dazed.

She had come here expecting to face anger, scorn, violence, and she was prepared for that; *this* left her breathless. She let her hands rest where they were. Her head was ringing. Now that they were actually touching, she felt the force of the man as never before. His personality was mesmerizing; his very flesh was electric with energy; his eyes held her transfixed; the flow of his words was irresistible. She had to struggle for the strength to speak, but then she found it and opened her mouth.

"I—" was all she had time to say, for there was an urgent knock at the door.

Bellmann let go of her hands and looked around. "Yes? What is it?"

The servant opened the door, and there stood Alistair Mackinnon. Sally sank back in her chair, half fainting.

He was terrified, that was plain. He was dripping wet—it was obviously raining hard outside—and the hand that held his hat was shaking uncontrollably. He glanced from Sally to Bellmann and back to Sally again, and then fixed his eyes, wide with fear, on the financier.

"I have come for—for Miss Lockhart," he said faintly.

Bellmann didn't move.

"I don't understand," he said.

"Miss Lockhart," said Mackinnon, tearing his eyes away from Bellmann and addressing her directly, "Jim

Taylor and I have come to—to help you home. Jim is—he's hurt, you know. His leg is broken. He couldn't walk in here; he's at the gate. We came because . . ." His eyes flashed back to Bellmann, and then to Sally again. "You can—come away now," he finished.

And she saw the courage that he'd had to summon up to enter the house of the man who'd been going to kill him, and found the strength to speak.

"It's too late, Mr. Mackinnon," she said. She forced herself to sit up straight, as straight as Miss Susan Walsh had done in her office, and with an effort that almost made her faint again she controlled her voice and said, "Mr. Bellmann has just asked me to marry him. I am on the point of deciding whether or not to accept his offer."

She sensed Mackinnon's incredulity. Keeping her eyes away from Bellmann, she went on:

"It depends on whether he can afford it. My hand in marriage will cost Mr. Bellmann three thousand two hundred and seventy pounds. That is the sum of money I tried to persuade him to give me some time ago. I had nothing to sell him then. But now that he has expressed an interest in marrying me, perhaps the situation has altered—I don't know."

Mackinnon was unable to speak. He seemed helpless in the electric charge that flowed between Sally and Bellmann. His eyes moved back to Bellmann, and then he jumped, startled, as Bellmann laughed.

"Ha, ha, ha! I was right—you *are* a match for me! Of course you shall have it. In gold? Now?" he said.

She nodded, and Bellmann got to his feet, feeling

on his watch chain for a key. When he'd found it, he opened a small safe behind the desk and, as they watched, took out three small sealed bags, threw them on the desk, and tore the seal off another, tipping it upside down. A flood of glittering coins spilled out on the blotter. He swiftly counted out two hundred and seventy pounds' worth, returned them to the bag, and pushed all four bags toward Sally.

"Yours," he said. "To the penny."

She stood. The die was cast now; there was no going back. She gathered the bags of gold and handed them to Mackinnon. His hands were shaking more than hers.

"Please," she said, "do this for me. Take this money to Miss Susan Walsh, of number three, Benfleet Avenue, Croydon. Can you remember that?"

He repeated the name and address, and then said helplessly, "But Jim—he's made me come here. I can't—"

"Hush," she said. "It's all over now. I'm going to marry Mr. Bellmann. Please go. Tell Jim . . . no, say nothing to Jim. Just go."

He looked like a lost child. With one last glance at Bellmann, he nodded faintly and left.

As the door closed behind him Sally sank down into the chair again, and in a moment Bellmann had surged forward to kneel at her side. It was like a dam breaking. He took her hands, and she felt as if all that power he had talked about, all those metamorphoses and alterations, had come to their final state in him: that he was steam power, electric power, mechanical power, financial power made flesh. He kissed her hands again and again, and his kisses were somehow charged with the sulfurous crackle she'd heard from the wires beside the railway lines as she walked through the valley to the house.

But it was done now. It was nearly finished.

"I am tired," she said. "I want to sleep. But before I lie down, I'd like to see the Steam Gun. Can you take me there and show me what it's like? It would be a pity to come all this way and not see it."

"Of course," he said, and rose at once to ring the bell. "It is a good time to see it. I love the works at night. We are making great progress with electric lighting, you know. What do you know about gunnery, my dear?"

She stood up and gathered her heavy bag from the floor. It was quite easy now, as long as her voice kept steady, as long as she didn't tremble.

"As a matter of fact," she said, "I know a good deal. But I am always prepared to learn more."

He laughed happily as they walked to the front door.

THE GUARD let Mackinnon out of the gate and locked it again behind him. Half running, half stumbling, clutching the bags of gold to his chest, Mackinnon made his way through the driving rain to the cab where Jim sat nursing the brandy flask, almost delirious with pain.

Jim couldn't take it in at first. Mackinnon had to go through it twice and then shake the bags so Jim could hear the coins jingling.

"Marry him?" said Jim thickly. "She said that?"

"Aye! It was like a bargain—she was selling herself for this gold! And I had to promise to take it to a lady in Croydon—"

"Her client," said Jim. "The one she lost the money for . . . in Bellmann's firm, see. . . . Oh, you bloody fool, what you want to let her do that for?"

"Me? I couldnae—it was her in charge, Jim, you know how strong she is—"

"No, I didn't mean that, mate. You did all right. You had the guts to go in there. We're all square now. I meant me. Oh, Christ, this leg, I don't know what I mean. I'm worried, Mackinnon. I think she's going to . . ."

He groaned again and rocked to and fro in his agony. The flask, nearly empty now, took a trembling journey to his lips, then fell to the floor of the cab, making the patient horse shake its harness. The rain was lashing down even harder outside. Mackinnon wiped the sweat off Jim's forehead with his sleeve, but Jim didn't notice.

"Help me out," he mumbled. "She's up to something—I don't like the sound of it. Come on, man, give us a hand . . ."

BELLMANN TENDERLY held the waterproof cloak around Sally with one arm and an umbrella over both of them with the other as they hastened down the gravel path toward the brightly lit building where the Steam Gun stood. He had given orders for the whole compound to be illuminated, and each light that came on gleamed yellow in a halo of moisture and splashing drops.

The building was called shed number one. As she'd

seen from the edge of the valley, it was isolated from the rest of the works, and they had to cross an open area of wet gravel, with the rain driving in hard, before they reached the shelter of the wall. A watchman, warned that they were coming, dragged the great door open on its rollers, and a blast of heat and light greeted them.

"Dismiss the men for half an hour," Bellmann told the foreman who came toward them. "They may go to the canteen and refresh themselves. This is an extra break; I shall take charge of the boiler myself. I want the building empty for my guest."

Sally stood by while the dozen or so men downed tools and left. Some of them glanced curiously at her; some looked neither at her nor at Bellmann. There was a muted, restrained quality in their attitude to Bellmann; she couldn't place it until she realized that it was fear.

When the last of them had gone, and the great door was rolled back in place, he helped her step up onto a platform overlooking the length of the building, turned to her, and said, "My kingdom, Sally."

It was like a railway engine shed. There were three separate parallel rail tracks, and on each stood what looked like a heavy freight carriage in the course of construction. The farthest one was still only a chassis, but she could see the massive iron framework that would hold the firebox, the boiler, and, she supposed, the firing mechanism. The central one was nearly complete, but for its shell: a mass of enormously complex pipe work, too intricate for the eye to penetrate, with a traveling crane on a beam holding part of the boiler suspended above it.

The third machine was finished. It stood in front of them on its rails, brightly lit, with a fire glowing in the heart of it which Sally could just make out through the window—like that of a conventional guard's van—at the rear. It looked like a perfectly normal goods carriage: a closed van made of wood, with a metal roof. In the center of the roof stood a squat little chimney, surmounted by a cowl. The only oddity was the large number of small holes in the side, which Henry Waterman had described to Frederick: row upon row of tiny black dots, looking from the platform like rivets or nail heads.

"Would you care to see it more closely?" he said. "If you like guns, this will fascinate you. We must keep an eye on the working pressure, or the foreman will be angry with us. They are testing the automatic grate tonight. . . ."

He led her along to the rear of the carriage, climbed up and opened the door, and then leaned down to lift her up and into the little compartment. It looked like a miniature version of what she had seen inside many locomotives, except that the firebox, glowing red, was at the side. The controls were slightly different, too: instead of driving pistons in their cylinders, this boiler supplied steam to different sections of the interior of the carriage, labeled chambers one through twenty, port and starboard.

Where the boiler was in a normal engine, there was a narrow passage that led into the heart of the machine. It was lit by the glow of an electric lamp.

"Where is the boiler?" Sally asked.

"Ah! The boiler is the secret of it," he said. "Quite unlike the conventional design. A masterpiece of engineering. Much flatter, you see, and more compact than the ordinary shape—it has to be, in order to make space for the gunnery. Nowhere but here could it be made so perfectly."

"Does the gunner sit here?" Sally asked. She was surprised to find her voice so firm.

"Oh, no. In the very center. Come this way."

Moving delicately, despite his massive frame, he edged sideways along the passage in front of her. Four or five steps took them to a compartment only big enough for one, with a swiveling chair and a mass of switches and levers on a polished mahogany board. An electric lamp gleamed overhead. Beside the chair, on each side of the compartment, metal racks reached into the darkness, and Sally could make out row upon row, coil upon coil, of glistening cartridges. The heat was intense.

"How does the gunner see out?" she said.

He reached up and pulled at a handle that she had not noticed. Out of the ceiling a wide tube, with a cloth-covered eyepiece, slid silently down.

"An arrangement of mirrors in here lets him see out the false chimney on top. He can see all around, three hundred and sixty degrees, a perfect view, by swiveling the tube. That was an invention of my own."

"So it's ready to fire?" she said.

"Oh, yes. We are ready to test it on the range tomorrow morning for a visitor from Prussia. You may come with me. I promise you, you will never have seen anything like it. I would like to show you the pipe work, Sally—all around this compartment there are altogether five and a half miles of piping! The gunner communicates with the engineer by means of a signal telegraph, and he controls the firing pattern with these levers here—you see? There is a Jacquard mechanism connected to the firing tubes, and by selecting the pattern from this diagram according to the instructions on the electric telegraph here, he can fire in any one of thirty-six different ways. Sally, there has been nothing like this weapon since the beginning of time. It is the most beautiful device the mind of man has ever conceived . . ."

She stood for a moment, feeling her head swim in the heat.

"And is the ammunition live?" she said.

"Yes. It's ready to go. Ready to fire!"

He was standing triumphantly, with his hands on the back of the swivel chair, in the only bit of spare floor space the compartment possessed. She stood at the entrance to the passageway, and she suddenly felt a great cold clarity sweep through her, a sense of freedom and release. This was the moment she had come for.

She reached into her bag, took her little Belgian pistol from the oilskin pocket she kept it in, and cocked the hammer with her thumb.

Bellmann heard the click. He looked down at her hand and then up again. She faced him squarely.

Fred's face in the rain; his bare arms in the candlelight; his laughing green eyes . . .

"You killed Frederick Garland," she said for the second time that night.

Bellmann opened his mouth, but she raised the pistol a little higher and went on:

"And I loved him. Whatever made you think you

could replace him? Nothing I have for however long I live will make up for him. He was brave and he was good and he trusted human goodness, Mr. Bellmann; he understood things you'll never understand, like decency and democracy and truth and honor. Everything you said to me in your study made me sick and cold and frightened, because I thought for a minute that you were right—about everything, about people, about the world. But you're not—you're wrong. You may be strong and cunning and influential; you may think you're saying the truth about the way the world works; but you're *wrong*, because you don't understand loyalty, you don't understand love, you don't understand people like Frederick Garland . . ."

His eyes were blazing at her, but she gathered the last of her strength and faced them and didn't look away.

"And no matter how powerful you were," she went on, "no matter if you controlled the whole world and gave everyone the schools and the hospitals and the sports fields you'd decided they wanted, and no matter if everyone was healthy and prosperous and there were statues of you in every city in the world—you'd still be wrong, because the world you want to create is based on fear and deception and murder and lies—"

He took a step toward her, his great fist raised. She stood her ground and raised the pistol higher.

"Stand still!" she said, and now her voice was trembling again, and she brought up her left hand to hold the pistol steady. "I came here to get the money I wanted for my client. I told you when we first met that I'd have it, and now I've got it. Marry you? Ha!

How *dare* you think you were worth that much? There was only one man I'd marry, and you've killed him. And—"

She found herself choked with a harsh sob as the thought of Frederick flooded back to her. Bellmann vanished in the starburst of tears, and she found Frederick close beside her again and whispered shakily, "Did I speak well, Fred? Did I do it right? I'm coming to you now, my darling—"

And she pointed the gun at the racks of cartridges and pulled the trigger.

JIM WAS clinging to the fence when the first explosion came, his other hand on Mackinnon's shoulder. They were making their way around the perimeter, since the guard refused to leave his hut. The rain was lashing down like thousands of tiny whips.

The first sound they heard was a muffled crack like thunder. It was followed only a second or two later by another, deeper boom, and as they strained to peer through the downpour they saw a sudden flare from their left, and a jet of flame leaped from the buckled doorway of an isolated building.

Instantly alarm bells began to ring. From the nearest lighted building, men ran out, only to dodge back quickly again as a volley of further small explosions followed the first two.

"She did it," said Jim. "She set it off. I knew she was planning something crazy. Oh, Sally, Sally . . ."

The building that had contained the Steam Gun was leaning over crazily. They could see it in the light of the lanterns held by the men who came crowding out again, in the light of the flames that were flickering

around the edge of the door. From the cries and
shouts, the air of panic, Jim could tell that they were
afraid of more explosions. The air was filled with the
jangling of bells—and then a siren began to add its
banshee howl to the din.

Jim shook Mackinnon's shoulder.

"Come on," he said, "they're opening the gate,
look—we'll find her, Mackinnon, we'll get her out—"

And he turned and hobbled back, like a crippled
demon. Mackinnon swayed, moaning with fear, and
then gathered himself and went after him.

THERE FOLLOWED three hours of fury. Three hours of
tearing at fallen beams, of flinging aside twisted pieces
of metal and broken bricks and shattered fragments of
wood, of burned hands and broken fingernails and
skinned knuckles, of sudden flares of hope and the
slowly growing weight of despair.

The fire brigade had been summoned at once, and
with the aid of the emergency crew on the site, they
had the main fire under control before long. It seemed
that the explosion in the first machine had set off not
only the rest of the ammunition on board but also the
supply that was stored nearby, waiting to be loaded.
The machine itself was unrecognizable; the one beside it was smashed beyond repair, the heavy crane
above having fallen on the center of it; the walls of the
building were still standing, by a miracle. Parts of the
roof had collapsed, and it was there that the rescuers
were searching, passing down pieces of masonry in a
human chain and easing great beams carefully aside so
as not to dislodge the rubble.

Mackinnon was working in the heart of it, side by

side with Jim. Something of Jim's demonic energy had passed into him, too, and he worked on despite pain and exhaustion and danger; and once or twice Jim looked across at him and nodded with grim approval, as if Mackinnon were an equal now, as if he'd passed some kind of test.

They found Sally under a corner of the fallen roof as the rain began to ease.

There was a shout from one of the North Star workers. He was bending low, waving his arm and pointing at a part of the fallen building they hadn't touched yet. Within seconds hands were mustered to hold up the length of wooden beam that had kept a section of the wall off her, and little by little, one by one, the pieces of rubble and broken iron that weighed it down were lifted off and passed away safely.

Jim, crouched as close as he could manage, reached in for her hand. Her blond hair was spread wide at his feet, streaked with dust and dirt. She was very still.

Then he saw her eyelids flutter. And at the same moment he found her wrist, with the strong pulse beating steadily. "Sally!" he said, and with his other hand stroked the hair off her forehead. He bent low and put his face close to hers. "Sally," he said softly, "come on, gal, it's all right now—we'll get you out. Come on, we got work to do back home. . . ."

"Jim?" she whispered. She opened her eyes and shut them at once against the lights, but she'd seen him and heard him, and she squeezed his hand.

"You silly bloody cow," Jim whispered back—and fainted.

23

The Orchard

IT WAS ONLY BECAUSE SALLY HAD BEEN STANDING IN THE passageway, and because Bellmann had left the door open at the rear, that she had survived. The first blast had thrown her clear, and when the exploding ammunition had ruptured the boiler, as she'd known it would, she was out of range of the worst effects.

Bellmann had been killed at once; they found what was left of him in the morning.

She was badly shaken but, apart from bruises and a sprained wrist, uninjured. Alistair Mackinnon telegraphed to Charles Bertram, who arrived within a day and took charge, arranging for Jim to be taken back to his own doctor to have his leg reset, finding a doctor for Sally, dealing with the inquiry into the accident.

For an accident it was universally taken to be. The papers printed the story that while Mr. Bellmann, the proprietor, was showing a guest around his factory, an unsuspected fault in a safety valve lead to a dangerous increase in pressure in one of the boilers. There was no mention of explosives; no mention of what the factory was producing. It sounded like an ordinary

industrial accident—tragic, of course, because of the
death of the well-known employer and benefactor, for
whom a memorial service was to be held in the parish
church.

So Sally went back to London.

AND, LITTLE BY LITTLE, she came back to life.

The first, and most urgent, problem was the business. Her own files were safe at Mr. Temple's, but
Garland and Lockhart, that living, growing thing she'd
loved so much, was shattered and broken. She had
renewed the insurance only months before, so replac-
ing the stock would not be too difficult; though, as she
knew, a business was much more than its physical
assets. She found a shabby studio in Hammersmith
and threw the staff into work, subsidizing their wages
with her own money until there was enough coming
in to pay them properly. She advertised in all the
papers, promising that outstanding orders and commissions would be fulfilled with no more than a
week's delay. She bought a studio camera, had new
stationery printed, took new orders. She bullied,
borrowed, bribed, hired, and drove the staff into
exhaustion—but it worked. Before a month was out,
the turnover had begun to pick up. Sally hoped that
the improvement kept up; her own money was
dwindling fast.

But worse than the loss of the business was the
blow that Webster had sustained. Everything he'd
achieved, his entire life's work in the field of photography, all the great and irreplaceable images he'd
captured on glass and paper, had vanished as if they'd

never existed. It was as if he'd lived his sixty years and done nothing.

Sally watched helplessly as he went through the motions of working—and then retired at night to the solace of the whiskey bottle. She knew he was tough; but she knew he'd loved Frederick like the son he'd never had, and she couldn't even guess what the loss of all his work meant to him.

Their biggest problem was premises. The studio she'd found in Hammersmith was too small for anything but basic portraiture, and it wasn't in a good spot; the nearest place she could find for the shop was in a dingy building three streets away, and having the two halves of the business inconveniently separate made extra work for everyone.

But if she took the time to search for somewhere better, and then they moved—that would all be time during which no money was coming in. During the daytime she pushed the problem aside, but it came back to her at night. In the dark she felt like a different person; tender-skinned and haunted, she lay awake and wept and whispered to a ghost.

One morning, as soon as she could, she took a train to Croydon and called on Miss Susan Walsh.

The old lady was seeing a private pupil when Sally arrived; but she was so shocked by Sally's appearance that she sent the girl away, telling her to come back later, and made Sally sit down by the fire and take a glass of sherry. Sally, cold, tired, and grateful, handed her a check for the amount she had won back from Bellmann—and burst into tears, much to her own fury.

"My dear child!" said Miss Walsh. "Whatever have you been doing?"

An hour later she knew the whole story. When it was over, she shook her head in amazement. Then she took the check and laid it on Sally's lap.

"I want you to invest this money in your firm," she said.

"But—"

The old lady stopped her protests with a steely eye.

"The last advice you gave me," she said quite sharply, "was somewhat unsound. I think you will admit that. This time, Miss Lockhart, I shall do as I think fit with my money. To my mind, Garland and Lockhart will be a safer investment than any shipping firm."

And she wouldn't be denied. If female emancipation meant anything, she said, it meant the right of one woman to support the work of another in any way she chose, and she would hear no more of the matter. Instead they shared lunch and parted the best of friends.

JIM SPENT three weeks in bed. He'd seriously damaged his leg during the search for Sally, and the doctor suspected that he'd walk with a limp for the rest of his life. He spent his time (in a spare room at Trembler Molloy's house in Islington) reading sensational novels, losing his temper at the thinness of their plots, writing a story of his own, tearing it up in a fury, cutting out and carefully sticking together a toy theater he'd sent Sally out to buy for him, trying out a plot with the little cardboard characters and losing his

patience with them, writing six separate letters to
Lady Mary and throwing them all away, tossing and
turning in his bed, heaving off the blankets, sweating
with pain, and drawing on the deepest wells of his
vocabulary to curse the whole state of things with an
intensity that might have blistered paint.

He might have sent a letter to Lady Mary eventually, but a fortnight after they came back to London he
heard from Mackinnon.

Mackinnon had decided, he said in his letter, to go
with his wife to America. There he would be able to
develop his art in a more spacious and forward-looking
setting than the English music hall provided, and
discharge his responsibilities as a married man without
the hindrances that had laid in his path heretofore. Or
that was how he put it.

Jim showed the letter to Sally.

"I wonder how long that'll last?" he said sourly.
"Mind you, he was all right in the end, old Mackinnon. He did his bit to get you out. And he didn't do a
bunk with the gold, like he would have done once.
Good luck to him—I suppose. But if he doesn't treat
her right . . ."

He wondered privately how Mackinnon had ever
persuaded that lovely, dreaming, tragic girl to share
the life of a music hall wizard and, for the matter of
that, how her father had reacted when he knew she
was really going.

But Lord Wytham had plenty of other trouble to
cope with. He had soon realized that Bellmann knew
all the time that Lady Mary was married, and was
daring him to admit it; and he knew that he hadn't

dared; and he suspected that he'd never see the money he'd asked for her. He'd been caught several ways. If he admitted he knew about the marriage, he'd lose Bellmann's money—but if he didn't, he'd lay himself open to a charge of conspiring to aid bigamy, and he couldn't decide which was worse. His only hope had been to feign ignorance of the marriage and to hope not only that news of it would somehow come out before long but that in the meantime he could make himself so useful to Bellmann that his position in the firm would be secure, at least.

But he felt uneasily that his usefulness to Bellmann was over, in any case. He could not understand the discussions at the board meetings he'd attended; he'd made all the introductions he could. Such influence in the civil service as he'd ever had was slipping away from him.

Then came the accident at Barrow. In the financial world Bellmann's death caused a sensation. Though the inquest labeled it accidental, rumors began to circulate that the North Star Castings disaster, as it was called, was closely connected with certain irregularities in Bellmann's other enterprises, which were now coming to light. A certain Mr. Windlesham, it was reported, was assisting the authorities with their investigations. The price of North Star shares plummeted. At the same time, apparently by coincidence, a number of government officials resigned or were quietly dismissed. Little of it reached the papers. Shortly afterward the firm collapsed altogether. Lord Wytham's bankruptcy followed almost at once.

Going to America with Mackinnon, Jim thought, was probably the best thing Lady Mary could do, under the circumstances. But he wished her well.

The North Star designers and engineers found work with other firms. Some of them went to work for Armstrong-Vickers, the famous arms manufacturers, but they didn't take the plans for the Hopkinson Self-Regulator with them; it was rumored that someone had broken into the factory and destroyed all record of them. The works opened again as a cooperative bicycle manufactory, but the workers lacked enough capital to make it succeed. It was sold again, and this time went back to the building of railway engines, at which it prospered.

As soon as Jim could get up, he hobbled out with a stick, found an omnibus to Streatham, and went to pay a call on Nellie Budd.

She'd recovered from the attack, with her sister Jessie's help, though she was thinner now, and she'd lost a lot of her vivacity. When he saw her, Jim felt glad about every blow he'd landed on Sackville and Harris. Jessie was back in the north now, Nellie said, but she was going to sell up down here and join her sister again. They'd patched up their differences. She was getting tired of the mediumship game, anyway. But when she'd recovered a bit more, the two of them were going to work out a mind-reading act and go on the halls together. Jim said he'd watch out for them.

So time passed.

And gradually Sally became aware of layers of

subtlety in the way the world worked; how nothing was clear or uncomplicated, how everything was patterned with irony.

Isabel Meredith, first. The two beings Sally had loved entirely, Chaka and Frederick, had both given their lives for Isabel. Sally had reason to resent her memory, but she couldn't. All she felt was pity.

And then photographs. Over the years Frederick had taken several pictures of Jim and many more of Sally; but there was no picture of him. Webster couldn't even remember taking one. He'd lived surrounded by cameras, lenses, plates, emulsions, and no one had made a record of that vivid, laughing face. There wasn't even a drawing.

And finally herself—and that was the biggest irony of all. She could hardly find words for it; but she knew she'd have to soon.

Then one day in late April, Charles Bertram announced that he had a surprise for them. It was a Sunday, mild and fresh and sunny, and he drove them down to Twickenham in a dogcart, refusing to say a word about their destination.

"You'll see what it is when we get there" was all he'd say.

It turned out to be an empty house with a large, overgrown garden. The house itself was covered in peeling stucco, but all the windows were intact and the proportions were lovely. It was seventy years old, Charles told them, clean, and dry—and haunted.

"The owner's a wealthy brewer," he said, unlocking the gate. "He can't let it at any price. Apparently there's a White Lady who wanders the corridors upstairs. She's perfectly harmless, but people do worry. Now if you'd step this way, lady and gentlemen . . ."

He opened the double doors into a sunny room overlooking the garden—and there was a table set for lunch, with cold pheasant, salad, wine, and fruit.

"Blimey, Charlie!" Jim said. "Good surprise, mate. Well done."

"First class, Charles," said Webster.

"I sent my man down ahead of us," Charles explained. "Sally?" He held out a chair for her.

She sat down. "Is it really haunted?"

"So the landlord claims. He's quite frank about it—I think he's given up expecting to let it. But look at the space!" he went on, opening the wine.

Webster was gazing out into the garden. "Is that an orchard down there?" he said. "And there's enough room on the grass there for . . . I wonder . . ."

"Rails," said Charles. "Parallel with the wall there, you see?"

Webster looked where he was pointing. "Yes, a proper setup. We could lay 'em as flat as we liked—and the sun's in the right place, too. . . ."

"Roof it over with glass," said Charles. "Then we could use it whatever the weather was like. And there's a lot of space behind the stable—I'll show you after lunch. Room to build a decent studio and a workshop, too. It'd mean hiring a full-time carpenter, mind you."

"You said the rent was low?" Sally asked.

"I've got the figures here. People don't want a ghost at any price."

"She's probably bored," said Jim. "We'll give her a job of work to do."

After they'd eaten, Charles said, "Sally—I've got something for you. It's probably not the right time, but there we are. I found it the other day. I thought you ought to have it."

He took an envelope from his pocket.

"I took it three or four months ago," he said. "We'd got a new lens for the Voigtlander, and there was no one else around to try it on, so I asked Frederick . . ."

She opened the envelope—and there he was.

It was a full-length portrait, wonderfully sharp and clear, with all the life and warmth that only Charles, apart from Webster, had seemed able to capture in a subject. Frederick was *there*—vivid and laughing and tense; it was a miraculous photograph.

She couldn't speak for tears, but she flung her arms around Charles's neck and kissed him instead.

"Thank you," she said when she could speak. "It's the best present I . . ."

Well, not the best, she thought a little later, on her own in the orchard. The best was impossible. You couldn't bring people back, despite the spiritualists. All that area of things was a mystery, half fraud and half miracle; better leave it alone and stick to real miracles, like photography. A rectangle of black-and-white paper, and it held all that life! She looked at it again, marveling. It wasn't enough, because it wasn't him; and yet it was, and it would have to do, because it was all the life he had.

And yet—irony again—it wasn't.

"Come on," she whispered to the picture, "it's time we told them."

She found them around the table, discussing the house—the number of rooms, the rental, the possibility of building on—and they made room for her as an equal, a partner.

She sat down and said, "I think we should take it. It's the best possible place, Charles; it's just what we want. I don't mind the ghost a bit. There's so much *room*. . . . I don't know why I'm saying this. I meant to say something quite different. So I'll say it now: I'm going to have Fred's child. Are you shocked? If he was alive, we'd be married by now. No, of course you're not shocked. There, I've said it. I'm going to have Fred's baby. And that's what I came in to say."

She was blushing. She set the picture up on the table, leaning it against the wine bottle. And then she looked at them—Webster first, then Jim, then Charles—and saw the same grin on each of them. Almost as if *they'd* done something to be proud of—silly great things.

"So there," she said.

Philip Pullman

completed a degree in English at Oxford
University in 1968 and has since written a
novel for adults (*Galatea*), a Gothic comedy
for children (*Count Karlstein*), and two books
for young adults—*The Ruby in the Smoke* and
its sequel, *Shadow in the North*. He is currently
working on a third novel to complete the
trilogy.

Mr. Pullman lives in Oxford, England,
with his wife and family.